Dollar Duchesses

Money for marriage into London Society

Three beautiful daughters of a New York
coal magnate are brought to London by their
socially ambitious mother, who seeks prestigious
marriages for her children—to British peers of the
realm. Titled men in need of funds to repair
their crumbling estates are drawn to these
wealthy young women. But can these matches
lead to something more than mere
marriages of convenience?

Read Lily and Aidan's story in
His Unlikely Duchess

Available now!

Look for Violet's and Rose's stories

Coming soon!

Author Note

I've been interested in the story of the Dollar Princesses for a long time, those young women who left the pampered world they knew to take on the challenge of a completely different one. I first found a love of history when I read through my grandmother's bookshelves as a child! She loved historical romance and historical fiction, and I discovered all sorts of queens through Jean Plaidy/Victoria Holt, village life in Austen, the moors and how annoying it was to be a governess through the Brontës, medieval court life in Anya Seton's *Katherine*, and (surprisingly!) lots of things from Barbara Cartland, including Victorian theatre, the Sepoy Mutiny and Elizabethan sailing ships.

One novel I found was based on the life of Consuelo Vanderbilt, Duchess of Marlborough. I couldn't believe it was true, this sad but fascinating tale of a young woman bullied into an unhappy marriage by her mother and then who rose above her circumstances to find real happiness and fulfillment. I wanted to visit Blenheim! When I found out she was a real historical figure, I ran to the library to find a biography of her life.

Lily is somewhat based on Consuelo (the ambitious mother, etc.), but her duke turns out to be very different from the real Marlborough! I hope at least some of those ladies found true love and happiness. If you're interested in more about the Dollar Princesses and this period in history, you can visit me at ammandamccabe.com. Happy reading!

AMANDA McCABE

—

His Unlikely Duchess

HARLEQUIN
HISTORICAL

ISBN-13: 978-1-335-50596-5

His Unlikely Duchess

Harlequin Enterprises ULC
22 Adelaide St. West, 40th Floor
Toronto, Ontario M5H 4E3, Canada
www.Harlequin.com

Printed in U.S.A.

Amanda McCabe wrote her first romance at sixteen—a vast historical epic starring all her friends as the characters, written secretly during algebra class! She's never since used algebra, but her books have been nominated for many awards, including the RITA® Award, Booksellers' Best Award, National Readers' Choice Award and the Holt Medallion. In her spare time she loves taking dance classes and collecting travel souvenirs. Amanda lives in New Mexico. Visit her at ammandamccabe.com.

Books by Amanda McCabe

Harlequin Historical

Betrayed by His Kiss
The Demure Miss Manning
The Queen's Christmas Summons
Tudor Christmas Tidings
"His Mistletoe Lady"

Dollar Duchesses

His Unlikely Duchess

Debutantes in Paris

Secrets of a Wallflower
The Governess's Convenient Marriage
Miss Fortescue's Protector in Paris

Bancrofts of Barton Park

The Runaway Countess
Running from Scandal
The Wallflower's Mistletoe Wedding

Visit the Author Profile page
at Harlequin.com for more titles.

Prologue

'I don't know why you still read that rubbish. Happy-ever-afters aren't real,' Violet Wilkins announced.

Lily Wilkins looked up from the book in her lap to smile at her younger sister. She had to laugh at Vi, who looked so disgruntled standing there at the gate to their mother's prized rose garden. Her arms were crossed over her rumpled shirtwaist and her scowl made her look much older than her sixteen years, despite the schoolgirlish braids and hair bows their mother still insisted on. Stella Wilkins would never admit to being old enough to mother quite so many growing girls.

Though, at almost twenty, Lily wouldn't be a girl much longer. She was already 'out' in Newport, and soon she would be in Manhattan, too, after a grand ball Stella was planning for the autumn. Lily shuddered to think what would happen after that.

'Of course I still read these,' she said, putting the book down on the marble bench beside her. 'And they're French novels, not fairy tales. No happy endings guaranteed.'

Just like in the real world. Lily had spent her whole

life watching her parents sitting at opposite ends of vast dining tables, barely tolerating each other's presence, smiling in public so no one would know 'Old King Coal' Wilkins, one of the richest men in New York, and his genteel Old South wife couldn't stand each other any longer.

That was the last thing Lily ever wanted, either for herself or her sisters. And that was why she took refuge in books. The fictional perils, dangers, adventures and, yes, romances of those heroines were preferable to daily life. Walks in the park, tea parties, letter writing, dancing with men who could only talk about Wall Street and horses...

Yes. Books were better.

'The French,' Violet said with a sniff. 'What do they know about fairy tales anyway?'

Lily laughed, her heart almost bursting with love for her redheaded sister. She had always tried to take care of Violet and her gentle twin sister, Rose. They had been her pride and joy ever since she saw them come into the nursery, tiny, pink-cheeked and howling. Almost as if they were her daughters rather than her sisters. The three of them had to stick together against the rest of the world, or they would surely be lost.

'What do you know of the French, then, Vi?'

'I know Monsieur Anatole's cooking, which is too salty, even though Mother is so proud she stole him from Mrs Vanderbilt. And I know Monsieur Worth's gowns, which are too heavy and itchy. I bet Frenchwomen *never* go walking or swimming, or play tennis, at all. I bet they don't even laugh.'

Lily noticed that Violet's hair was still damp in its untidy braids, dark red glinting with gold in the sun. She was fiddling with her beloved 'Talbot's Mousetrap' camera, as usual. Photography had become Violet's passion and she was constantly begging to take portraits of family and friends, or wandering the seashore taking pictures of the waves. 'Were you swimming in the cove again? If Mother catches you…'

Violet laughed and kicked out at a clump of dirt. 'Mother is much too busy planning next week's dance to fuss about my swimming or my camera. It's *you* who should be careful now, Lily.'

Lily frowned. She couldn't quite trust Violet when her sister got that 'I have a secret' light in her changeable hazel eyes. Where Violet's twin Rose was calm and serene, always so careful about her lessons and concerned with proper behaviour, Violet had other concerns. Concerns such as always knowing exactly what was happening in every corner of the vast Wilkins household and taking a photo of it if she could.

Lily had no idea how Violet did it and Violet never told her secrets. *Forewarned is forearmed*, Violet would always say as she skipped away.

Their mother, who was always very excitable anyway, and much prone to fainting fits and crying jags, had been preoccupied for weeks, putting together a grand dinner and ball that she intended to be the sparkling highlight of the Newport summer season. It was easy to hide from Stella Wilkins when her every energy was focused on besting Mrs Astor, but sometimes she would suddenly remember Lily should 'help' with the arrangements. That Lily was a vital part of her great social plan.

Heaven help Lily then.

'Has Mother been asking for me, Vi?' Lily said, reaching for her book again. As if French princesses and castles on the Loire could save her. She'd learned long ago that nothing could save her, or her sisters, but herself. She was the key to their freedom.

Violet gave her a sympathetic grimace. 'She's talking to Papa in the library. He just got here from the city a few hours ago.'

'Oh, no,' Lily moaned. It was never a good sign when her parents actually spoke to each other. Her father seldom even came to Newport, since the seaside was a ladies' world and men were only meant to pay the bills and come in for dinners or balls or to sail a yacht when needed. When their father did venture out of his New York office, he mostly stayed hidden in the library.

If he was *talking* to their mother...

Something serious indeed must be going on.

'Were they speaking about Adam Goelet again?' Lily asked in dread. Her mother had been pestering her to 'be nice' to Mr Goelet for months. After all, Stella would say with tears in her eyes, he was the only son of her father's closest business associate, heir to much of Madison Avenue and estates in Pennsylvania, and 'not so badlooking' at all. If one overlooked his unfortunate squint and perpetual onion breath—and the fact that even Lily could see he clearly preferred the company of his male friends to any lady.

Violet kicked harder at the dirt. 'I think she's quite forgotten about poor Mr Goelet.'

Lily would have hoped that was a good thing. But she knew their mother all too well. Ideas were much too sticky in Stella's head, and she wouldn't give up one scheme unless she had another to replace it. Especially when it came to her daughters and their marriages.

'So what are they talking about now?' Lily said.

'I'm not quite sure, but I think you should go listen for yourself.'

Lily sighed. She didn't want to leave the sanctuary of the quiet rose garden for the chaos of a house embroiled in party preparations, but she knew she had to eventually. If she didn't at least try to make Stella happy, her mother could curtail her visits to the Women and Children's Hospital again, or to one of her other charities, and some days that was all that kept Lily sane, being able to be of some use outside the hothouse of the Wilkins house.

She rose from the marble bench and quickly smoothed the navy dimity skirt of her sailor-style dress. 'No, don't worry, Vi. I'll find out what's going on, you and Rose don't need to worry.'

Violet gave her a relieved smile. 'I know you will, Lily. We never worry when you're here.'

'And I never worry when I know you're keeping watch. Shall we work on my photograph after tea? The light will be good then.' Violet brightened and Lily gave her sister a quick hug, then hurried towards the house. 'Go and check on Rose. I'll see you both at tea.'

It had grown later than she'd realised, she noticed with dismay as she rushed across the manicured green expanse of the lawn. Rose Garden Cottage, as her mother had named the seventy-room house, gleamed a golden rose in the waning sunlight, all red brick and pale stone, rising above the roll of perfect gardens and the distant crash of the sea against the cliffs. The silk curtains weren't drawn yet over the windows, but Lily knew they soon would be. Maids would be hurrying to finish pressing evening gowns and grooms would be polishing up the carriage horses.

She had spent too long with her book.

Lily found Rose hovering just inside the French doors that led on to the terrace. Rose, like Violet, was a small, slender girl, but her red hair was neatly braided and twisted about her head, her white muslin dress spotless, her skin fair and not freckled. But her hazel eyes were just as wide and worried.

'Is Mother in the library still?' Lily asked her, trying to smile carelessly as she checked her own reflection in the nearest gilt-framed mirror. Unlike her sisters, she had plain brown hair and dark eyes, but her posture had been perfected by years with a German governess and a back brace, horse riding lessons and corsets. She had learned long ago that a straight spine and a serene smile hid much.

But not from her sisters. 'Yes, with Papa,' Rose said, her eyes wide. 'There were…raised voices.'

'Not to worry, Rose Red,' Lily said, kissing her cheek. 'Probably just a problem with the peach ices coming in Papa's refrigerated train car or something.'

Rose laughed, but Lily knew she wasn't fooled. Nor was Lily. But she still marched down the corridor, past the marble tables from Versailles and the van Dyck portraits of someone else's ancestors, past the towering flower arrangements in alabaster vases and maids bobbing curtsies, to where the tall double doors of the library waited.

Normally no one went into the library. That was the one room out of all of the rooms at Rose Garden Cottage that was their father's. Today, though, Lily could hear her mother's voice floating past the thick oak panels.

'… I won't stand for it, do you hear me, Coleman?' her mother was saying, her usual dulcet South Carolina tones hard and brassy. 'You've always left our girls' education to *me* and I have worked myself to the bone to make sure they are a credit to us. My own health has been broken, but that doesn't matter to me. Only the darlin' girls matter. And now we have the opportunity I've been praying for…'

Lily's father's voice answered, a rough rumble too

low for Lily to understand. Whatever he said made his wife wail.

'You don't care about us at all! I tell you, I shall die if you don't…'

Lily thought it would be much better to get this over with, before her mother's maid came running with the smelling salts. She quickly knocked and pulled the door open.

'You sent for me, Mother?' Lily said brightly, even though officially no one had 'sent for her'. She studied the library in front of her: the carved dark panels of the walls, the red brocade curtains, the tapestries copied from a set at Hampton Court and her parents grouped around the tall, ivory-inlaid desk; her father in his velvet chair, his gouty leg propped on a footstool, his mutton-chop whiskers, once darkest jet, now half-grey, his spectacles slipping down his nose; her mother standing in front of him, tall and slim still after twenty-five years of marriage and three daughters, her pale hair piled atop her head, striped chiffon and silk floating around her. A handkerchief was pressed to her eyes.

This was what Lily had seen over and over in her parents' marriage, ever since she was a tiny girl trying to keep the peace so her sisters wouldn't hear the quarrels and start crying. It was precisely what she never wanted for her own life and definitely not for her sisters'.

Her mother turned to her and held out a slim, white hand, sparkling with diamonds and pearls. 'Thank the stars you are here, Lily my darlin'!' Stella Wilkins cried. Lily hurried to clasp her hand, hoping to hold her mother steady. 'You must help me talk some sense into your papa. We have a golden chance here and he wants to toss it all away.'

'Not toss it away, Stella,' Lily's father muttered, shifting his aching foot on its stool. 'Just wait a year or two. What's the hurry?'

'Hurry!' Stella shrieked. 'Lily is already nearly twenty. All her friends are married. We must seize the chance now.'

Lily swallowed hard, afraid this was about Adam Goelet again. 'Perhaps you should tell me what is happening, Mother?'

Stella clutched her hand even tighter and led her to the brocade sofa near the window. She didn't look at her husband again, but smiled brightly at Lily. 'My dearest girl, it is quite, quite wonderful! You remember that my mother went to school in England when she was a girl? She told me about it so often.'

Stella gestured to the portrait in the shadows on the panelled wall, of a stately, golden-haired woman in massive, pink silk skirts and puffed sleeves, marble columns behind her, magnolia blossoms in her hand. Lily's grandmother. 'Of course,' Lily said. It had been all her grandmother had ever talked about when Stella would take Lily and the twins to South Carolina when they were children—the glories of England she had seen in her golden girlhood, before her genteel Southern world fell apart.

Lily had never minded those stories, though, for the long history of England, the romance of it, was most fascinating. The castles and monuments, the battlefields and museums. She'd pored over books about it all, peppering her grandmother with questions.

A tiny spark of excitement kindled to life deep inside, but she dared not let it take hold, not yet. Too many things disappointed in the end.

'Well, I had a letter from the daughter of one of her English schoolfriends,' Stella said. 'Lady Heath, her name is, the widow of a viscount. She spoke most kindly of the old friendship and offered to meet us if we ever came to London. Lady Heath has many connections, even to the royal court, and meeting her could be so beneficial to you girls. Don't you think?'

The excitement grew. Was this escape, then? An end to Newport and Fifth Avenue, to her mother's constant struggle to belong, to outdo everyone else? Was she going to see England at last? But she glanced at her father, still trying to find a comfortable position on his stool. 'I would certainly like to see London,' Lily said cautiously. 'The centuries-old buildings and museums...'

Stella tossed a tearful look at her husband and her hand tightened even more on Lily's. 'Of course you would. You are such a good, scholarly girl. Papa, though, is being ridiculously obstinate.'

'It's a long way, Stella. You wouldn't let them go when they were younger—why suddenly now? That's all I am saying,' Coleman Wilkins said wearily.

'They were not ready before now! And England is not too far for Jennie Jerome, is it? Or Consuelo Yznaga,' Stella cried.

Lily saw in a flash what this was all *really* about and she felt like a fool for not realising immediately. It wasn't about her grandmother, or culture or education. It was about marriage. Stella seemed to have something bigger in mind now than the Goelet money.

Jennie Jerome was the daughter-in-law of a duke now. Consuelo Yznaga would one day be a duchess herself. Her mother wanted a coronet for the Wilkins family, too.

Of course she did.

Lily felt a sudden wave of fear, washing away that tiny spark of excitement. She had known she couldn't hide in her books for ever, but—to jump into English society, a pool whose depths she could not fathom? Everyone would be watching, everyone would know why she was there in London and she was sure to disappoint her mother again. 'Mother, I don't know. Perhaps Papa is right, perhaps I am too young…'

'You are almost twenty! And the twins are almost seventeen. They need polish so badly,' her mother wailed. Stella collapsed on to the sofa, her face buried in her handkerchief. 'There is no more time. If you were settled, the other girls would be safe, too. No one could touch us!'

'It's all right, Mother, I promise,' Lily said soothingly. She reached out and rubbed her mother's silk-covered shoulder, meeting her father's gaze above Stella's head. In his eyes she saw her own feelings: resignation. They would go to London. But Lily had no idea what would happen then. She only knew she couldn't be afraid. Rose and Violet were counting on her to help them make their own choices for the future and she would never let them down.

Chapter One

London—*the next springtime*

There were two hours, thirty-eight minutes and four seconds left before she could run away.

Lily carefully studied the clock set high on a marble pedestal in Lady Crewe's ballroom. It was a lovely clock, all gilt and pastel porcelain flowers lavished around enamelled numbers that kept perfect time. A lovely clock in a lovely ballroom, one of the few in the London town house, with its polished parquet floors crowded with satin slippers and patent dancing pumps, tall windows set in the blue silk walls, half-open to let in the cool breezes from Green Park, and arches of glossy greenery and fragrant hothouse gardenias. An orchestra was hidden in a gallery high above their heads, playing lively waltzes and polkas, the music blending with waves of laughter. One wall was lined with mirrors, reflecting the dancers back to themselves, and reflecting Lily in her pale pink satin gown trimmed with antique lace, her grandmother's pearls around her neck.

Lady Crewe's invitations were much sought after, Lady Heath had assured Lily's mother. She was friends

with the Prince of Wales and many of his Marlborough
House set. They set the style now, with their fine clothes
and dashing manners. It was a great triumph to be asked
there as a newcomer, an American, and Lily certainly
couldn't refuse her mother when Stella was so overcome
with triumphant delight. It was what she had been working towards ever since they arrived in London and started
tiptoeing carefully to tea parties and charity luncheons,
meeting the right people, undergoing the closest scrutiny.

Lily sighed, shifting on her own satin slippers as she
leaned on a pillar in her hiding place behind a bank of
potted palms. She'd seen so little of what she was dreaming of in London, no museums or historical buildings,
just drawing rooms and park pathways, where she sipped
tea and led her horses down bridle paths, trying not to
hear the whispers, or see the speculative glances. *Another dollar princess, come bounding over to snatch up
a coronet—how much does she have, do you think?*

This ball was no different. She smiled and laughed
with her sisters in their rented bedroom as they helped
her dress, concealing from them how she longed to hide
every time she ventured out to face that curiosity.

She'd danced twice before she could scurry away and
find this quiet spot. She peeked between the green fronds
again, studying the gowns, since she had promised to
tell Rose and Violet every detail. Violet longed to photograph it all, though so far she had been confined to the
park with her camera. The fashions in London, except
for Americans like herself who had already married their
English husbands, were not as grand as in New York and
Newport, not as crisp with silk and lace newness, not as
bright in their colours. But the swirl of them all together
along the length of the floor was lovely, like the stained-
glass windows of an old church.

Much lovelier to watch than be trapped in the middle of it all.

The beautiful clock suddenly struck the hour, playing a tinkling little song as the porcelain cupids cavorted, startling Lily from her close studies of the dancers. She laughed as she remembered how Violet had accused her of reading fairy tales, and she had declared there were no happy endings. But did the chimes mean the coach of her dreams was suddenly going to turn into a pumpkin, like Cinderella's did?

She envisioned all the dancers, in their bright gowns and black suits, their old jewels, suddenly sprouting gigantic orange heads and the idea of it made her laugh harder. She pressed her gloved hand tight over her mouth, trying to hold it all back. It would never do to give away her hiding place! If Mother or Lady Heath found her…

'Laughter at Lady Crewe's ball? Shocking,' a voice said behind her. The voice was deep, as smooth as a length of velvet, full of suppressed laughter.

Lily whirled around, her heart beating fast, startled at being found out in her hiding place.

For an instant, she felt quite frozen at the sight of the man who stood there, half hidden by more of the leafy palms. He was quite, quite beautiful, almost unreal, like something in one of her books, suddenly sprung into real, vivid, colourful life.

Like all the other men in the ballroom, he wore the regulation suit of evening clothes, severely tailored black coat, white cravat pinned with a small cameo, and cream-coloured satin waistcoat, but on him it all seemed so very…different. So intriguing.

He was taller than most of her dance partners, much taller than her own meagre five foot three, with entic-

ingly broad shoulders and lean hips, long legs encased
in close-fitting dark trousers.

His hair was a gold-tinged brown, almost tawny as if
he spent much time in the sun. Lily couldn't see how that
was possible in such a grey place as London. It gave him
an enticing glow, a warmth she feared she wanted to get
closer and closer to, as if he could melt the ice around her
at last. Unlike the other men's tightly pomaded coiffures,
it fell in unruly waves over his brow and the velvet collar
of his coat, and was enticingly soft-looking.

He didn't seem as if he belonged in the sparkling, ar-
tificial hothouse of the ballroom. Lily thought he should
be on the deck of a ship, prowling through the sea mist,
or riding a wild horse madly across the open fields, taking every fence amid joyful, unfettered laughter.

Or grabbing a sighing, melting woman up into his
arms and kissing her passionately until she swooned.

Oh, yes. Lily could picture *that* all too well.

He ran his hand through his hair, rumpling it even
more, and smiled at her. Lily swayed at the brilliant sight
of it and reached out to brace herself on one of Lady
Crewe's flower-covered arches. Dear heavens, but he was
beautiful. She had never seen eyes so very green before,
like their hostess's emerald necklace, deep and dark, set
in a lean, sculpted face touched with the gold of the sun.

Who was he? She was quite sure she'd never seen him
before, for he would have been impossible to forget. He
was probably untitled, some poor younger son, and her
mother would disapprove of Lily 'wasting time' with
such a man. *Such* a man, one she could only have imagined in a book before.

Now here he was, dropped right in front of her, smiling down at her. Her heart pounded, drowning out the
chatter, the music. She couldn't breathe. Surely he could

hear it, too, pounding through the silk and lace of her new gown?

She glanced back over her shoulder at the ballroom, half sure she'd nodded off in her hiding place and was dreaming. She felt cold and burning up at the same time, as if she had a fever. She shivered and wrapped her arms tightly around herself as she watched the dancers. It was all exactly the same out there. But she wondered, with a daring, hopeful, fearful spark, if suddenly everything had changed.

She closed her eyes tightly for a moment. When she opened them, he was still there. Not a dream after all, but a wonderful, wonderful reality.

She laughed again. She just couldn't help it.

He was just as gorgeous on second look, with an enticing dimple set deep in his clean-shaven cheek, but now his brow was creased in a small frown. He watched her with cautious, narrowed eyes, as so many people in London did.

Lily went cold all over again. *Of course*—he was Prince Charming and she was still the gauche American who didn't know the proper thing to do, no matter how much she read and studied. At home, she was considered the careful paragon of politeness, but here she always seemed to put her foot wrong.

It had never been of consequence before, not really. After all, no matter what her mother thought or hoped, Lily didn't intend to marry and stay in England, not if she could help it. Not if she could find another way to set her sisters up in life. But now, with this man, it seemed to matter so very much.

She bit her lip uncertainly. She hadn't been introduced to this man; she knew very well it was most improper to speak to him, whether at home in New York or here in

London. But she suddenly realised she'd been standing there in silence, like a veritable ninny, punctuated only by bursts of laughter. Surely he thought she was a lunatic.

That was the last thing she wanted Prince Charming to think about her.

'I am sorry,' she said at last. She felt her cheeks burn all over again when she heard how breathless she sounded. She swallowed and started again. 'I know it's rude to laugh and also to hide behind the decorations. I do hope you aren't related to our hostess.'

He smiled again and his eyes crinkled enticingly at the corners. Lily was startled once more by how very green they really were—quite unreal, in fact. It made her feel even sillier, even more giddy. 'So that I would tattle on you for running away? That would be most hypocritical of me, since I am obviously doing the same thing.'

Lily laughed. 'So you are. Most wicked of you not to dance.' She peeked towards the row of gilded chairs along the blue silk walls, where girls sat like flowers amid their white and yellow and pink skirts, whispering to each other behind their fans or watching the dancers with wistful eyes. Surely any one of them, proper pedigreed English ladies, would kill to have one dance with a man like this, untitled or not.

But he was here with her, in their own quiet little world, and Lily found she never wanted to leave this flowery bower. Never wanted to stop looking at him.

'Well, I have been gone from England for some time, so I fear my manners have become terribly barbaric,' he said.

Lily tilted her head to the side as she studied him again. That explained the touch of sun-gold in his hair, the warmth of his skin, the unfashionable lack of any beard. Had he been on a sunny island? The plains of remotest Africa? She longed to know more, to know *everything*. She had only known him for a moment, but she already wanted so, so much more.

She had never felt that way before.

'We have that in common, then,' she said. 'I am finding myself very slow to learn the manners here, too. As soon as I think I know them, they change on me.'

He laughed that deep, velvety sound that seemed to slide over her skin. 'You are American?'

'How can you tell?' she asked, chagrined. 'I left my Stetson hat at home tonight. I was told it was not at all *de rigeur.*'

He shook his head, that smile lingering. 'Your gown is the height of fashion and could not be lovelier. It's your accent. I spent some time in America myself.'

He thought she looked *lovely*? Lily bit her lip to keep from giggling, but she couldn't stop the warmth that flooded through her. 'Where in America, sir?'

'In Colorado, mostly. An astonishing place.'

'Colorado?' Lily was surprised. Most foreigners never went west of Boston, as indeed she herself never had, except for visits to their grandmother in Charleston. Yet she had read so much of the West, of the vast mountains and glowing deserts, and was fascinated. 'How amazing. I've always wanted to see such things; they don't seem as if they could be real in the paintings. But Mama says it would be much too dangerous in such a lawless place.'

His smile widened, that dimple deepening, and Lily was thrilled to see he looked quite rakish. She could see him in some Western saloon, striding up some mountain. 'And she would be absolutely right. The mountains can be frightfully dangerous. But lots of fun just the same. London isn't much for fun, I fear.'

Lily laughed. She was even more intrigued by him.

One thing was for certain, she felt more comfortable, more alive, here with him in these few moments than she had in all the grey, English days so far. 'I should love to see it one day. Though perhaps I should learn to shoot before I do. I'm sure lawn archery games in Newport aren't really sufficient practice.'

'I'd be happy to assist in such endeavours at any time.' He still smiled down at her, amazingly, and showed no signs of wanting to run away from her American manners. 'But since I can't whisk you off to Colorado tonight, maybe I could beg for a dance instead?'

'A dance?' Lily suddenly felt the cold touch of uncertainty again. She glanced towards the dance floor. The polka was ending and a new waltz forming, couples taking their places. She glimpsed her mother standing with Lady Heath on the other side of the room, her amethyst tiara glinting fiery purple as she craned her neck, looking for someone. No doubt looking for Lily.

'I fear we haven't actually been introduced,' she said. 'My mother would not approve.'

His dimple deepened and he leaned closer. He smelled delicious, too, like something spicy and clean. 'I'm afraid it would take too long to find someone to introduce us and I'm much too impatient a man to wait for the next dance.' He reached out and took her gloved hand in his. He bowed low over it, making her laugh. 'How do you do? My name is Aidan and I promise I have no wicked intentions.'

Lily pursed her lips, pretending to be doubtful. He did make her feel so very daring. Perhaps she couldn't run away to the Colorado mountains, but she could surely dance with a man who only had a first name.

And a lovely name it was. *Aidan.* She turned it over in her mind, the musical sound of it.

She gave a little curtsy. 'How do you do, Aidan. I am Lily.'

'There, now we are introduced. Well enough for a dance, anyway. If you'll do me the honour?'

She could only nod, afraid she would burst into delighted laughter if she spoke. He offered her his arm and she slid her own on to it lightly. As he led her out of their hidden bower on to the dance floor, she could feel the taut strength of him under her touch. He was surely no lazy club-sitting English gentleman.

She could hear the whispers rise up behind her as they took their place on the floor, just as they always did, but now she didn't care at all. They could titter about her American money and American manners all they wanted, as long as she could look into Aidan's green eyes.

They found a space at the edge of the gathered couples and Aidan laid his hand lightly on her waist, drawing her closer. She could feel the heat and strength of it through her satin gown, her corset, and she leaned towards him.

The orchestra launched into a Viennese waltz. Lily's many, many dancing lessons, spinning around her mother's ballroom with the funny little Italian dancing master while her sisters applauded from the musicians' gallery, were the only thing that guided her steps now. She couldn't think about the intricate steps, the spins and twirls, the patterns around and between the other couples. She could only think about, only see, the man who held her.

The room blurred around her and she held tightly to his shoulder. He spun her around faster and faster, making her laugh, and his smile was all too fascinating as he looked down at her. She wanted it to go on and on.

Only as the music wound to a stop, when the giddy whirl slowed and ceased, did she become aware of anything other than those intensely green eyes watching her, the warmth of his touch on her waist. Without the music and the swish of all those yards of silken skirts, she could hear the whispers again.

'…the new American girl,' someone nearby said with a muffled giggle. 'Coal mines, they say. Her mother must be so proud now.'

There were other voices, other words, all around like a fractured kaleidoscope, but somehow the titter seemed amplified in Lily's ears. It was certainly nothing she hadn't heard a hundred times since they arrived in London. She had learned to pretend she couldn't hear them, that they couldn't reach the world in her head, and usually they couldn't.

But that was before she met Aidan. Now, the embarrassment, the knowledge that he would hear, would know, that he might think she was here to trade dollars for titles, made her want to sink into the parquet floor. She dared to peek up at him and he smiled down at her.

'Miss Wilkins, dear, there you are,' she heard Lady Heath say, her cut-glass voice full of determined cheer. 'I am glad to see you are enjoying yourself tonight.'

Lily stepped back from Aidan. It felt so cold without his warm touch and the real world crept even closer. She turned to find Lady Heath, her mother's 'sponsor' in London society, watching her with a bright smile. Her dark blue gown and pearls, her simple blonde hairstyle, were all in the best, quietest taste, but her dark eyes saw everything.

'And you, Duke,' Lady Heath continued. As Lily watched, shocked, she gave Aidan a low curtsy. 'You have always claimed to be such a poor dancer. I fear no one will believe you now.'

Aidan's smile turned rueful and he ran his hand

through his hair, tousling the waves all over again. 'Lady Heath, you have found me out. But I am only a passable dancer made better because I found such a lovely partner.'

'I'm glad to see you have made the acquaintance of my young friend Miss Wilkins,' Lady Heath said, a hint of censure in her voice, though her smile never faltered. 'If I had known the Duke of Lennox was here...'

The Duke of Lennox? Shocked, Lily instinctively backed away from him. He looked nothing like any duke she could ever imagine. Too young, too handsome, too... free. And she had been dancing with him! Now surely the whispers would really flow. The American hunting for a duke...

No wonder everyone was staring. This was what they were all sure she was after from the moment her family arrived in England. A title—a *ducal* title—bought and paid for.

And for a moment she had been silly enough to think this was a fairy tale. That he could touch her hand and everything else—her mother and all her expectations; the English nobility, who looked at her as if she was some exotic creature in a zoo; her sisters, who relied on her so much, waiting for her back at their rented house—could all vanish. That she was just Lily and he was just Aidan, the man with the beautiful green eyes, who made her laugh and danced so wonderfully.

But he was a duke. That most sought-after, most elusive gem that her mother would seek at any price. Did he think that of *her*, too?

She dared a quick peek at him. His expression, which had been so open, so laughing in their hidden bower, was closed behind a polite smile. He didn't look at her.

'Lily, darling, there you are!' her mother trilled, coming up to slide her arm around Lily's waist. 'Lady Heath and I have been looking for you everywhere, but I see we needn't have worried.'

'Duke, may I present my friends, Mrs Coleman Wilkins of New York City and her daughter, Miss Lily Wilkins?' Lady Heath said smoothly. 'Of course, you have already met. Your mother would scold me terribly if she could see how I have been neglecting you, not making sure you have all the important introductions, Duke.' Lady Heath smiled at Mrs Wilkins. 'The Duchess was my friend at school. I have known her son since he was in leading strings.'

'Mama would be enchanted by your new friends, Lady Heath, as I am. How do you do, Mrs Wilkins? Miss Wilkins?' Aidan said as he bowed over her radiant mother's hand before turning to Lily.

Lily still couldn't quite think of him as a *Duke*. His hand still felt so warm on hers, so strong. But his smile was so horribly polite now.

Her mother gave one of her trilling Southern laughs and waved her painted silk fan. 'We have heard of you, of course, Your Grace, even all the way across the Atlantic. I've read that your home, Roderick Castle, has parts dating back to the thirteenth century and that King Charles II once hid in the stables as he fled that dreadful Cromwell. And that you have your own Wren chapel! It must all be terribly thrilling.'

Lily was astonished, but she knew she shouldn't be. Of course her mother would have read up on her quarry before coming to England. The Duke laughed and Lady Heath's smile became the tiniest bit strained.

'It seems you know more about my home than I do, Mrs Wilkins,' he said. 'There are parts that are very old indeed, though. My brother and I used to play hide and seek behind crumbling old stone walls. Perhaps one day you will come to Kent and see it for yourself. I would love to hear your opinion.'

Lily's mother laughed again, and her fan waved even more furiously. 'Oh, Lily and I would adore that! We've seen nothing yet outside London and Lily loves history.'

The Duke looked down at Lily. His eyes were darker, but she looked deeply into them, seeking any hint of the man she had just danced with. 'Is that so, Miss Wilkins?'

It *was* so. Lily thought of the stacks of books in her room, of all the places she longed to see, to ask about. But she was too burningly aware of the polite way he looked at her now, of the whispers that rose and fell like ocean waves behind her back.

'Yes,' was all she could say. She immediately wanted to slap herself for being a ninny, but her tongue wouldn't come untied.

'I've been away from England a long time myself, Miss Wilkins,' he said. 'I find I have much to rediscover.'

'Perhaps your mother will soon give a party at Roderick, Duke, so we can all rediscover it,' Lady Heath said. 'I know she has missed you a great deal.'

Lily saw an unreadable glance pass between them and Aidan seemed to retreat from them even further. But before they could say anything else, they were interrupted by their hostess, who stepped to the front of the room.

'Ladies and gentlemen, if you would care to find your partners for the quadrille,' Lady Crewe said. The dance before supper, when everyone would pair off for the meal.

'Oh! Lily does so enjoy a quadrille,' Mrs Wilkins said, with a pointed look at the Duke.

Lily felt a rush of panic. She didn't want him to be *forced* to dance with her now, not after that lovely first dance! That one memory she had before he found out who she really was.

'I fear my head aches terribly, Mother,' she whispered.

'And I fear I have kept my new friends out for too many late nights,' Lady Heath said with a laugh. 'Let me call my carriage for you at once, Mrs Wilkins. It will take you both home. We must be sure Miss Wilkins feels entirely the thing for the opera tomorrow night. It is Signora Malomar's last appearance in London, you know, and they do say the Prince of Wales will be there. Excuse us, please, Duke.'

Lady Heath firmly took Mrs Wilkins by the arm and led her away through the crowd. Lily turned to follow when she felt a gentle touch on her hand. Though it was fleeting, it was as warm and alluring as summer sun.

She looked up at Aidan, at the *Duke*, and at last he smiled at her again. Really smiled at her. 'I hope we shall meet again soon, Miss Wilkins,' he said quietly.

'Old King Coal,' Lily heard someone say nearby and she shivered. Were the whispers, or his eyes, stronger? 'I do hope so,' she whispered and slid her hand away. She rushed after her mother, trying not to run like some wild American, not to seem as if she was fleeing from them. At the door she glimpsed a lady, golden-haired, beautiful, a small half-smile on her face surveying the ballroom as if she owned it. Lily quite envied her that feeling of belonging.

Then the lady's smile faded a bit and Lily followed her gaze. The beautiful woman watched the Duke.

'Lily, do hurry! If you must insist on leaving...' her mother called impatiently.

'Oh, yes, I'm coming,' Lily answered, and turned away from the gorgeous woman who watched the Duke with narrow-eyed, intense interest. As if she knew him well, as if he was hers.

But even as the crowd closed in behind Lily, a thick

jungle of satins and diamonds, she thought she could still feel him watching her. And part of her, the unruly part that always had to be so tightly locked down, wanted nothing more than to run right back to him.

Chapter Two

'So, you have met my new little protégée?'

Aidan, Duke of Lennox, didn't turn around at the sound of Lady Heath's amused voice. He stood on the Crewes' terrace, looking out over the darkened gardens at the expanse of Green Park beyond. It was quiet there, apart from a few whispering couples stealing a moment alone, and no one stared at him with speculation in their eyes. *Been away so long...his poor mother...when the brother died...*

He liked the quiet better. It reminded him of the mountains, of the vast, silent, majestic places where he was just a man before nature and not a duke. But he found this hiding place wasn't nearly as interesting as the one he had found behind the potted palms in the ballroom.

'Your protégée, is she, Lady Heath?' he said, as non-committally as possible. He knew any words of his, especially ones concerning marriageable young ladies, would find their way directly to his mother at Roderick Castle.

Lady Heath laughed and came to lean beside him on the cold marble balustrade. She gestured towards the thin, exotic cheroot between his fingers, sending its sweet-scented, silvery smoke out into the night. 'Your mother would be appalled at such a habit, you know.'

He smiled down at her. Even though she was his mother's bosom bow, the Duchess's partner in helping keep the Prince of Wales and his set happy and spending money neither of them possessed, he had always been very fond of her. She was like his honorary aunt, kind and funny, and he was glad to see her again.

Even if she did have that hard, matchmaking gleam in her eyes he had come to recognise all too well since his brother had died and he became the Duke.

'Are you going to write to Mama to tell on me, Aunt Eleanor?' he said.

'Not if you give me a tiny little puff, darling.' Lady Heath laughed as he handed her the cheroot. She inhaled delicately and coughed. 'Perfectly vile. From one of your mountains?'

'Of course. A dreadful habit, I know, and I intend to give it up very soon. They're American—like your new friend.'

Lady Heath smiled through the smoke. 'She's rather sweet, isn't she? Not at all like the last one I took on. It was all I could do to keep that one from dancing on the table tops, or calling the Prince "Tum-Tum"—surely only *you* could ever do that with impunity. Though she did marry a baronet in the end. I have higher hopes for Miss Wilkins.'

Hopes like a ducal coronet? Aidan stared out into the night, but he didn't really see the pinpoints of carriage lights beyond the park, the rustle of the wind in the thick green trees. He only saw Lily Wilkins, her wide, soft brown eyes, her shy smile. Lady Heath was right—Miss Wilkins was sweet. Very sweet. That was why he should stay away from her and why he was so drawn to her.

'What did you think of her, Aidan dear?' Lady Heath asked quietly.

What had he thought about her? He had thought he wanted the dance to go on longer, so he could keep touching her, feeling her sway towards him. But then he had heard who she really was—an American coal heiress.

American money was becoming the saviour of many an old house. Aidan had seen all the despairing estate reports on Roderick Castle—roofs leaking, floors buckling, artwork sent off to auction. Roderick was his responsibility now, centuries of Lennox history on his shoulders, and he had come back to save it any way he could.

Maybe even marriage to an heiress.

But he hadn't expected Lily Wilkins, the sweetness of her. Or the biting bitterness at what he had to do.

'She was rather nice,' he said. 'A very fine dancer.'

Lady Heath gave a satisfied little smile. 'I think she would rather stay at home with her books, but all in all she's not bad, rather biddable. She has two younger sisters to think of and her mother is certainly most insistent that Miss Lily fit in here in London.'

He wasn't sure someone as pretty and fresh as Lily Wilkins could ever 'fit in' in the old, grey ballrooms of London, nor in the dashing new set of the Prince of Wales, but that was a good thing. He had never fit in, either. 'And has she?'

Her smile widened. 'You tell me, darling. You were the one dancing with her. Everyone will be chattering about that tomorrow.'

Aidan groaned. He had almost forgotten in his months of wandering free in the mountains how fast a choice bit of gossip spread through society.

Lady Heath laughed. 'The burden of a duke. Come visit me soon, Aidan dear. I am dying to hear all about your grand adventures. Perhaps I shall have a party and invite Miss Wilkins. You can gauge her manners better then.'

Aidan knew he shouldn't. It would only fan the gossip even higher, yet he found himself saying, 'I will, thank you, Aunt Eleanor.'

'Don't thank me. It will be quite the feather in my cap to have the Duke of Lennox in my humble little drawing room.' She handed back the half-smoked cheroot. 'We should return to the ball, I think. Miss Wilkins is gone, but the other pretty debs will want a dance.'

'That's quite what I'm afraid of.' Aidan took one more inhale on the cheroot, but the sharp bite of the smoke didn't quite distract him from what waited in the ballroom. When he was younger, before he left England, the ladies had sought him out—but now it was different. Now their intentions were much more honourable, but he wasn't sure his were.

If only the pretty Miss Wilkins was there to dance with him again, with her intriguing eyes staring up into his.

He laughed at his own folly. Adorable Miss Wilkins might be, and charming in her soft innocence, she had a part to play here, too. As much as they both might like it, there was no escaping what they were.

He ground out the cheroot and offered Lady Heath his arm to lead her back to the ballroom. He wondered exactly how long he had to stay before he could politely make his escape. All his time away from England had made his social skills rusty.

Supper was not quite over, but a few people had drifted back into the ballroom, milling around whispering and laughing in a haze of champagne punch. Some of them came to greet Aidan, to welcome him back to London, invite him to tea or dinner or a shooting Friday to Monday once the Season was over. The orchestra played a low, buzzing symphony above their heads.

'Who shall you dance with next, Aidan?' Lady Heath whispered. 'Miss Whiting-Hayes? Or Lady Arabella Martindale?'

'None of them are as pretty as your American protégée,' Aidan teased. 'Or as you, Aunt Eleanor. Maybe you would dance with me?'

She laughed. 'My dancing days are past, I fear. But I am glad you think Miss Wilkins is pretty. I do say that—'

Suddenly, the door at the top of the dining room opened and a party of people appeared after their supper. Aidan froze at the sight of them, for in their very midst, like a rose in red and black velvet, was Lady Rannock.

Melisande. He'd known he would have to see her again, of course, for her name was always prominent in all the society news. Lady Rannock at Marlborough House, at the Goodwood races, at Chatsworth, dancing, hunting, riding new-fangled bicycles. But he hadn't foreseen it would be so sudden, so unexpected.

That she would still be so beautiful, this woman who had once laughingly thrown him over because he was not the ducal heir, then tried to run back to his arms. The woman who had broken his poor brother's heart so terribly.

Melisande's pale, silvery hair glistened in the candlelight, piled high and held with a ruby tiara. She was laughing at something one of her companions said, her head tilted back so her rosy skin caught the light. Two men leaned close to her, clinging to her every word, and neither of them were the elderly Lord Rannock.

Aidan watched her as if caught in a dream—or a nightmare. For an instant he could only remember how she had once made him feel, so young and foolish. So free. And then the way she betrayed him, and worse, betrayed poor Edward. Now—now he only felt strangely numb. As if he stood in the middle of a freezing mountain ice storm.

He was no longer that stupid young man.

Melisande looked up and saw him. Her famously brilliant smile flickered, turned downwards at the edges, before it flamed even brighter. She waved a gloved hand at him and Aidan turned away.

'You remember Lady Rannock, I'm sure,' Lady Heath said drily. 'She has been asking your mother about you lately.'

'Has she?' Aidan murmured. 'I can't imagine why.'

'Was she not a great friend of yours once? And of Edward?'

Edward—his brother, who was meant to be the Duke. Yes, she had certainly been a friend of his. Aidan glanced down at Lady Heath sharply, but she just gave him an innocent smile.

'Lady Rannock can surely wait,' she said. 'You promised me a dance, I think.'

Aidan laughed. Yes, seeing Melisande was a surprise, surely just the first of many, but he was older now. Harder. 'And you said your dancing days were behind you.'

'I think there's life in these old feet yet.'

He led her on to the dance floor as a mazurka formed and Lady Rannock was lost in the crowd.

But it wasn't Melisande's sky-blue eyes he thought of when he finally escaped a few hours later to his bachelor rooms. It was Miss Wilkins and the soft, shy light of her dark eyes as she looked up at him as they spun in the dance.

Chapter Three

Lily felt the pierce of light through the haze of her dreams, unwelcome and cold, and heard the swoosh of curtains being pushed back, the clink of china on a silver tray. *Morning*—how awful. In the bliss of sleep, she'd still been dancing, gliding over a parquet floor as if her slippers had wings, carried higher and higher on a cloud of song by a pair of strong arms. Nothing could touch her there, hurt her, she was so wonderfully free. No longer alone.

And when she peeked up in that dream world, there was a pair of gloriously beautiful green eyes smiling down at her, only her. Only *her*, Lily, not the coal heiress. There was nothing in the world but the two of them, dancing and dancing...

'Your tea, Miss Lily? Mrs Wilkins wants to see you in the morning room as soon as you're ready,' her maid, Doris, said, tearing apart the last shreds of that lovely dream as if it was a piece of old tulle. 'Lady Heath is calling later.'

Lady Heath. Lily knew why *she* was coming. To gloat over Lily's dance with a duke in front of all London society. In her dream, he was just Aidan, of the beautiful smile, the gentle touch on her hand, the strong shoulders she held as they waltzed. But really he was a duke. Her mother's highest quarry.

Lily longed to groan and pull the satin quilts over her head, to ignore Doris, her mother, Lady Heath, London society, everyone, and dive back down into dreams. But she knew very well that a lady wouldn't behave that way. And she'd been taught, above all things, all her life, to be a lady.

She opened her eyes and pushed herself up against her pillows to face the day. Doris held out a steaming cup of tea with one biscuit—always only one—on the edge of the saucer and Lily smiled up at her. It wasn't Doris's fault Lily felt all at sea that morning, as if something deep and fundamental had shifted. Doris had been her ally for years, ever since she became Lily's personal maid when they were both only sixteen. Her mother had wanted a French maid, of course, not a girl who had started as a housemaid at the Newport cottage, but Lily had always liked laughing with Doris and begged and begged for the promotion. For once she had got her way and now she had a friend to depend on behind the scenes.

'Thank you, Doris,' Lily said hoarsely and reached for the tea. It was blessedly hot and strong, giving her strength to face the morning.

Doris went about tidying the room, picking up the ballgown discarded across a *chaise* and shaking out its rumpled folds. How magical it felt wearing it last night, sweeping its satin train across the floor with Aidan!

'How was the ball, then, Miss Lily?' she asked, checking stockings and petticoats for any tears that could be mended. 'Not as boring as you feared?'

'No. Not boring at all, in the end.' She smiled as she thought of that music, that dance.

'I knew you'd like it, once you were there! Did the Prince of Wales come?' Doris was obsessed with royalty and cut out every newspaper snippet she could find about Prince Bertie and Princess Alexandra for her scrapbook. Their glamor brightened even a grey day.

'No. I don't think he could possibly go to every house where he's invited.' She felt bad when Doris looked terribly disappointed by the lack of royal sightings. 'But Lady Heath thinks she can get me on the list to be presented at the next royal Drawing Room. She says that since the Queen has become so quiet, Princess Alexandra usually presides.'

Doris brightened, no doubt buoyed up by the thought of the ostrich feathers and embroidered trains she would be in charge of arranging. Maybe there would even be a glimpse of her idol, the beautiful Princess, in all her jewels. 'Now, that *would* be grand! She does look so lovely, the Princess. But a bit sad in her photographs.'

Lily thought of the rumours of the Prince's many affairs and thought, if the gossip was true, it was no wonder his wife was sad. Were all English noblemen like that? All *dukes* like that? 'I would imagine she's not always entirely happy. She's a long way from her homeland and family in Denmark. No matter how much she's envied, everyone has sorrows.'

'Now, that's the honest truth, Miss Lily. I wouldn't trade places with her for a thousand dollars, but I wouldn't mind a peek at her wardrobe.' She picked up the pair of satin dancing shoes and clucked over stains on the white fabric, then checked the almost unmarked soles. 'Did you dance much last night? Or did you hide in the corner like last time?'

Lily laughed. Poor Doris had had to listen when Lily's

mother lectured her after the last ball for not making enough *effort.* 'You do know me too well, Doris.'

Doris shook her head, the lace trim of her cap trembling. 'The best way to get away, Miss Lily, to get your own life, is to find someone nice to marry. Your mother can't boss you, then, when you have your own house.'

Lily knew Doris was quite right. Marrying might have its pluses and minuses, but it was essential if she ever wanted her own life, ever wanted to be able to help her sisters find their own independent lives away from their parents. And an ocean between her and Stella wouldn't come amiss sometimes. But the thought of a marriage without real love made her want to sob. Like the Prince and Princess.

She gulped down the last of her tea. Crying would do no one any good at all. 'Well, Doris, you'll be happy to know I *did* dance a few times and I didn't even hate it.' In fact, for a few moments, it had been utterly blissful. But that was *her* secret for now. Probably her own secret for always. The time she danced with a handsome adventurer and he turned out to be Prince Charming. Well, Duke Charming, which in England seemed even better.

Doris beamed. 'That's more like it. I knew England would be more fun than home.' She draped the gown over her arm, along with the frothy lace petticoats. 'Now, I'll go see about your bath. Don't forget Mrs Wilkins wants to see you. She'll be in a flurry with Lady Heath coming.'

Lily sighed. 'When is my mother *not* in a flurry? But you're right, we'll have to hurry. I'll wear that new eau de Nil morning dress. Mother can't find fault with that, it's quite new.' And green would make her think of Aidan's eyes.

Once she was alone, Lily finished her biscuit and studied the chamber around her. It was a rented room in a rented town house, so nothing was her own, but that was not much different from home. Her mother arranged every room in Newport and New York, choosing every carpet and vase and cushion. But Lily thought she rather liked this English room better, with its cosy fireplace and flowered chintz upholstery on every chair and *chaise*. She wondered if she might choose something like it for her own room one day, when she had made her escape.

She thought of Doris's words. If she wanted to get away, to have her own house, make her own decisions, she would have to marry. And marry carefully, to someone who would be kind and understanding, and not just another tyrant to replace her mother.

She leaned over to reach under the edge of her mattress, the only place her mother didn't regularly search, and pulled out a small, red leather notebook. She'd kept the journal for as long as she could remember, especially since coming to Europe, writing all her confused thoughts about the new place and where she fit into it.

She flipped through the pages, covered with lists of what to do and not to do in English etiquette:

> *The charm of good housekeeping lies in a nice attention to little things, not a super-abundance; at table, the hostess should always wear her brightest smile, no matter what occurs.*

There were sketches of castles and ancient bridges and the river. On the last page was a list of gentlemen who had asked for dances or sent her flowers and what Lady Heath said about them all.

The last name was Lord James Grantley. The younger son of a duke, so of course her mother rather liked him even though she would have preferred an elder son, and

Lily thought he did seem nice. He studied sixteenth-century poetry, knew all sorts of history and languages and had lovely brown eyes. She'd put a little star by his name. If she *had* to marry in England, he seemed like just the sort of man she should look for.

She'd hoped to see him again at the Crewe ball, but instead there was the Duke.

Lily frowned as that wondrous dance came flooding back to her. The dazzlement of his eyes, the thrill of his touch. That was how her parents first came together, in a rush of infatuation. Long before her father was 'Old King Coal', he was a law clerk who once danced with a golden-haired Southern belle at a church social and they fell madly in love. That was the story he told everyone and look where an *amour foudre* took them. Separate suites at opposite ends of enormous houses, quarrels and brusque letters. Lily didn't want that for herself and especially not for her sisters. Better someone who could be her friend than someone who evoked such emotions, someone who could like *her* as well as that coal money.

But, oh—the Duke's green eyes…

There was a quick knock at the door and Lily just had time to shove the book back under the bed when her sisters rushed in. Even they looked different here in England, older, taller, their red hair swept up into silver combs and ribbons, their navy serge skirts sweeping the floor. They would be ready to marry, too, sooner rather than later.

Violet ran to jump on the bed next to Lily, sending pillows flying, while Rose followed more sedately to perch on the edge of the dressing table stool.

'Oh, Lily, how was the ball? Do tell us everything!' Violet cried. She snatched the remains of the biscuit from the teacup saucer and stuffed it in her mouth. 'Did you dance all night? I wish I had been there to photograph it all!'

Lily laughed and hugged Violet close. No matter what happened, no matter who she married, she would always have her sisters. How she loved them! 'Not all night, but once or twice. Really, it was all a bit boring and stuffy.'

Violet sighed. 'I can't believe it would be *boring*. Music and gossip, and handsome men falling at your feet! Staying at home practising our French is what is boring. Rose and I are old enough now to be out here in England, why can't we go to balls, I'd like to know? My art will never be inspired this way.'

'Because we don't know anyone in London, so Lily has to meet them for us,' Rose said. 'I think a large ball like that sounds utterly terrifying.'

'I would have much preferred reading French with you two, anyway,' Lily said. Except for her dance with Aidan. But that was her secret for now.

'But once you choose one of your lovely English suitors and have a vast medieval manor house of your own, we can stay with you and go to parties as much as we like, right?' Violet said.

'Who told you I have English suitors?' Lily asked.

'Mother, of course,' Violet answered. 'Isn't that why we're here? To captivate London with your beauty and find a fine English suitor who will be much more cultured than any New York boor?'

'I don't think Lily should ever marry anyone she doesn't like,' Rose said softly. She fiddled with one of the silver combs on the table, a worried expression on her perfect oval face.

'Certainly she shouldn't,' Violet said. 'But surely the men here *must* be more interesting than the ones at home?

The way they always natter on about their yachts and their Wall Street offices...'

'The ones here aren't usually any better,' Lily said. 'Except they natter on about cricket and shooting.' Apart from Aidan. He had made her laugh, made her forget where she really was. Not a word about cricket or shooting.

Doris came into the chamber, the evening gown gone and the green morning dress carefully draped over her arm. 'Your bath is ready, Miss Lily. And Mademoiselle Clemence is looking for Miss Violet and Miss Rose for their lessons.'

Violet rolled her eyes. 'Must we?'

Lily nudged her off the bed. 'You must, if you want to catch a medieval manor with your fine accomplishments. But go along with you both! My bath will be ready soon and I need to make my own plans.' It was better than sitting in the morning room with their mother and Lady Heath, analysing all that went right and wrong at the ball last night. Time to start the day.

Lily tiptoed down the stairs of their house, her kid leather shoes muffled by the old Axminster carpet, and she wished she could run back to her room. To lock the door and escape into her books, forget London and all the expectations landing on her shoulders.

She turned at the landing and hurried down the last of the stairs into the entrance hall. Not that her mother had such terrible taste when it came to gilded cages, Lily thought as she glanced around. Just like their New York house and Newport cottage, this town house was decorated in beautiful, up-to-the-minute fashion. But here, it had an English flavour that was different. As in Lily's bedroom, the colours were lighter, brighter, just a bit shabby at the edges. Portraits of people she did not know, in stiff satins and gleaming pearls, gazed down at her from the moiré-silk-papered walls and fresh white roses were arranged on every table along with silver and porcelain ornaments. Liveried footmen waited by the front door.

This was the sort of cage Stella had designs on locking Lily in for ever—English, historical, correct, elegantly shabby. Only, with *real* family portraits, real silver and china and silk touched by the hands of the same family for generations. And she, Lily, would be expected to be part of that, a link in some old family's chain. Could she do it? Did she *want* to do it?

What were her choices?

Lily stopped in front of a looking glass, Louis XV, framed in gilt, and smoothed her loose Newport knot of waving dark hair. She shook out the skirt of her green dress, with its high lace collar and ruffled lace sleeves, and pinched at her cheeks that looked so pale after her dream-filled night. She pasted a bright smile on her lips, determined to get through the day as pleasantly as possible.

Through the half-open door of the morning room, she heard voices. Lady Heath's crisp tones, her mother's Southern drawl. But her mother didn't sound entirely happy.

'...such a triumph for her, dancing with the Duke of Lennox of all people! But she wouldn't make the most of it. I've told her, she needs to jolly these boys along a bit. Men like a girl who flirts just a little, who seems interested in *them*.'

There was the clink of fine, thin china. 'In America, maybe, Stella dearest, but we are in England, looking at English suitors. Englishmen do also like a girl who laughs and teases—just look at Prince Bertie! He comes alive in the company of such women. But not always in the ladies they marry. They want to marry ladies just like dear Lily. Quiet, well-dressed, sensible, intelligent. A woman who can look good in a coronet, or smoothly run your dinner parties from the foot of the table no matter who the guests might be. She's quite perfect here, really.'

'I should hope so,' Stella said with a sniff. 'I've worked hard enough for years, since the day she was born, fitting her for just such a position.'

So she had. Lily remembered with a shudder the iron posture brace, the hours of drilling in French, the going over and over *Debrett's*.

'Was it for nothing?' Stella went on. 'We've only had proposals from an impoverished French *comte* and the untitled son of a viscount! All very well, but…'

Lily frowned, an image of Henri in Paris flashing in her mind. All his hand-kissing and elaborate compliments…he'd made her laugh, even though his moustache was rather too elaborate. He had proposed? Why hadn't she known? And Mr Lewis, said son of a viscount? He did come from a good family, but spent most of his time talking to her about cricket. And there had been Mr Goelet at home. Stella seemed to like him at first, but then when the England trip came about she had turned on him, the poor boy.

That was when Lily had realised her parents had something more in mind for her.

But what did *she* want? She could hardly begin to know. Giving her own opinions had been discouraged since she was toddler. She only knew she wanted to find happiness for herself and her sisters.

'Well, she did certainly score a great victory last night,' Lady Heath said, satisfaction in her creamy English voice. 'The Duke of Lennox! And he danced with no one else. They're all surely still chatting about that today.'

'Oh, yes,' Stella said with a happy sigh. 'The Duke of Lennox! How handsome he was. They did look well together.' Lily was sure her mother was having rosy visions of Lily and the Duke in velvet robes, processing through Westminster Abbey.

She closed her eyes and tried to imagine it herself, but all she could see was his hand held out to her, his smile as he looked into her eyes.

'Tell me more about him, then,' Stella said and there was the splash of more tea being poured.

'He was the second son, not meant to inherit Roderick Castle. His brother, Edward, was such a paragon, so perfect at Oxford, quite brilliant. He could have been a first-rate Classicist if he was not meant to be the Duke! The boys' father died rather young, you see, after sadly frittering away so much of the old Lennox fortune. It was up to his mother to try to sort it all out when the boys were young. Edward was dutiful, but Aidan did turn wild. Sent down from Oxford for running in such a fast set! Gamblers, pranksters—and even worse.'

'Worse?' Stella gasped and Lily nearly echoed her.

'But then he went off on some archaeological expedition for the British Museum, travelling all over America and the East. And Edward fell in love with the Honourable Melisande Milwood, was expected to marry her, even though…'

'Even though what?' Stella whispered, clearly thrilled.

'Miss Milwood was caught kissing Aidan before he left. At a tea party.'

Stella gasped and Lily felt her stomach lurch at the gossip. 'So Edward was going to marry his brother's cast-off goods?'

'So it seemed. The Duchess was against it, of course, violently so. Then poor Edward died, swam too far off-shore on a trip to Blackpool. Melisande married a Scottish lord, Lord Rannock, and went off to hide herself among the heather...until this Season, when Aidan came back to London at last.'

'Do you think...?' Stella sounded uncertain for the first time. 'Do you think they will revive their old romance?'

'I shouldn't think so,' Lady Heath said firmly. 'Lady Rannock is still married and, anyway, she has no money. If Roderick Castle is to be restored to its former glory, or even made not to fall in, that would never work. And she's not as young as she once was, either. Lennox will need heirs.'

Lily bit her lip, feeling queasy at so much news at once. So the Duke needed a bank balance and a baby—and an heiress to give him both. Did he expect that of her? It hardly seemed likely of the man she'd met on the dance floor, but she was still learning the English way. Maybe it would always be beyond her.

She made herself smile again and stepped into the room as if she'd just arrived. 'Mother.' She kissed the older woman's powdered cheek and sat down on one of the tapestried chairs on the edge of the seat, her ankles crossed, back perfectly straight, chin parallel to the floor, just as she'd been taught. 'And Lady Heath, how lovely to see you today.'

'And you, Lily! How rested you look this morning,' Lady Heath said.

'Have some tea, my dear,' Stella said, pouring from the Sèvres teapot. 'Darling Lady Heath has been telling me of a dinner she's planning, such fun.'

'Just a very small one,' Lady Heath demurred. 'My

tiny abode can bear nothing grand! But the Prince of
Wales has said he could possibly attend, which is quite
the triumph for poor little me. He only requests that some
of these "lovely Americans" attend!' She sighed. 'The
Prince does so enjoy all things American, ever since he
visited New York in the last decade. Your mother has
graciously accepted my invitation.'

Lily felt her breath tighten in her chest. 'The—the
Prince?'

'Yes, and you must sit next to him, of course, and wear
that darling new blue tulle gown,' Lady Heath said. She
drew out her ever-present red morocco leather frame,
filled with little slots where cards could be placed to
make a seating plan. 'See, here will be the Prince and
you, Lily. The Archbishop here and Lady Wondera here.
Lord and Lady Stoneman here—they are so dull, but
Bertie insists on them, for they are great bridge players.
Your mother here and the Duke of Lennox here. The
Duchess can go here.'

The Duke on Lily's other side. Of course. *This* was
what the dinner party was really for. To throw her at the
oh-so-eligible, oh-so-penniless Duke. Of course, she had
already danced with him, laughed with him. But that was
different. It was just for them, two people; she hadn't even
known who he was then. Now it would be Miss Wilkins
and the Duke, with everyone watching them. Speculating about a money match.

Even the Prince of Wales would surely know.

Lily shivered to think of a whole evening stuck between a prince and a duke, trying to think of something
interesting to say, to keep smiling as if she did not care.

'Oh, Lady Heath,' she said beseechingly, 'may I not
sit a bit further down? Maybe…there?' She pointed to
another chair, labelled 'Lord James Grantley'.

'Nonsense!' Lady Heath insisted. 'The Prince will want to see *you*, as I am sure will the Duke. He looked so happy dancing with you last night.'

'But I—' Lily said.

'Don't be such a ninny, Lily!' her mother snapped. 'This is exactly why we came to London. To meet the best society. It's almost the end of the Season; there's not much time left. You cannot turn coward now. Think of your sisters! If *you're* properly established, it will be ever so much easier for them. I've surely brought you up to face any situation. The time to strike has come!'

Lily knew when she was cornered. She gently touched the Duke's place-card. 'Yes. Of course.'

Her mother and Lady Heath went on chatting, talking of which dishes to serve at the dinner, which wines, which flowers. When Lady Heath expressed a concern at the price of champagne, Stella said, 'Oh, my dear, never worry about that! Coleman will happily pay for any wine you want to order!'

Lily sat back to sip at her cooling tea, pretending to listen, but she could only think of the Duke. Would that one dance ever stop haunting her?

Chapter Four

To Aidan's surprise, the dining room of Lennox House wasn't empty as usual when he came down to breakfast. Usually, plates of eggs and toast were laid out on the Chippendale sideboard, beneath the pale squares on the blue wallpaper where paintings once hung. But today there were covered silver warming trays and the table was spread with a white damask cloth and laid with the old Sèvres coffee service.

His mother sat at the end of the table, her silvery-chestnut hair gleaming under a little feathered tip-tilted hat, her pale blue silk morning dress bright in the dusty light from the windows that desperately needed cleaning. She daintily lifted a forkful of kedgeree under the awed study of two housemaids. When she waved them away, they bobbed quick curtsies and left the room.

'Darling!' she cried, her voice as clear and judgmental as church bells. 'There you are at last. Coffee?'

Aidan glanced at the sun filtering through the windows, then at the ormolu clock on the sideboard. It was still early. His mother never roused herself from her own rooms at Claridge's before one at least. His suspicions were immediately stirred.

'Mama,' he said, not moving from the doorway. 'This is a surprise.'

'Oh, darling, surely a mother needs no excuse to visit her only remaining child? Or to visit her old home.' She glanced around the dining room, her sharp-as-glass green eyes taking in the dust on the carved wooden chairs, the worn upholstery cushions. 'Though it is surely not much as I remember it. How merry this place was in our day!'

Her day was much of what ailed Lennox House and Roderick Castle now. His father had spent money as though it was water, leaving them no cushion at all when land values went down. His mother still spent, but Aidan didn't have the time or energy to argue with her. He had been up too late even after returning from Lady Crewe's ball, thinking of Lily Wilkins and her sweet smile. What would breakfast be like with her to talk with him across the table? It was a strangely pleasant image.

He sat down next to his mother and let her pass him a cup of coffee.

'Is Lord Shelton abroad right now?' he asked. The Earl of Shelton was Agnes's longtime lover and now future husband. 'I heard he went to Baden-Baden for his gout.'

She laughed lightly. 'Oh, yes, Arthur *does* love his baccarat! Gout is only his silly little excuse, I'm afraid. He will be back next week.' She reached for the jar of marmalade and carefully studied the handwritten label. It was from Roderick, as usual. 'But I do admit that, while he is away, I've run into a teeny-tiny bit of trouble with my milliner. I wonder, darling, if you could help your old mama in her moment of need?'

Aidan remembered the piles of bills on his desk, growing steeper every day. He gulped down the blessedly strong coffee. 'Mama, you know how the estate stands. This house is close to going on the market and my agent is taking a very close look at the staff at Roderick. The downturn in rents might mean selling some land.'

A frown flickered over her cherubically pretty face and she waved his words away as if such troubles were mere clouds on a sunny horizon. She'd grown up the youngest daughter of a viscount, the wife of a duke, a great beauty and social favourite, and never saw any reason to change her thinking. 'I vow, I can't believe I've lived to see the day when a duchess should worry about her milliner!'

Aidan took another gulp of coffee. 'Believe it, Mama.'

Her bow mouth hardened. 'There is a very easy solution, you know.'

'Oh, yes? Pray tell me, Mama, what an army of agents hasn't been able to find.'

'Because they are *men*. Men are always blind to the practical solutions of life, to what is right before them.' She poured a dollop of cream into her cup and stirred at it carefully. 'I heard you danced with a certain Miss Lily Wilkins last night at the Crewe ball.'

Ah. So that was why his mother had appeared in his house for the first time since he returned to London. Gossip must be raging across town like wildfire. He wished he was back in the jungle, alone, with Edward still in his proper place and Aidan in his.

Though he wouldn't mind if Miss Wilkins was in the jungle with him. Alone in a small tent, her smile glowing up at him…

He pushed away such thoughts and made himself remember who Lily Wilkins really was. An heiress. And he was a penniless duke. 'I might have danced with several girls last night.'

'Lady Heath told me you only danced with one.' She

put down her cup with a little click. 'Do you know how very rich her father is?'

Aidan knew how Miss Wilkins's eyes gleamed with laughter, like a dark star when he spun her around. How small and slim and delicate she felt under his hands. How it was like coming across a fairy hiding behind the pillars of the ballroom, an unexpected gift, a moment away from his worries.

'No, Mama,' he said shortly. How swiftly the dream of a pretty girl died, like sunshine drowned in a hailstorm. He couldn't escape who he really was, no matter how he tried.

'Well, I know it is vulgar beyond thought to mention such things, but you say we are in dire straits. Even I can understand that.' She waved her hand, gleaming with ruby and amethyst rings, around the bare room. 'Your father and your brother were utter darlings, of course, but they had no head for money matters. I would have hoped you were different, Aidan, with all your travels.'

'My work has hardly fitted me for running a ramshackle estate. Or any estate at all.' He had been brought up to know he was not the heir, that he would have to make his own way in the world and he had done that. His travels, through deserts and jungles and mountains, made him able to speak several languages, learn new customs and deal with different people, battle heat and disease and hostile warriors. It was Edward who was meant to be the Duke, to save Roderick.

But Edward was gone. And Aidan had never faced a challenge like assuming the responsibilities of a duke before.

For once, even his mother looked a bit abashed. 'Maybe your education was different from your brother's…'

'Yes.' Edward had done all that was expected from

him and done it beautifully. He had excelled at Oxford, where Aidan found his youthful hijinks got him into trouble all the time. Edward had been the serious one, the focused one, the Duke. Edward was the one who would have won Melisande in the end. Edward, who was gone for ever.

'But now you are the Duke of Lennox. And, if I do say so myself, a very handsome and dashing one. Your poor brother was a shadow to you in that way! And such an impractical heart, rest his soul.' She sighed, as if remembering Edward's love for Melisande. 'You are even famous, Aidan. The brave explorer! Ladies love that.' Her eyes narrowed. 'And Mr Coleman Wilkins is very rich indeed.'

'So your solution for Roderick Castle is that I should marry the man's daughter?'

She frowned at him. 'Oh, pooh, Aidan! How coarse you are becoming. London is not the jungle, you know. Any lady would be fortunate to be the mistress of an estate like Roderick, as I well know. I had many suitors when I was a young lady and I chose your father.' She reached again for her cup and set it back down when she realised she'd sent the maids away. 'An American is not ideal, I admit. Look at the Manchesters' daughter-in-law! She plays the banjo, I believe, yet their roof at Kimbolton was falling in and now it's all tickety-boo. The Prince of Wales seems to like Americans very much indeed and one need hardly pay attention to the old Queen's opinions these days. The Wilkins girl would learn about Roderick, I'm sure.'

'And what if the lady has other ideas for her future?' He remembered how sweet, how shy Lily had seemed as she ducked behind the palms of the ballroom. He didn't want to be the one to crush that sweetness under the heel of a dukedom.

His mother laughed. 'Don't be silly, Aidan! Why would the Wilkinses be here in London otherwise? I hear there are two other daughters, as well, and a fine marriage for the oldest would set them all up. It would solve our troubles in no time.'

Aidan arched his brow at her. 'And set Arthur up for baccarat once you marry?'

'You leave Arthur to me, darling, and worry about your own future married life. And Roderick. I know you care about the estate.'

God help him, but he did. Roderick was in his blood and he would do anything to make sure its people were secure and happy, to see the house as glorious as it had been in his grandfather's day. But enough to marry a sweet fairy girl just for her hard, cold dollars? 'There must be another solution.'

'Such as what? Selling it all off bit by bit until there's nothing left? Just a shell of a house for the future, tenants and servants who have depended on the estate for generations left to starve?'

Aidan scowled, but he had to admit his mother had a point. Roderick was in dire straits and would only get worse if he could not act quickly.

'Much easier to marry, Aidan, and in one "I do" have enough to ensure Roderick's future,' she said firmly. 'You have to marry and have an heir anyway, and Miss Wilkins will do as well as any other girl. I hear she's even quite pretty.'

'She is,' Aidan muttered. 'Very pretty.'

His mother nodded. 'Lady Heath is having a little dinner party. They say the Prince himself will attend. Miss Wilkins is her newest protégée, you know.' Aidan

knew what that meant. Lady Heath had been augment-
ing her meagre income for several Seasons now, welcoming Americans into her home, gently coaxing them
into social shape. 'The last one married an Italian count,
I think, with a glorious Tuscan villa. We must move fast
to secure Miss Wilkins.'

Aidan hated the sound of that—move fast to snare the
unsuspecting prey. Poor, pretty Miss Wilkins. If he only
had a heart to offer her, a proper life, but he'd abandoned
such notions years ago.

Yet—he had to admit that the thought of seeing her
again, seeing her smile, touching her hand, was not at all
unpleasant. In fact, he looked forward to it.

'What do you propose?' he asked cautiously.

His mother gave one of her satisfied, catlike smiles,
as if she had made him see *sense*. As if he would follow
her blindly, as his father and brother had.

How little she knew him.

'As I said, Lady Heath proposes to give a dinner party,'
she said. 'One does hate to travel all the way to a place
like Bayswater, of course. Surely even Lady Heath could
afford some place a tiny bit more fashionable? But needs
must. I will make sure we have invitations and you will
go and dazzle the girl.' She pursed her lips in thought.
'Perhaps I should have a small gathering, as well? A garden party, maybe. Just to take a look at the Wilkins girl
first. If she is *really* unsuitable, best to see now.'

Aidan gave a humourless laugh and took a gulp of
his cold coffee. 'One dinner party and she'll fall at my
feet, eh?'

'Don't be absurd. If she's acceptable, I'll have a house
party at Roderick. The Season is winding down anyway
and any American girl would be quite dazzled by the

place. Between your fine eyes and the house, it should do the trick.'

She was probably right. Not about his eyes, but Roderick, though past its highest glory, was romantic and filled with history. The marble corridors, the brocade-draped chambers, the rolling gardens—they were all lovely in their way. Even he remembered that about the house of his childhood. And Lily Wilkins seemed like a girl who would enjoy history.

'It's not in fit shape for a party,' he said, remembering the damp spots on the ceilings, the shabby carpets, the missing paintings.

'Oh, Aidan, ye of little faith! Roderick can be stage-managed in no time. Miss Wilkins, and more importantly her mama, will love it. Any girl would want to be Duchess of Lennox. And married to a handsome English explorer!' She took a happy bite of her toast. 'Trust me, darling. This is the best solution.'

Aidan wasn't sure he *could* believe her. When it came to his mother, he trusted very little indeed. But he did want to see Lily again. To see his home come alive again in her eyes.

Yes. He wanted to see her very much indeed.

Chapter Five

Lily sat very still in front of the dressing table mirror as Doris fixed her coiffure for Lady Heath's dinner. She was lucky that, though her tresses were dark and not fashionably golden, they were thick and waving, not requiring the pinch of extra hairpieces pinned in. Doris busily wielded the curling tongs and fastened ringlets into place, held with diamond star-shaped clips. The air smelled of singed hair and violet powder.

Though Lily dared not move her head or risk Doris's artistic wrath, she stared out the window as the daylight faded and gaslights winked on, one by one. The days were growing shorter now, London getting quieter as families began to leave town as the Season waned and country houses opened to prepare for the shooting. Time was growing short to do—well, something. Anything, or leave England empty-handed. Lily felt that tension all around her, the crackling anticipation of her mother and sisters and Lady Heath that *something* had to happen at last so they could all move forward again. But she herself felt frozen, like that tiny, ancient amber fly they had seen at the American Natural History Museum.

She couldn't move forward and she couldn't go back.

Lily sighed and longed to pound her fists on the lace-draped table, making the silver brushes and pots and boxes she'd no part in choosing herself rattle and crack. She had always been a quiet sort, dreaming her secret dreams, she knew that. Happiest in her books, her daydreams, half ignoring her mother whenever she could, half following when she had to. Yet she had never thought of herself as indecisive, either, a girl to dither at the crossroads. She knew what she wanted—her own home, her own purpose, the means to help her sisters find their own lives—and she'd been sure one day she would know how to do it.

Lily twisted her hands together to keep from lashing out. Well, here she was, dithering at the crossroads. She'd known before they even left Newport that part of her mother's grand design in going to Europe was to marry off her daughters well, starting with Lily. Preferably for high titles that would make the Knickerbocker matrons of New York who had rejected Stella Wilkins sorry indeed. As 'mother of a countess', or even 'mother of a duchess', she wouldn't be snubbed again. As Stella often lamented, it was too bad all the Royal Princes were already married or too young.

It was easy to shrug all that off at home. Here, now, was a real-life duke right in front of her. A duke who Lady Heath said had his roof falling in, just waiting to be shored up with American dollars. A duke who was more handsome and dashing and fascinating than any man she had ever imagined.

Lily closed her eyes and saw him again. The Duke of Lennox. Aidan. How easy it was to laugh with him, dance with him. How hard everything else seemed.

But did it have to be? He had a shadowy past, with his brother and Lady Rannock, and an estate in need of repair. She should be wary of all that, she *was* wary, but the man himself was so attractive. Too attractive.

When she'd hidden away to read tales of England, of King Arthur and his chivalrous knights, the Crusades, Miss Austen's villages, the Brontes' grey skies and governesses, she had built a vision of England in her mind. An image of grand houses that were a part of history and family and immortality. A part of a neighbourhood, a net woven that encompassed everyone in it, bound them together.

Yet she had not thought a great deal about the real people who must live in such houses, beyond an image of such history. She'd vaguely thought they must be grey and fusty, bound to the past. Aidan wasn't like that at all. He was golden and vibrant, so alive. So full of secrets, too.

Her mother and Lady Heath might think that by plopping her down next to the Duke at dinner all would be well. But Lily was not so sure. Aidan seemed like a man who knew so much, had seen so much. Was he bored with London life, with young ladies like her?

Perhaps it was true and he could be the key to the new life she longed for. She had to think of her sisters. What kind of life did *they* deserve? A wealthy man's wife in America, even one miraculously accepted by Mrs Astor, had no real role to play in the world. Those ladies faded away into their own plush houses, into the shadows. In England, Lily had seen, a lady could do more, even bound as she still was by marriage and family. Ladies in London had salons, literary societies, political groups, ran charities, helped others. Surely fiery Violet and gentle Rose would fare better here, with her to help them—and protect them from their mother, as there was no one to protect Lily.

She thought again of Lord James Grantley, of how intellectual and kind he had appeared, how he had seemed the sort of man she should look for. So different from Aidan, with his golden sun-god looks, intimidating title and his past.

When Lord James touched her hand, it had been— pleasant. Sweet. Not at all like when Aidan had touched her and she felt the crackle of fire against her skin. A breathless thrill. But surely it was Lord James who could give her what she needed? And she did not even know the state of *his* roof.

She took a deep breath. She had to stop dreaming now and start *doing*. Taking control of this England plan herself. Starting tonight.

'There, Miss Lily. What do you think?' Doris said.

Lily dragged herself away from her distractions and turned back to the mirror. For an instant, she didn't recognise herself. Usually her hair was caught back in a simple twist, maybe decorated with a flower or two as all young ladies did. Tonight, Doris had copied a guide from a ladies' magazine and done it *à la Alexandra*, a style made popular by the Princess of Wales. It was drawn high and curled, fastened with those diamond stars and framing her brow with a loose fringe. It made her look older, sophisticated. But not at all like herself.

'Oh, Doris,' she murmured. 'You've quite outdone yourself. It's very—well, stylish. But surely it's a tiny bit…er…mature for me?'

'Mrs Wilkins's orders for the evening. And she says you're to wear this. I've specially pressed it and everything.' Doris nodded at the bed, where a gown of silver brocade trimmed with midnight-blue velvet and swansdown waited, rustling stiffly.

Lily stared at it, open-mouthed. It was not the blue

tulle Lady Heath had suggested. It was a creation from
Monsieur Worth in Paris; her mother had insisted on including it among the piles of simpler silks and muslins
and tulles suitable for a young lady. It had a deeper décolleté than anything else Lily had worn and was more
elaborate, richer.

'I can't wear that,' she protested. 'It's just a small dinner party! I will feel…too much.'

'Your mother said so, Miss Lily,' Doris said firmly.
Doris was her friend, but even Lily had to admit that
Stella paid the wages. 'It's the only gown I've pressed.
And just look at those gorgeous sleeves! You will be the
most elegant lady there.'

That was what Lily was afraid of. No deb she had seen
in London could be called 'elegant'. But she saw she had
no choice. The minutes were ticking away on the little
Louis XVI clock on the mantel and they would have to
leave soon or be late. No one could arrive after the Prince,
Lady Heath had said. Between tardiness and looking like
the Queen of Sheba, she would have to choose Sheba.

Lily sighed and stood up to unfasten her lace dressing
gown. Doris bustled around her, tightening her corset,
lowering the elaborate gown into place, straightening
the velvet sleeves. It was stiff and itchy against her skin.

'There! Now see, Miss Lily, you do look beautiful,'
Doris said, her voice filled with the satisfaction of a job
well done.

And it *was* well done, Lily saw as she glanced in the
full-length mirror. Doris would make a fine lady's maid
to a titled Englishwoman. Every fold of the heavy, elaborate gown was perfectly straight, every jewel exquisite.
She looked like a fashion plate, from the diamond stars
in her hair to the tips of her white satin shoes.

She looked like a duchess. A young, scared duchess.

The door flew open and her mother rushed in, dressed just as perfectly for her role as 'a proper duchess's mother' in amber cut velvet and a topaz and diamond parure. She held a large satin box stamped *Garrard* in her gloved hands.

'Oh, Lily!' she cried, her accent as rich and smooth as honey in her satisfaction. 'You look stupendous. I always say you just don't make use of your looks as much as you should.' She reached out to adjust one sleeve, smoothing the swansdown trim. 'And I have the perfect finishing touch. Your dear papa had it sent over to me last week, but I think it suits you better.'

Lily, shaking with trepidation, unlatched and lifted the lid. Resting on a bed of rose satin was a pearl necklace, but *what* a necklace. It put her plain double strand to shame. Six strands of perfectly matched milky orbs, interspersed with bars of sapphires and diamonds, with a clasp of diamonds in the shape of a fleur-de-lys.

'Mother!' she gasped.

'And there are earrings, too!' Stella pointed out long pearl drops suspended from more sapphire fleur-de-lys. 'They belonged to a French *emigré* from the eighteenth century. And now they're *ours*. Can you believe that, darlin'?'

She took out the heavy necklace and with Doris's help fastened it around Lily's neck. It lay there, cool and heavy.

Lily pressed her fingertips against one of the pearls. The diamond bars bit into her skin. 'Mother, none of the other debs will be dressed like this…'

Stella's pretty face hardened. 'We are *lucky*, Lily. Never forget that. My family lost *everything*. We were utterly dispersed after that dreadful war. And here we are

in England, meeting dukes and duchesses, even princes!
You should be proud. You *must* be proud.'

'I am proud, Mother.' And she was—though perhaps
not of the same things her mother was.

Stella beamed and squeezed Lily's hands so tightly her
clasp bit into her daughter's fingers. 'Wonderful. Now,
we are going to have a lovely evening. A successful evening. Yes?'

Lily nodded, and tried to smile. It was always easier
to just smile with her mother—even when her lips could
barely make the motion.

How, how, could she face Aidan tonight?

Eleanor, Lady Heath, gave a satisfied smile as she
examined the table decorations one last time. She might
not live in a fashionable neighbourhood; she might not
have the money for the finest food or the most elaborate
flowers. Poor Leonard, her handsome Army officer who
unexpectedly inherited a title from his uncle before he,
too, perished most inconveniently, hadn't left her with
a sixpence. But she had her brain, her originality, and it
made her bread and butter.

Tonight's party, more than any other, had to be absolutely perfect. She studied her dining table with a criti-
cal eye. The candlelight cast a golden, mellow glow over
the room, gleaming on the silver and the masses of white
flowers, disguising the shabby wallpaper, the cheap artwork. The air smelled sweetly of rose oil, the wine—a
fine vintage, gifted from one of the heiresses she had
assisted—was decanted on the sideboard, the company
would be delightful.

She moved slowly along the table, moving a fish fork
here, a crystal goblet there, twitching the damask cloth
into place. At the head of the table, she studied the care-

fully penned place-cards. Next to herself was the Duke of Lennox, and to his right Lily Wilkins.

She slid the two cards just a tiny bit closer together. Not subtle, she had to admit, but in this matter there was no time for subtleties. She had the chance to put those two together in an intimate setting and the Season was too swiftly drawing to a close.

If she could help arrange such a spectacular marriage as the Wilkins millions and the Lennox strawberry leaves of a ducal coronet, her career would be made. Her drawing room would be the destination of every American heiress, every impecunious peer, from London to Edinburgh. It had to go perfectly.

Eleanor tilted her head as she considered Lily Wilkins. It was lucky the girl was as she was: pretty, well read, well mannered. She needed little enough instruction in English etiquette. It was easy to introduce her to anyone without fear of embarrassment on a hostess's part. Yet there was that worrisome glint she got sometimes in her doe-like eyes, that flash of something like…rebellion.

Eleanor sighed. She knew such things too well from her own wild youth. But Stella Wilkins was sure to dampen down any such sparks immediately.

As for Lennox, there should be no problem there, surely. Handsome young dukes were thin on the ground indeed. Dukes that were famously dashing adventurers were even rarer. Unique, even. What lady could resist?

Eleanor touched one gloved fingertip to the edge of the place-card. There was still the gossip about Lady Rannock, it was true. Once she and Lennox had been rumoured to be quite in love, even though she was meant for his brother. Would they coax their flame back into a bonfire now? But Roderick Castle was falling in. No love affair, no matter how passionate it once was, could patch leaky roofs.

No, Miss Wilkins would do very well indeed. And with the gratitude of Stella Wilkins, Eleanor might even be able to move to a more salubrious address.

'Is everything to your liking, Lady Heath?' her butler asked.

'Oh, yes,' Eleanor purred. 'Very nice indeed.'

Chapter Six

Lady Heath's house, unfashionable neighbourhood or not, was everything Lily might like for herself, she thought as they were helped from their carriage and hurried up the shallow stone steps to the red front door. The house was narrow but cheerful and pretty, pale rose brick with light shining invitingly from every sparkling window, the sound of laughter and piano music floating out to the tree-lined street.

Lily couldn't understand what was wrong with the neighbourhood, for it all looked quite respectable, with a small park across the way and quiet houses to either side. In fact, if she had her choice, if she was not bound by 'Old King Coal's' money, she might like to live there herself, with books and music and chintz chairs as in their rented town house.

But that sort of thing for her was as far away as the moon and it was no use worrying about it. She followed her mother into the small entrance hall, where the scent of hothouse lilies was strong and the laughter echoed a little louder. A footman came to take their wraps.

'I'm glad to see Lady Heath can keep a servant,' Stella sniffed.

'Oh, Mother, she *is* a lady,' Lily whispered. 'She hardly scrubs the floors. And this all looks quite respectable.'

'Respectable. Yes.' Stella's gaze swept up the narrow staircase with its polished banister and old Persian carpet runners, the marble-topped table with its arrangement of lilies and silver tray for cards. 'She *is* good at appearances, as we all must be.'

Lady Heath appeared in the doorway from where that laughter emanated and smiled. Her gown, cream-coloured satin trimmed with touches of crimson, her hair swept up and caught by another lily, shone brightly in the old-fashioned candlelight. 'My dear Mrs Wilkins, Miss Wilkins. I'm so glad you could come. Do have a glass of sherry before dinner. Miss Banks was just entertaining us with some Chopin at the piano. Perhaps you could favour us so after dinner, Miss Wilkins? I hear you are very talented.'

'Oh, she would love to, Lady Heath, I'm sure!' Stella replied happily, as if she had not just been criticising Lady Heath's house. 'I do hope we're not too late?'

'Perfectly on time, Mrs Wilkins. And how lovely you both look! Such spectacular gowns. Do come in.'

Lily nervously smoothed her skirt and her elaborately curled hair, wishing again she had worn her regular tulle or plain silk. She didn't feel like herself at all.

'Do stop fidgeting, Lily,' her mother hissed. 'Smile!'

Lady Heath's drawing room, though small, was attractive, with its piano and paintings and dainty decorations, but Lily barely noticed it. It looked as if they were the last to arrive, with a crowd gathered around Miss Banks at the piano. Just as Lily had feared, she was dressed quite wrong. Older ladies like her mother were in heavy satins and brocades, but girls her own age, such as the piano player, wore white and pale pink and daffodil-yellow tulles with dainty single strands of pearls.

Yet she forgot all that when she saw the Duke of Lennox standing near an open window, listening to a lady in grass-green velvet who chatted to him vivaciously as he listened with a half-smile on his lips. He nodded to Lily as he caught her staring and raised his glass to her in a little salute.

Lily felt her cheeks flood with heat and she glanced away. Her fingers twitched as if they wanted to reach for him again, to let him sweep her on to the floor and into a looping, twining circle of dance. She took a glass of sherry from a butler's tray and tried not to gulp it down.

'Miss Wilkins!' another lady said and Lily turned to see Miss Mary Banks, the pianist's sister, smiling at her. 'What a charming gown. I'm sure it must be Monsieur Worth. My mama is such a tyrant, she won't even let my sister and me enter his salon yet! She says it must wait until I marry.' She patted her own pink gauze skirt. 'Is it all terribly luxurious and wonderful?'

Lily laughed, glad of the distraction from the Duke, and told Miss Mary all about the red velvet fitting rooms of Worth's salon, the glasses of champagne and plates of *foie gras*, the lengths of beadwork and lace everywhere. She said nothing of the tedium of long hours of standing perfectly still while heavy satins and velvets were pinned around her, while her mother debated with the couturier himself over feathers and braid.

'I do hope I'm not interrupting,' a voice said and Lily glanced up to see Lord James Grantley smiling at them shyly.

'Oh, you must know our cousin, Lord James Grantley,' Miss Mary said. 'Jamie, I am glad to see you've dragged yourself away from your studies for one evening of fun. He is studying Hebrew, Miss Wilkins, though he already knows Latin and Greek, not to mention French and Italian. I don't know how you keep it all in your head at once!'

Lily smiled at him and thought of how restful and easy his calm good looks were next to Aidan. 'You do sound rather like my sister Rose, Lord James. She is teaching herself Spanish right now and last month it was Sanskrit, though I don't think she will go to India. She's always off to the British Library.' She took a sip of her sherry and wished she did not envy Rose quite so much. She could escape into her reading, but people like Rose and Lord James had whole worlds open to them through their studies. Just as Violet did with her camera.

'How frightfully clever she must be,' Miss Mary said, though her tone clearly said a clever young lady was most odd indeed.

'Do you read much yourself, Miss Wilkins?' Lord James said. 'I thought from our last conversation you were literary.'

'Whenever I can, though mostly poetry and novels, and Shakespeare now that we're in England,' Lily said. She remembered how she had thought of Aidan as some poetic hero, some medieval warrior setting off for unknown climes. She took another, longer sip of the wine and tried to ignore her mother's little frown from across the room.

'I will send you a little treatise I wrote on *Love's Labour's Lost*, then,' Lord James said. 'It may be quite dull, of course, but perhaps it would be of some interest.'

'I would enjoy that,' Lily said.

There was no time for more conversation, for a sudden hush descended on the drawing room and the Prince of Wales appeared. Lily had glimpsed him once or twice, but up close she realised he wasn't much like she would imagine a *prince* to be. He was not tall and was rather portly, his pale hair thinning, except for his beard, and his pale eyes small. But his smile was kind enough and he nodded affably as everyone bowed and curtsied low. 'Good evening, everyone,' he said, in a surprisingly German-accented voice.

Lily thought the Duke of Lennox would have made a much more poetic prince. But Prince Bertie did have a presence, a confidence, a barely leashed sense of fun and an attractive smile that took in everyone. She could see why society flocked around him.

'Shall we all go in to dinner?' Lady Heath announced.

Lord James glanced at Lily and opened his mouth, as if he would offer to escort her. Miss Mary had already left her side with another young man. Lady Heath's soirée did seem far more informal than the usual strictly regimented affairs Lily had become accustomed to in Paris and London—and Newport, of course; no place was ever more formal than Newport. But Lady Heath hurried over to her, the Duke himself in tow.

He looked frozen, as if caught in the wake of an implacable ship, and Lily felt quite the same. She felt her cheeks turning hot just to be near him again, especially now that she knew the gossip about his past.

'Miss Wilkins, would you be a dear and go in with Lennox?' Lady Heath said with a gentle, impossible-to-refuse smile. 'Lord James, I see the elder Miss Banks has left the piano now. I am sure she is quite longing to practise her Latin.'

'Certainly, Lady Heath,' she murmured. The Duke offered his arm and she slid her gloved fingertips through the crook of his elbow. She tried not to breathe too deeply of his warm scent, not to look into his eyes. She just hoped she could keep from shaking too much.

They followed the others through the open doors into the dining room. It was as charming as the rest of the house, with sunny yellow walls glowing in candlelight, the scent of white flowers in the air. Lily wished she could admire more of it, but she was all too achingly aware of the Duke at her side. Of how very perfect he looked, how at ease and confident, and how *uneasy* she felt. Wrong in her silly, expensive gown, her elaborate pearls, wrong in herself.

They sat down at their appointed places next to Lady Heath and across from the Prince himself. A footman shook out the starched damask napkins for their laps just as a watercress soup was brought in and spooned into the gold-edged bowls. Lily glanced down the table to find her mother beaming like a thousand suns and Lord James at the very end of the table. She dared not look at the Prince!

'There are no palms to hide behind, I fear,' Aidan whispered, gesturing to the room around them. 'But there is that Japanese screen in the corner…'

Lily laughed, though she tried to hide it behind her napkin. She didn't want her mother, or anyone, to think she was flirting. But it was hard not to smile at him despite everything, not to lean into his warmth, his delicious scent of lemony cologne and starched linen and leather.

For one moment, he was just the man she had met in her hidey-hole at the Crewe ball, not *the Duke*. She could almost forget everyone's stares at them as they tried to eat their soup, though they all tried to pretend they weren't looking, thinking, whispering. Was she going to buy a title with her American dollars? Only Lady Heath herself seemed to pay them no mind, all her attention on the Prince as they chattered about racehorses.

She could not, though, forget about Aidan. How handsome he was, how his quiet, deep voice echoed inside her as he talked of inconsequential matters like London museums and restaurants. How his sleeve felt when it brushed her bare arm, the wool soft and warm. She thought of the lady she glimpsed as she was leaving the ball, with her golden hair, her confident smile, the way she looked at him. Could Lily ever, even after years in England, feel such confidence?

'Was it this difficult?' she asked, gesturing to the elaborately laid table, the watchful eyes. 'On your travels?'

'Oh, no, much easier.' He smiled down at her as the soup was taken away and replaced with the fish course. 'I was merely shot at with poisoned arrows and caught fever in the desert once when there was only whiskey and feverfew to see me through. It was quite wonderful, compared with being dropped back into London society.'

Lily laughed aloud; she couldn't hold it back. 'But surely, Duke, you were brought up to all this. Princes and gossip. It's all as new to me as—as a poison arrow.' She resisted the urge to tug at those blasted pearls, the ones that felt as if they were strangling her. Even if she did marry the Duke, what a terrible duchess she would make! But to look into his eyes every evening... 'In fact, I might enjoy the poison arrows rather more.'

His smile quirked at the corner of his lips in a rather adorable way. 'I'm wounded that we English have nothing to tempt you at all, Miss Wilkins.'

She was tempted by *him*. By that smile, the sound of his voice. Like an infatuated, silly little girl. And she feared her mother was only tempted by the ducal title. 'Oh, I wouldn't say that. England does have its beauties, things I've only read about before. The Tower, castles, gardens, art. I liked the avenues in Paris, but I never quite felt as if I was walking in true history as I have here. Tracing the footsteps of people long gone. I simply haven't had the chance yet to see all I would like.' She suddenly realised that many of those historical footsteps would have been his own ancestors. He was part of this place, part of history itself.

It was a sobering thought.

'You have only just arrived, then?'

'Oh, no. We've been here most of the Season.' And in that time, aside from a few moments to escape and explore museums and Hyde Park, she had mostly seen ballrooms and couturiers. 'But I would like to see the countryside, too. The gardens and hedgerows, the old castles and battlefields. I've always loved reading history.' She felt silly even saying it, as those places must be familiar and dull to him. 'But such things must be commonplace to you. Lady Heath tells me parts of Roderick Castle date back to Henry VIII's time.'

'Yes, it was rebuilt during the sixteenth century, with some additions in my great-grandfather's time. But we have a tower that is even older, perhaps thirteenth century. And our garden was designed by Repton, with a chapel by Wren himself.'

'It must be beautiful.'

'Yes, in its way,' he said shortly and Lily wondered if she had said something wrong. Did he not like his home? Perhaps it held sad memories of his lost brother. The brother who had loved a lady who loved Aidan. The reminder of the gossip made her swallow hard and look down at her plate.

The fish was cleared for a sorbet and Lily suddenly realised that Lady Heath had not done the usual thing and signalled for everyone to turn to conversation with

their other dinner partner. It was most odd, but Lily was
too enthralled with the Duke to think more of it.

'I would imagine your own homes are much finer than
poor old Roderick,' he said. 'One does hear that every
bedroom in a Newport mansion has its own bathroom!
Not to mention central heating.'

'Oh, yes, but they are all new,' Lily exclaimed. 'The
homes here have such stories behind them. When you
walk along a gallery or sit in a chair, how easy it must
be to imagine all who were there before you.' She didn't
mention the fact that so much of the decor in her mother's house was old, taken from English and French homes
that were suffering from lack of dollars. The spirits didn't
seem to travel with them then.

Aidan smiled at her, that wonderfully crooked smile.
'You are a poet, Miss Wilkins? A historian?'

Lily blushed and stared down at her plate. 'Oh, no. I
just like to read about history. I'm no scholar like Lord
James over there.'

He glanced down the table at Lord James, his smile
fading. 'Nor am I, Miss Wilkins. More a doer than a
thinker. Are you and Lord James friends?'

'I—not really, I just enjoy hearing of his studies. I
never had the chance to learn such things. My governess
was more in the French and watercolours line.' Though
her mother had always made sure there were also lessons
in etiquette and precedence, curtsies and posture, all for
the chance to move forward in her world. 'I wish I had
the chance to be a…a doer.'

'And what would you like to do, Miss Wilkins, if you
had the chance?'

Lily glanced at him in surprise. No one had asked
her that before. Yet he looked genuinely curious. She'd
been *told* what to do for as long as she could remember;

her dreams had so far only been that—secret dreams. 'I would like to ride, I think. I had to leave my horse behind in America and I've not had the chance of a good gallop since.'

His smile returned, like sunshine bursting from behind grey clouds. 'Well, I'm not sure I could provide a really good gallop anywhere in London, but a ride in the park could be possible. If it's not the fashionable hour at Rotten Row, there might be a quick canter. Perhaps you would care to join me tomorrow? If your mother approves, of course.'

Lily wasn't at all sure she'd heard him correctly. Had he really asked her to ride with *him* in the park? Truly? She felt her stomach lurch in excitement, nervousness, fear.

She glanced down the table at her mother. Stella was smiling as she talked to the archbishop beside her, looking her usual supremely confident self. *Of course* her mother would give her permission for such an outing. Was that not why they were in London? What the dances and the Worth gown and the pearls were for?

She suddenly remembered the conversation she had overheard between her mother and Lady Heath. Aidan was the most eligible man in England, with an ancient title. An ancient title and no money for his castle roof. Lily sighed, deflating a bit.

Yet her longing to escape her mother's stuffy house, her watchful gaze, was so very great. She thought she would scream and go mad if she couldn't get out into the fresh air. And to be there with Aidan, just the two of them...

She nodded. 'I would enjoy that. Thank you, Duke. I'm sure my mother would not mind.'

'Excellent, Miss Wilkins. I look forward to it.'

'Well, ladies, shall we?' Lady Heath rose to her feet to lead the women to the drawing room while the men had their port and cigars. Lily gave Aidan a quick smile and hurried to follow, wishing she could stay with him.

As Lily sipped her coffee while the other ladies chatted, she stared out the window at Lady Heath's darkened little garden. She could see the pale outlines of flowers and the glow of city lights beyond the wall. She knew she wouldn't be alone there for long; she could hear the chatter of the other ladies behind her along with her mother's bell-like laugh. Stella did love to chatter with friends, but Lily knew even that wouldn't keep her occupied for very long. Not when she knew her mother was just aching to interrogate her about the Duke.

The Duke. Lily closed her eyes and pictured him again as he sat beside her at dinner. His crooked smile, his easy talk, making her feel comfortable again, at ease, forgetting all about the room around them. The Prince right across from her. It did seem silly to keep thinking of him as 'the Duke'. He looked like no duke she had ever imagined. She'd pictured them all like old paintings of Wellington, stern and old and beak-nosed, lofty above all of them. Aidan wasn't like that at all.

Aidan. That was how she found she thought of him. It was a musical, fanciful name, one that suited him. Not that she would ever call him that to his face. Even fine, titled English ladies called him *Duke*, in those light, flirtatious, English voices of theirs.

She wondered what that beautiful, golden-haired Lady Rannock called him. Or had once called him, before they were parted.

'Lily, darling, whatever are you doing lurking over here by yourself?' she heard her mother say, as she knew she soon would. Stella linked her arm in Lily's, leaning close as if in maternal affection. The rich scent of French perfume surrounded them. Lily thought of how Aidan—she *could* call him that in her mind—smelled of lemon and starch and fresh air.

'Just having a breath of air, Mother,' she said and took a sip of her coffee.

'Very wise, before the gentlemen and the Prince join us.' Stella leaned closer and whispered, 'The Duke looked quite enchanted with you, darling! Whatever did you talk about with him? Not your poetry, I do hope.'

Lily thought of what they had talked about, about his invitation to ride in the park. There had been horses, history, houses—nothing too fascinating, she would have thought. She wasn't a lady who could enthral with feminine wiles. But she had enjoyed it all, very much. Too much. 'His home at Roderick Castle, I think. History.'

Stella sighed. 'Oh, history. How fascinated these English seem to be with their fusty old stories. Yet they are not a patch on my family's old home in South Carolina, I would think. Still, I'm glad to see you were taking an interest in a party at last. We must keep it up, darling. Lady Heath says his mother, the Duchess, has been looking high and low for an eligible new Duchess of Lennox. I wish she could have been here tonight to meet you. No one else has to offer what *we* do.'

Lily widened her eyes in mock ignorance. 'And what is *that*, Mother? Grandpa's old plantation?'

Her mother frowned, but quickly smoothed her lips. It would never do for a Wilkins lady to make wrinkles.

'Your beauty, of course, Lily. I saw it the minute you were born, when your elegant little fingers wrapped around mine. You could be one of the great beauties of the age if you would just make the most of it. You're far lovelier than those Professional Beauties the Prince likes so much.'

Lily glanced at her reflection in the window, her dark hair, her pale, small face. She thought her mother's words were mere wishful thinking. The Professional Beauties, ladies of the Prince's Marlborough House Set whose photos were sold in shop windows, like Jennie Churchill and Patsy Cornwallis-West, were gorgeous and elegant, full of grace, famous and admired. She had no answer for them.

Luckily, Lady Heath rose to her feet at that moment, drawing their attention. 'Miss Wilkins, would you possibly favour us with a piece at the piano? The gentlemen are taking so long with their port and those vile cigars, we shall grow quite bored!'

'She would love to, Lady Heath,' Stella answered. Lily nodded with a smile. At least music was something she always enjoyed, could always lose herself in, and behind a keyboard she could forget the wrongness of her clothes, the awkward glances, the whispers.

She sat down at the piano and sorted through the music there. She found a piece she already knew fairly well, a Chopin nocturne, and launched into the slow, sweet opening chords. Soon, she really could forget all else, losing herself in the bittersweet emotions of the piece, imagining a long, star-twinkling twilight where so much was finished, so much yet to begin.

The melody built and built, like night gathering in, until finally it ended in one last, lingering note. The sound of applause brought her back to earth again and she glanced up, surprised to see she was still in Lady Heath's candlelit London drawing room, not wandering through a warm summer's night. Her mother beamed, as she always did when Lily played, and Lady Heath looked quite satisfied. The Misses Banks applauded, but frowned, as if they feared their own performances were somehow overshadowed.

And the Duke—Aidan—stood near the dining room doorway. He did not applaud, but she couldn't look away from the expression on his face. He seemed so far away for a moment, caught in a whole different place and time. She wondered if he saw a different night sky in his mind, the vast, empty, glittering night of a desert.

'That was lovely, my dear,' Lady Heath said.

'Indeed, indeed,' the Prince agreed. 'You could grace the Albert Hall itself, Miss Wilkins. How accomplished you American ladies are!'

'She was taught by Monsieur Zywyny himself, the relative of Chopin's own teacher,' Stella said. 'He declared she should be a concert pianist! Her father and I are quite amazed at her talent. We are terribly tone deaf ourselves. But then, Lily is remarkable, if I do say so myself.'

'Mother...' Lily murmured, feeling her cheeks flame as she shuffled through the pages of music. 'I am only quite mediocre.'

'The Duke is also most talented at the piano, though he is far too modest to admit it,' Lady Heath said, tossing a smile at Aidan. 'Perhaps you and Lily might favour us with a duet?'

Aidan laughed and Lily wished she could sink into the parquet floor beneath the piano and vanish. 'I am quite out of practice, Lady Heath, after all my travels, though I admit your piano does look most tempting.'

'Then I insist you must try it,' Lady Heath said. 'I am sure it will be most delightful for us!'

'Thank you, then. Shall we, Miss Wilkins?' he asked with a smile.

Lily smiled shyly and nodded. They sat down together before the keyboard, pressed together on the narrow bench. She hoped she wouldn't tremble and fumble the notes, not now, not with everyone watching, not with Aidan beside her.

'The Schumann, *Variations on a Theme*?' he said. 'Do you know it?'

Lily nodded, and he smiled. 'Very well! One, two—go.'

Their fingers flowed into the Schumann. Lily sensed everyone watching them avidly, whispering behind fans, but she paid them no attention now. The music demanded all her focus, trying to follow Aidan's lead. She felt his arm brush over hers, his hands over hers, around hers, following her, as the music wound about her. The music and Aidan seemed as one.

As they crashed together into the finale, perfectly together, they were laughing with the joy of music.

'Beautiful,' Aidan said and Lily glanced up, breathless, to find him smiling down at her. He kissed her hand as the guests clapped for their performance.

'Brilliant, Duke, brilliant! And you, Miss Wilkins, so charming,' the Prince himself said. 'What a treasure you have found, Lady Heath.'

'I certainly think so,' Lady Heath said. She beamed at Lily, but all Lily could see, all she knew in that moment, was Aidan.

Aidan took a deep inhale of his cheroot as he enjoyed the quiet of Lady Heath's small garden. As he had told her at the Crewe ball, it was a terrible habit he had picked up in the wilds of an American gold field and he would give it up very soon. Especially once he had a wife to please. His mother certainly complained about it enough.

But for now, it gave him an excuse to escape the noise and clamour of parties. He was a duke, Roderick Castle

would need a mistress, his family name required a social life and he needed an heir. But how to choose? How
to change his life irrevocably again, just as it had been
when Edward died?

Aidan took another deep inhale, enjoying the sharp,
metallic bite of it at the back of his throat that tossed him
back into happier days. Days when he could wander as
he pleased, talk to whomever he pleased, with no thought
to the outside world.

For just a moment, he wondered if he could find a wife
who would be content to look after Roderick Castle and
Lennox House while he went back to South America.
Certainly, enough of the couples he knew spent precious
little time together. Once the heir was born and the estate secure, a couple whose marriage was made of convenience and land and family names could go their own
ways. No one cared, as long as it was discreet.

His own parents' marriage had been like that. And
now his mother was going to marry her long-time lover.
But Aidan had never wanted a life like that himself, one
of expectations, conformity, convention, loneliness. It
was one of the things that had driven him off on his
travels. In the jungle, he was only a man, only himself
and what he could make of his day. Yet he had never
counted on being the Duke, to be in charge of handing
Roderick Castle over to the next generation, intact, part
of that unbroken chain. In charge of the welfare of hun-
dreds of people.

He didn't want to be the one who lost it, the one who
sold the land bit by bit, scattered the artistic treasures,
let the leaky roof fall in. It would be dishonourable to
abandon all that his forebears had worked for, all that the
tenants and servants worked for now.

But how to save it all?

He thought of Lily Wilkins, her soft white hands flying over the piano keyboard, her shimmering dark eyes as she looked up, startled, as the music faded. Lily Wilkins of the absurd pearls and elaborate gowns, the shyness and uncertainty of her smile.

Miss Wilkins of all that coal gold.

Aidan took one last drag of his cheroot. As he put it out under a marble planter he heard a burst of giggles. Not wanting to be surrounded by a gaggle of debs, he dashed behind the planter and hoped he could become invisible.

'That gown!' he heard someone say smugly—one of the Misses Banks? 'My dears, have you ever seen anything of the sort on someone younger than forty?'

'I heard it was from Monsieur Worth,' another lady said, in a rather wistful tone. 'It must have cost a thousand pounds!'

'And those pearls…' The first lady sniffed. 'So ostentatious. But what can one expect from an American? They probably even dress that way for breakfast.'

Aidan realised they had to be speaking of Lily. A rush of fierce protectiveness washed over him, the need to defend someone vulnerable. And he knew, beneath the priceless pearls, she *was* vulnerable.

'She didn't give anyone else a chance at the piano, either,' another young lady said. 'I've been practising my Mozart for ever so long.'

Aidan again pictured Lily's hands flying over the piano keys, her eyes closed as if she was one with the notes, floating up and up into the night sky. No one would even think of leaving an instrument when they were so caught by its spell. And he could have listened to her all night.

'I thought she was very nice,' someone else said. The other Miss Banks? 'So easy to talk to! Indeed, her manners were all they should be.' Someone made a loud, startled huff, and she went on, louder. 'Better than *some*, I must say.'

'Well, I never! Who would think my own sister would defend such a ruffian? Perhaps she will invite you to her grass hut when next you are in New York.'

'I'm sure she could buy all of Mayfair with those pearls,' another lady said. 'No grass huts needed.'

'And I doubt she would go back to New York, anyway,' the first Miss Banks said. 'My mother says that Mrs Wilkins is the new Clara Jerome, hunting English husbands for her daughters. I doubt Miss Wilkins would settle for some mere younger son like James Grantley, either, do you?'

Aidan froze. Grantley? Was he a serious suitor for Lily's hand? And did she like him in return?

'She'll have to dress better, then,' one of them snorted. 'Surely our English gentlemen have more refinement than to want wives like that?'

Aidan had heard quite enough. Title-hunting Mrs Wilkins might be, and mercenary his own mother might be trying to be, but Lily did not deserve to be gossiped about. Her shy smile, the way she looked up at him with her dark eyes, the way her soft fingers conjured up magic on a piano, the way it felt when he touched her hand— when they were together he did not feel as if either of them were hunting for anything except another moment to be alone. To be just Lily and Aidan.

He stepped out from behind the planter into the light that flowed from the open French doors to the drawing room. He could hear music, a fumbling little waltz—so it seemed Lily *had* given someone else a turn at the instrument. The low rumble of the Prince's laugh, Lady Heath's silvery giggle, Stella Wilkins's flat vowels… Four young women stood clustered by the door, a fluttering, cooing flock of pigeons in white and pale yellow, fans fluttering as they whispered behind them.

'Ladies,' he said with a careless smile and a low bow. They all looked startled and all but the younger Miss Milbank guilty and flushed. 'Lovely evening for a stroll, is it not?'

He sauntered back into the drawing room and saw to his relief that many of the guests had departed, including the Prince and the Wilkinses. As much as he wanted to see Lily again, to take her hand and shield her from the knives of any whispers, he was glad she wasn't there to see him discomposed in any way. To laugh at his protectiveness.

He suddenly couldn't bear the polite party any longer. Couldn't bear London, the people, the noise, the expectations. He longed for the vast silence of the open spaces he once roamed so freely, just himself, Aidan, a man. No titles at all, nothing that anyone there could care about.

The only moment he had felt that freedom in society was when he sat at the piano with Lily, their movements as one, the notes wrapping around them like magical ribbons, binding them together.

He made his way to the hall to call for his carriage. Then he decided to send it back to Lennox House empty, as he wanted to, *had to*, walk. He would go mad without some real exercise.

'My dear Duke,' Lady Heath called. 'Leaving already?'

'It does grow late, Lady Heath—Eleanor,' he said, trying to smile, to pretend that this life, this *ducal* life, was perfectly normal to him. 'I've imposed on your lovely hospitality long enough.'

'Not at all.' She gave him an understanding smile, a gentle touch on his sleeve, and he remembered their

conversation at the Crewe ball. 'It was most kind of you
to entertain us at the piano. I fear my poor instrument
is too neglected, and I do forget how talented you are.'

Aidan laughed. 'My father never forgot. He always
declared a piano was no fit pastime for a gentleman. I've
enjoyed being able to play again. And I had a great deal
of help tonight with the duet.'

'Miss Wilkins. Yes. She is a surprising young lady.'
She fluttered her painted silk fan. 'I confess I find myself feeling quite protective of her sometimes.'

Just as Aidan had, when he heard that gossip about
her. Why did he want to race to her, catch her up in his
arms, wrap her in silk and crystal apart from the rest of
the world? 'She's very charming. In fact, you might be
glad to hear we are going riding in the park tomorrow.'

'Indeed?' Lady Heath's brow arched above her fan.
'I certainly *am* glad to hear that. You two could very
well suit.'

'Because of her money and my falling-in roof?'

She laughed. 'Because you are both unique, independent, romantic souls. And lonely, I think. Perhaps you
can do each other some good.'

'I don't know about romantic,' he muttered. 'But I
thought you just might approve. I'm sure my mother will
be happy, too.'

Lady Heath's fan fluttered in front of her suddenly
uncertain expression. 'Duke—Aidan.' She took a step
closer. 'I know you may not take much heed of my words
now, but I have known you and your family for a long
time, and I—' She broke off and shrugged as if she
couldn't quite find the answers.

'Yes?' he said gently.

'I worry about you. About how different your life must
be now, all the responsibilities Roderick Castle must

bring. But Lily Wilkins *is* a sweet girl. A sensitive one. I wouldn't want either of you—well, hurt, in any way.'

He kissed her hand and gave her a smile. If this marriage came off, it would be to her credit—and helpful to her income. But she sounded so truly concerned, for both of them. 'You are a good friend, Lady Heath, and that is a rarity here in London. Trust me, I do not want to see Miss Wilkins hurt, either. It's just a ride in the park for an afternoon.'

'Oh, my dear. Believe me…' She shook her head sadly. 'In our world, it is *never* just that.'

Chapter Seven

Lily twisted in front of the looking glass, trying to study herself from every angle. Her new dark green riding habit, trimmed in black braid, was from Busvine tailors, where they said that famous horsewoman Jennie Churchill bought all her habits, and it was quite *à la mode*. Yet Lily wasn't entirely sure about it.

It was certainly beautiful. The luxurious cashmere wool fabric, the perfect cut of it, the deceptive simplicity. Yet it was also quite *daring*. It fit against her like a glove, perfectly smooth against the specially made chamois leather underpinnings. It showed no skin at all, not like the deep décolleté of a Worth evening gown, but she felt much more exposed than ever.

What would the Duke think?

She closed her eyes and remembered their duet at the piano, as their hands moved as one, shoulder to shoulder as they created the magic of the tune. How wonderful it had been to feel so close to him, to feel they were only themselves! Only two people. The gossip forgotten, the past gone.

Until the song ended.

'It's absolutely beautiful, Miss Lily,' Doris said,

twitching at the long train that would drape over Lily's left leg once she was in the saddle.

'Do you really think so?' Lily asked, twisting again. It did feel much freer than her corsets!

'Like a proper English countrywoman, I would say.'

Lily laughed. 'At least we won't be riding to hounds today. I doubt my rusty skill would ever be up to it. One challenge at a time.'

As Doris handed her the new matching hat, tall-crowned, glossy black silk with a wisp of lacy veiling, Lily's mother rushed in. Unlike Lily, Stella still wore her morning peignoir of blue velvet and chiffon.

'Aren't you nearly ready, Lily?' she demanded. 'He'll be here at any moment!'

'Yes, Mother, almost.' Lily smoothed the already impeccable skirt and twirled around. 'How do I look?'

Stella slowly circled her, eyes sharp as a hawk with a rabbit. 'Quite correct. Lady Heath was right to send us to Busvine. I do wish a young lady could wear a bit of lip rouge—they do say Lady Randolph Churchill does and it looks most fetching below the edge of the veil. But we must do what is proper. What a duchess would do.'

Lily was quite sure a duchess could do as she liked. She remembered her fancy gown at Lady Heath's dinner, the other girls' pink and white tulles, their cameo pendants and single strands of pearls. Surely those English girls had been taught from birth how to be proper duchesses. But it was never any use to argue with her mother.

But for the first time, she actually considered those words—what would, what *could*, a duchess do? She would have duties, of course, many of them. But it seemed there was freedom, too. The choice to do what she liked, wear what she liked, make friends where she liked, make sure her sisters could marry as they chose. There was freedom in it, as well as restraint.

And if the Duke who gave that freedom happened to look like Aidan...

Lily bit her lip as that secret smile threatened to form, the smile she always had when he came into her mind, curse him. She had always considered dukes to be old and fusty, but he was young and vibrant and wild and *alive*, shimmering with light from his very fingertips. Nothing stuffy or mouldy about him in the least, nothing snobbish. Surely that old gossip was only that—gossip? The past was past.

He was going riding with *her*.

Lily put her hat carefully on to the smooth, coiled plaits of her hair and pinned it into place. She lowered the veil and smiled. Maybe, just maybe, she could soon have more choice in her life than she had ever realised.

She picked up her gloves and riding crop, and hurried out the door, feeling strangely lighter than she had in an age.

Rose and Violet hovered near the banisters on the landing, positioned to stare down into the entrance hall. Though they had done that for as long as Lily could remember, first huddling near her as they watched their mother sail out for an evening in satins and furs, now to wave Lily off, they suddenly looked...different to her. Older. They would be in her position soon enough, going to parties and meeting gentlemen. Before then, she had to get herself into a position to help and protect them. They were not children now and neither was she. She had to be equal to whatever fate tossed at her.

'What are you two doing there?' Stella said sternly. 'You should be at your art lessons!'

'We want to see the famous Duke!' Violet said, equally

stubborn as their mother. 'Is he as handsome as the newspapers say, Lily? Perhaps I could take his photograph!'

'Yes,' Lily answered firmly. 'He most certainly is handsome.'

'And a handsome duke must have good-looking friends,' Violet said, a speculative gleam in her hazel eyes. 'If you're nice to him, Lil, he might bring those friends around one day.'

'Lily is *always* nice to everyone, Violet,' Rose protested. 'And I would rather hear about his travels than gawk at his manly shoulders. He was in the Sahara, you know, and in a canoe down the Amazon.'

'You must learn to be more delicate in your conversation, Violet,' Stella admonished. 'But I suppose you are not really wrong.'

A knock sounded at the front door and they all jumped. Lily felt her stomach lurch with nervousness and she straightened her hat and her tight sleeves. It would all be fine, she promised herself. She would surely not fall off her horse and make a cake of herself in front of him!

The butler opened the door and there he was. Truly there, before her, in the flesh. The Duke. Aidan. He swept his hat off and his gold-streaked hair was tousled, gleaming in the sunlight. He smiled and his green eyes crinkled adorably at the corners.

'The Duke of Lennox calling for Miss Wilkins,' the butler said.

'Oh, Lily,' Violet whispered. 'I didn't know he would be quite like *that*.'

Lily took a deep breath and forced herself to walk, not run, down the stairs. Not that she *could* run in her new, brightly polished boots from Batten.

'Miss Wilkins,' he said with a smile, pushing an errant lock of hair back from his brow. Lily found that her gloved fingers itched to do that for him. 'It looks like a fine day for a ride. Mrs Wilkins, I promise I will take the greatest care of your daughter.'

Stella smiled serenely. 'I would not have expected anything else from a gentleman such as yourself, Duke. My dear Mr Wilkins says you can always tell the quality of a man by the boots he wears.' She gestured to his own Batten creations; unlike Lily's, they were battered and creased, though carefully polished. 'It's clear you use them for work. Will you join us for tea after?'

'Thank you, Mrs Wilkins, I would be honoured.'

Lily followed him out of the house and was immediately glad to be out in the fresh air. To be outside with *him*. He glanced up at the sky as he replaced his hat and flexed his shoulders under the fine black cloth of his riding jacket. It was a grey day, rather overcast, but she didn't care. He cast his own light, a human Apollo come down from Olympus—or from the marbles at the museum.

A groom waited with the horses, a bay gelding and a grey mare with a soft white star on her forehead. 'Is this one for me?' Lily said in delight, crooning softly to the horse as she stroked its velvety nose. It nuzzled into her, making her laugh. Horses were her best delight at home, her one escape, and she'd been sad to leave her own behind.

'Her name is Star, appropriately. She does seem to like you, Miss Wilkins,' Aidan answered with a smile. 'Though I confess they're only hired. The Roderick stable was sold soon after my father died, not being entailed. He was most avid about the hunt and the turf.'

Lily nodded. Yet another sign of the Lennox poverty. 'I know little about racing, I fear—Mother thinks it so unladylike.' Or maybe she just didn't like the time her husband spent at the track—and the actresses he took there. 'But I do know a smart horse who wants to gallop when I see one. Don't I, Star?'

'Shall we go, then? Before the rain sets in.'

Lily nodded and, to her surprise, rather than waiting for the groom to help her into the saddle, Aidan lifted her himself. His hands were warm, strong and secure around her waist, his fingers sliding against the fine wool and doeskin. He raised her straight through the air, as if she weighed no more than a feather, and settled her perfectly into the side-saddle. He helped her adjust the long train over her legs and made sure she was comfortable before he found his own horse.

Lily fussed a bit with her train, making sure it draped down gracefully to cover both legs completely. She glanced up and saw her sisters' faces at the upstairs window. She waved and they waved back merrily.

The park was quiet at that hour, the bridleways empty but for a few other serious riders and some groundskeepers at the flowerbeds. The walkways were lined with black-cloaked nursemaids and their noisy charges rolling hoops or peeking from lacy prams.

'How pretty it all is!' Lily exclaimed. 'I've never noticed those flowers before, or the sky beyond the treetops, all green and gold and blue. It's all so much in flower still! We usually only come out in the carriage in the afternoons and you can't see anything past the other coaches.'

'Ah, yes, the fashionable hour,' he said. 'My mother never sets foot on the ground when she's in town. She must make quite sure her hat is finer than any of her friends.'

Lily laughed. 'My mother is just the same. She *lives* to be bowed at by Princess Alexandra when the royal car-

riage drives past.' She imitated the little royal bow, right
and left, wave, wave, that the Princess was famous for.

'By Jove, but you have it down just right, Miss
Wilkins,' he teased. 'You should be royalty.'

Lily shook her head. 'I fear I would be quite terrible
at it. All the stares and whispers, every moment just perfectly correct, every smile to each person prescribed.
Though maybe being a duke is rather the same? Someone told me the Lennox title is much older than the Ha-
noverian royal one.' Lily sighed when she remembered
all those dull evenings pouring over *Debrett's*.

Aidan's smile faded. 'Yes, it's from before the Civil
War. Ours, you know, not the one you had in America.
But the first known ancestor came over from France with
the Conqueror and Roderick land is in the Domesday
Book. But that's all dull stuff for such a fine day when I
promised you a gallop!'

Lily didn't find it dull at all, but she studied the open
stretch of empty bridleway before them. 'I'll race you!'
she cried.

He laughed and urged his horse faster, gaining on her,
leaving the groom quite behind. Together, they hopped
over a shallow dip and Lily felt as if she was flying. All
her doubts were left behind in that moment. There was
no one around the paths at that hour and they could just
gallop and gallop.

Lily laughed again as she pulled far ahead of Aidan—
just before a low-hanging branch snatched her hat from
her head. She drew up sharply, laughing even more.

Aidan caught it from the tree and tossed it to her just
as a drop of rain hit her nose. 'I declare you must be the
winner, Miss Wilkins,' he said as they drew up their
horses near an empty bandstand. Prince Albert peered
down at them from his gilded perch in the distance be-

fore the red-brick hall. Other than that, there were only flowers and trees, and the grey stretch of sky above, to see them.

'No, I think it's a tie,' she answered, still laughing in delight as she put her hat back on. 'That *was* wonderful! I haven't felt so free in simply ages.' Or ever, truly. Even while riding at home, she was carefully followed.

'Free, yes—and, I'm afraid, rather damp soon.' He glanced up at the sky, which Lily could see was darkening ominously. More droplets of rain landed on her cheeks through her veil.

Aidan swung easily and gracefully down from his saddle and helped Lily from hers. Hand in hand, they raced for the shelter of the bandstand just as the clouds split open. Lily stood by the wrought-iron railing and watched as he tethered the horses, sent the groom away and came to join her. The rain pattered on the tin roof and surrounded their little shelter with a silver curtain. Aidan took off his hat and shook his damp hair, tousling it by running his gloved fingers through it. It tumbled over his brow in unruly waves.

Lily felt a trembling surge in her stomach as she stared at him, yet she couldn't look away.

He grinned that wonderfully crooked smile of his and said, 'I think we might be here for a while.'

Lily wondered if he was sorry about that. Sorry he couldn't just drop her at her door and be done with her for the day. 'I don't mind at all. I could stay here for hours, outside in the fresh air, no curtsying lessons or French grammar to study.' And she could. It seemed the perfect place, with the faintly metallic-smelling breeze sweeping around them, the sound of the rain, the moisture on her cheeks. And Aidan, standing so close to her their shoulders brushed, giving off an electric spark she craved more of. She eased her veil up on to her hat and took a deep breath. 'But if you have important appointments, Duke…'

'I don't. Not a single appointment to keep that's more important than this one.' He sat down on the railing next to her, one foot propped on the ironwork, one carelessly swinging free. He smiled down at her, a lazy, sweet smile that made her think perhaps he *would* rather be there than anywhere else. Just as she would. 'And perhaps, Miss Wilkins, when we are here alone, you might call me Aidan? Every time someone says "Duke" to me, I look for my father or brother.'

Lily nodded, sad for the reminder that he had lost his brother so recently. 'You must miss him—and your father—very much.'

He glanced away, frowning thoughtfully. 'My father I did not know very well. He was always busy, looking after Roderick, attending Parliament, travelling abroad. But my brother—yes, I do miss Edward, very much. He was a kind, gentle soul and very dedicated to his studies and his duties. A much better Duke than a wanderer like myself could ever hope to be.'

And Edward had been in love with Lady Rannock—who loved Aidan? Lily could barely fathom that, if gossip was true. It was too sad. How it must haunt Aidan now. 'I do envy the places you must have seen… Aidan.' She blushed to say his name aloud, the one she had only held in her mind since they met. It suited him—ancient, Celtic, unusual. 'But I think being at a place like Roderick Castle must be an adventure of its own. I love to read and when I lose myself in some ancient tale, like Chaucer, or a modern novel like Sir Walter Scott, I try to imagine what it must all be like. To walk hills your ancestors walked centuries ago. The oldest houses I knew growing up were no older than me! They still smelled of new wood and paint.'

'Roderick Castle *is* an extraordinary place,' he said, his face turning serious. He stared across at Prince Albert, but seemed far away. Far away from *her*. 'When you move from one corridor to another, each built in a different time by different people, you see the progression of—well, of England, I suppose. The sort of lives they lived, what they needed and what they thought was beautiful. What they wanted to hand down and down. Their portraits always watching us. The people who need us, generation after generation, relying on us, helping us. It's part of me, but also feels distant from me, in some strange way.'

Lily could see that he really did love it, no matter how he might have loved his free travels as well. She wondered what that was like, to have a home like that, to know you were part of something. That you were important. 'It must be so wonderful to belong to something bigger than yourself in such a way.' And to be able to help the people on his land. She could see that it was important to him, never to let down those who relied on him.

'It is…interesting, Miss Wilkins. Impossible to describe, really.'

Impossible to explain to someone who did not grow up to know it all like the back of her hand? Someone not part of all this? 'Do call me Lily, please. If I can call you Aidan, you must call me Lily.'

'Lily.' The soft sound rolled gently off his tongue and he smiled down at her. 'You spoke of freedom, the freedom of being out here, of going for a ride. Do you sometimes feel imprisoned, then?'

Lily considered this. Maybe it was the rain, the soft patter of it over their heads, the feelings of being alone

with him in this strange new world. Just the two of them.
Not a duke and 'Old King Coal's' daughter, just Lily and
Aidan. It all felt wonderfully intimate, secret, as if in here
she could tell him anything.

'At home, I feel I'm never alone, never have the chance
to even keep a thought to myself. To know what *I* want
to do,' she said. 'New York and Newport were even more
restricted for young ladies than I've seen so far in Europe,
with servants always at my heels, even going to Bailey's
Beach or the milliner and the bookstore. I don't get to
wear what I like, or eat what I like, or arrange my chamber how I like. It does seem different here in some ways.
Ladies—married ladies—have real duties and responsibilities. A job, if you like, just as you men do. I am sure
your wife or sister, if you had one, your mother, they have
things they must do on the estate, things they must fulfil
at Court. It would be nice to feel so useful, so needed.'

Aidan leaned his chin on his fist and studied her
closely, as if he took every word seriously. As if he was
interested in what she said. 'If you *could* think of what
you wanted to do, Lily, what would it be?'

She searched carefully for words, conscious every moment of his green eyes on her.

'I think… I should like to help people. As you do on
your estate. To work together with them to make sure
we all have what we need. What can make our lives better.' She laughed self-consciously. 'And to grow roses.
I do so love roses. The varieties I've seen here in England are so lovely, so much variety between each sort.
We visited Kew Gardens one day. Mother and my sisters were thoroughly bored, so we didn't go back, but I
could have stayed there for weeks, pestering the gardeners with questions.'

Aidan leaned back against the railing, folding his arms

across his chest and the rain fell behind him in silver streamers. 'My grandmother used to grow roses. Her gardens at Roderick were famous. She won all sorts of ribbons and trophies, but I fear it's a shambles now.'

'Really? But I'm sure there are some left, just waiting to be brought back to glorious life. I should like to see it.'

'Would you really?'

'Oh, yes! And the medieval tower you told me about.' She leaned closer to him. 'May I tell you a secret, Aidan?'

He leaned towards her until they nearly, temptingly, touched. He still smelled of linen and lemons, of wool and faintly of horse. 'I do love secrets, Lily.'

'I very much dread going back to New York,' she whispered.

'I can understand that, if you're followed everywhere there.' He leaned just one, teeny tiny inch closer and she wondered if he would perhaps kiss her. 'And I dread—' He broke off and leaned back.

Lily swallowed a cold, hard knot of disappointment. 'Dread what, Aidan?'

'Never being caught in the rain like this again,' he said hoarsely.

She reached up to touch his face, trailing her fingers over his finely carved features as she marvelled at him. He made her feel so strangely safe with his quiet strength, but at the same time she was dizzy with feelings she'd never known before and couldn't understand.

'Lily,' he whispered, and then he did what she longed for. He kissed her.

She went up on tiptoe to meet him, twining her arms around him so she wouldn't fall from this dream. So he wouldn't leave her. His arms closed around her waist, pulling her even closer to him.

She marvelled at how they seemed to fit together.

Their mouths, their hands, their bodies, as if they were made to be just like they were now. She parted her lips instinctively and felt the tip of his tongue sweep over hers. Lightly, enticingly, then the kiss turned frantic, hungry, full of burning need.

Until a loud crash of thunder rumbled overhead, reminding her where they were.

He stepped back from her, his arms falling away from her body. She shivered, suddenly so cold, sad, as if she had just been dropped from a great, dizzying pink cloud on to the hard earth again. She didn't know where to look, what to say, what to think.

She only knew everything, absolutely everything, had changed in some unfathomable way in only an instant.

'I think the rain has stopped,' he said gently, his voice rough. They glimpsed the groom hovering discreetly in the distance with the horses.

Lily opened her eyes and looked up at him. His eyes were vividly green, but he, too, looked terribly sad as he looked down at her. 'My mother will probably be missing me,' she said. Though she knew Stella wouldn't, not really. Her mother was probably hoping Lily had eloped with the Duke to Scotland.

Not that such a thing was possible, she knew that. She could see now that he needed a different sort of wife than her, an English wife who could know what the work of his title required and jump right into it. Not a pampered American girl.

She found her hat where she had dropped it on the wooden planks of the floor, now with the veil sadly torn and the brim crushed. She pinned it back on as best she could and let him help her back into her saddle. Star seemed none the worse for wear for her dampening and pawed at the ground as if ready to gallop again. Aidan gently adjusted her train and for some reason his careful movements made her feel even more sad.

'Thank you, Aidan, for listening to me,' she said, afraid that might be the last time she would say his name. 'For listening to my ramblings.'

He gave her a crooked, sad, little smile and touched her gloved hand for one lingering moment. 'Lily. It was certainly my pleasure.'

Chapter Eight

When Lily came down to breakfast the next morning, she was surprised to find her mother already there,
dressed in an elaborate bronze taffeta morning gown, a
plate of eggs and kidneys in front of her, along with all
the morning newspapers. A teetering stack of invitations,
creamy cards just waiting to topple and scatter, stood by
her coffee cup.

Fortunately, they had been to the opera the night before and there'd been no time for Stella to interrogate Lily
about her ride with Aidan, or why he didn't come in for
tea when they returned. But Lily knew questions were
coming and she wished she didn't have to face them after
a sleepless night. She'd lain awake so long in the darkness, feeling his lips on hers again, the surge of emotion
she had never known before, the excitement she'd never
imagined. What did it mean? Did it mean *anything*?

Trying to explain it to her mother would just make it
all the more complicated.

She fetched her eggs and toast from the covered dishes
on the sideboard and sat down gingerly across from her
mother. A cup of coffee was left at her place and a jar
of homemade marmalade from Lady Heath's stillroom.

Aidan, so easy to talk to, so comfortable to be around. But *he* seemed to admire Rose herself, sweet, quiet Rose.

'Being Lady James wouldn't be quite as much fun as being a duchess, or so Violet says. Duchesses can do whatever they like. But I think you should choose whom *you* like best.'

'We should all be free to do that, darling Rose.' And a duchess could help free her sisters, too. Everyone would seek them out; almost all choices would be open to them. They wouldn't be beholden to their mother with Lily there to help them. 'Sometimes, though, we simply don't have that freedom.'

'It's terribly unfair. Think of all we could do if only we had men's dangling bits...'

Lily laughed in shock as she held up her hand. 'Rose! What a thing to say. It sounds like Violet.'

'Well, she *did* say it first, but she's not wrong. If we were men, we could go to college, sail the seas, be politicians or doctors or writers of important books. We could do anything, go where we like. Do you want to stay here in England?'

'I don't know.' Lily considered all she had seen of England: the old houses, the green fields, the ancient churches. 'Maybe.'

'You should write it all in your book,' Rose said, gesturing to the velvet notebook on Lily's lap. 'The good *and* the bad parts of it all. About England and the Duke, even about Lord James.'

'If you can help me,' Lily said.

'Of course.'

They opened the book and were busily scribbling ideas when they heard Lady Heath arrive.

'My dears!' Lady Heath cried, sweeping into the library as she pulled off her embroidered rose-coloured

'Lily, darling, we're to have luncheon with Lady Heath today. I'll have Doris lay out your blue velvet suit.' Luckily, Stella seemed to be in a good mood. Planning Lily's wardrobe always cheered her up. 'And you will never guess what arrived with the morning's post!'

'An invitation to dine and sleep at Windsor with the Queen?' Lily teased.

Her mother gave her a stern glance. 'Don't be flippant, Lily, it is not becoming in a young lady. But I will say such an invitation might indeed be in your future. The Duchess of Lennox has invited us to a tea party in the garden of Lennox House!'

'The Duke's mother?' Lily said, stunned, a forkful of egg suspended in mid-air. She quickly put it back down at her mother's frown, but her breath felt caught deep inside of her. What would her mother say if she knew he had kissed Lily? She would be booking Westminster Abbey for the wedding right away.

Could this really be happening, now, to her? Could the Duke really be seriously interested?

And what was he interested *by*, really? Her—or those American dollars?

The doubt ached deep inside of her, simply because she found herself so very fascinated by *him*. Looking forward to every moment she could snatch with him.

'Yes, indeed, the Duke's mother. They say she was once a great beauty and will probably be married again soon, to an earl.' Stella frowned at the stiff, cream-coloured card beside her plate. 'Though an earl is not as good as a duke.'

'No.' Lily remembered all Lady Heath's careful lessons. Barons, viscounts, earls, marquesses, dukes. But then there was the age of the title to consider when arranging precedence, age of title holders, all sorts of things. And what about archbishops?

She shook her head. She would make a very bad duchess, she feared. If only it was all just kissing in the rain.

'You'll need a new gown,' Stella said, pouring out more coffee, as if to fortify herself for garden party battle plans.

Lily thought of her grand Worth gown and the simple organzas of the other young ladies. 'Oh, no, Mother, please. Surely my lavender muslin will do very well. It's very pretty and it has such a lovely matching hat.'

'Nonsense. Everyone says the Prince of Wales likes Americans so much because we have dash and style these dour English ladies sadly lack. I've seen it myself now.' She studied Lily closely over the gilded edge of her cup. 'We can't do much about the lack of dash, I suppose, but we *can* work on the style. Show them what we've got.'

Lily lowered her gaze and took a nibble of toast. It was true she didn't often feel *dashing*, except when riding a horse, or when Aidan smiled at her. Violet was the dashing one and Lily had never minded that.

Until now.

'The party is too close to order a new frock,' her mother said. 'You could borrow my green brocade—I haven't worn it yet—and my emerald earrings. It will have to do…'

Lily followed her old habit of no longer listening as her mother made plans, of escaping into her own thoughts. Her mother never required anyone else's opinion, anyway. Instead, she took herself back to the park, to the rain, to Aidan's green eyes, to the touch of his hand.

After breakfast, she ran into the small library as her mother summoned all the maids to look through ward-

robes and jewel cases. Lily took out her little velvet journal and made notes instead, writing down every detail she remembered of their ride in the park so she could never forget it.

When Rose peeked around the door, Lily could still hear the clamour from upstairs. She waved Rose inside, who gratefully shut the door and curled up next to Lily on the sofa.

'Is it true, Lil?' she said softly. 'You're going to a party with a duchess?'

'Yes, the invitation came this morning. That's why Mother is scouring her jewel boxes to deck us out like two Christmas trees.'

'And you went riding with him yesterday, the Duke himself. I saw him from upstairs. He was very handsome.' She frowned thoughtfully as she toyed with the silk fringe on a cushion. 'Will you marry him?'

Lily laughed. One ride, even one world-changing kiss, was far from matrimony. No matter what her mother thought. 'Darling, riding and tea in the garden hardly constitute a proposal, even here in England.'

'But it must be close. That's what Lady Heath says. A gentleman never endangers a lady's reputation by paying her too much public attention. And we know it's what Mother dreams of above all else—to be the mother of a duchess.'

'She would like it, certainly. Mrs Astor would *have* to call on her then,' Lily said, trying to be light.

'But what do *you* want, Lily?' Rose said. Lily could never hide from her, the most serious, the most watchful of the Wilkins. Rose was quiet, but wise. 'You did rather like Lord James Grantley, I thought. He sends such pretty bouquets.'

'Yes, he does seem very nice,' Lily said. And so unlike

gloves. Her pink walking suit gleamed in the grey light, simple and elegant and perfectly English. Lily wished her mother would listen to Lady Heath's fashion advice more. 'What on earth is the uproar I hear upstairs? Are you all packing to move to a new house without telling me?'

'Mother and Lily are invited to the Duchess of Lennox's garden party,' Rose said. 'And Mother is just planning what to wear.'

Lady Heath arched her brow, but her English nature didn't give any thoughts away. 'The Duchess? How exciting. She used to be famous for her parties, but she has been rather quiet since her eldest son died. This is a very good sign.' She sat down across from them and smoothed her gloves on her lap. 'Your day in the park with the Duke must have gone well, Lily dear.'

'He was...very charming,' Lily stammered. She looked down at her notebook, trying not to blush again.

'And I am sure he found *you* charming, too.'

'I could not say,' Lily managed to choke out. Rose peered up at her, too closely.

Lady Heath shook her head. 'Lennox is not like other, more typical, English gentlemen. He has had his own rather exciting career, has seen much of the world. He could never be content with a typical English girl. Perhaps you, Lily, are just what is required.'

Her dollars required to mend English houses? Lily didn't want to ruin the magic of her day in the park with Aidan with such thoughts, but they were always there. Those doubts. If only she could truly trust in Aidan? Know he was true? 'I am not at all exciting.'

'You do yourself too little credit, my dear,' Lady Heath said.

'Indeed she does!' Rose declared. 'She is so smart, and ever so pretty. And kind.'

'You see how clever Rose is? She does see so much,' Lady Heath said with a laugh. 'She will be the next Duchess after you, I am sure. How well you will both look in the strawberry leaves of a ducal coronet! Now, tell me, what are your mother's plans for the garden party wardrobe?'

Lily sighed. 'I said my lavender muslin would do very well, but she declares I must borrow her green brocade and emeralds.'

Lady Heath clucked her tongue. 'Oh, no, my dear, that would never do! The game has quite changed now. Everyone has seen how American you are. Now they must see how English you *could* be...'

Chapter Nine

Lily smoothed the skirt of her lavender muslin and creamy lace sleeves, which Lady Heath had persuaded her mother was the *correct* thing to wear to a garden party, and tried to sit still on the carriage seat. She felt so very nervous about this invitation, more than any other party she could remember. What did the Duchess's attention mean? What would Aidan say to her when he saw her today? What would *she* say to *him*? What did she want to happen? She hadn't heard from him since their outing to park, though he had sent a lovely bouquet of violets.

She closed her eyes and tried to take a deep breath. Doris had drawn her corset tight that morning and the high, lacy neckline of the dress seemed to close around her. At least she was not swathed in her mother's expensive brocade and emeralds. She would look more like the other young ladies, less likely to stand apart.

As Lady Heath had said, *more English*. She would fit in, even though she was American.

What would being 'more English' mean? Would Aidan like to see that in her? It had felt so different being alone with him in the rain. So easy, no questions racing around in her brain. With a crowd watching the two of them, speculating, gossiping…

She shivered, and opened her eyes to smooth her skirt again and straighten her hat. The tip-tilted confection of white straw and satin roses was pinned firmly to the up-sweep of her hair, but it felt tipsy.

'Oh, Lily, do stop fidgeting,' her mother said crossly. Though she, too, kept fussing with her own ribbon-edged sleeves and her cashmere shawl. Stella Wilkins always knew her worth in America, but she had never been to a duchess's garden party before. 'I've been at such pains all these years to raise my daughters to be graceful and poised.'

'I think Lily looks very graceful,' Rose said.

'And poised,' Violet added. 'It's really *us* you need to be worried about, Mother.'

Since it was a daytime event and the whole family had been invited, Violet had wheedled and cajoled until Stella declared she had a headache and gave in, allowing the twins to attend the party. Lily thought they looked very charming in green and white muslin and silk, though Rose looked a bit nervous. Violet's eyes shone with ex-citement and of course she had her camera in tow.

'Your turn will come soon enough, Miss Violet,' Stella said with a warning shake of her gloved finger. 'But don't you dare ruin your sister's chances with bad behaviour today! Our family's whole future depends on this.'

Lily did not want to be reminded that the burden of the Wilkins name rested on her shoulders. Luckily, the car-riage slowed and came to a stop before her mother could launch into a full lecture. Lily peeked out the window at the house in front of them and saw it was quite grand, much larger than any other London house she had seen. All pale stone, looming red-brick chimneys and large windows, gazing out as if to judge the passers-by beyond its wrought-iron gate.

She bit her shaking lip and reminded herself, *grace and poise*. This was just a large house, no different from her parents' dwelling in New York.

A footman in dark green livery opened the carriage door and helped her out on to the pavement. A blue carpet was laid from the door for guests to walk on and she could hear the echo of laughter from somewhere just out of sight. She glimpsed a stern-looking butler waiting at the black-painted front doors.

The twins took Lily's arms, linking one of them on each side, as if they sensed her hesitation. 'It does look very pretty,' Rose whispered.

'And so grand!' Violet said. 'Just think, Lily—this could be just *one* of your houses.'

'Oh, do hush,' Lily murmured, the butterflies in her stomach fluttering even harder.

Their mother sailed past them, up the marble steps and handed their invitation card to the butler. 'Ah, yes, Mrs Wilkins and the Misses Wilkins,' he said, his voice just the deep, stentorian tone a butler *should* have. 'Do follow me. Her Grace is already in the garden.'

They stepped into the house, cool and shadowed after the warm day, and Lily couldn't help but notice that though the house was indeed very pretty and large, with a soaring rotunda overhead reached by a sweeping, marble-balustraded staircase, it seemed strangely unreal. Empty, echoing, still. As if it simply waited.

'No wonder this has to be an afternoon party,' Stella whispered, sounding more her confident self now as she looked around the empty, black-and-white-tiled hall, the quiet sitting rooms beyond. 'How could you have a din-

ner party or dancing in such a place? Not a chair or painting to be seen!'

The butler led them through open glass doors at the
end of a corridor and onto a pale stone terrace. Unlike
the inside of the house, the garden was a riot of colour,
flowerbeds overflowing with red, pink, yellow and white,
with little iron tables dotted on the grass and a croquet
game in progress. Ladies in gowns coloured to rival the
flowers sat on the dainty chairs or strolled the white
gravel pathways, their parasols bobbing in the breeze.

Lily studied the groups gathered on the terrace and
the lawn, but she didn't see Aidan anywhere. She didn't
know if she was relieved or quite disappointed.

'Mrs Wilkins! And your charming daughters, yes? I
have heard so much about them.' A lady came towards
them with an outstretched, lace-gloved hand and a smile,
and Lily knew it had to be the Duchess. She was tall and
slim in a gown of cherry-coloured striped silk and a large
white hat, her hair still golden in the sunlight, her eyes as
green as Aidan's. 'Welcome, welcome! Would you care
for some tea? Or champagne? Or perhaps your younger
daughters would like to join the croquet with my nieces?'

'Oh, yes, Mother, please!' Violet begged and Stella
nodded. The twins let go of Lily and abandoned her to
her fate, joining the crowd of laughing young ladies on
the croquet lawn.

Lily so wished she could join them, but instead she
was trapped where she was. She curtsied to the Duchess,
and tried to smile. *Grace and poise.*

'And you are Lily Wilkins, of course,' the Duchess
said, studying Lily closely with those vividly green eyes.
Lily realised that even though they were the same colour
as Aidan's, they were like winter ice, where his were
like a summer's day. 'How well your name suits you,

my dear. You are quite as pretty as a flower. Will you sit with me for something to drink? I do long to hear all about American life. My fiancé, Lord Shelton, says we shall travel there one day!'

'Thank you, Duchess,' Lily said and exchanged a glance with her mother. Stella gave a little nod and she and her mother sat down with the Duchess at one of the little iron tables at the edge of the terrace, just under the shade of a blue awning. It was laid with a silver tea service, a tiered tray of enticing, glistening raspberry tarts and tiny salmon sandwiches that all looked quite untouched, like a painted still-life. The Duchess was all lightness as she poured tea and chatted with Stella about Newport, its yachts and dances, but Lily had the distinct sense they were being very carefully studied.

'How different you must find our little city,' the Duchess said with an airy laugh. 'So quiet and slow! I should so love to see your New York, it sounds terribly exciting. And rather naughty, I dare say.'

'New York and London are not dissimilar at a certain level of society, Duchess,' Stella said, a note of coolness creeping into her Southern vowels. Lily knew that tone well; it meant be cautious. She stuffed a tart in her mouth. 'But I would be most happy to host you at any time, in New York or Newport, so you could see for yourself.'

'How kind you are, Mrs Wilkins,' the Duchess said. 'I am sure I *will* have the chance to travel soon, once I see my dear son settled and he does not need my assistance any longer. New places would be good for my health, as well, or so my doctor says.'

'I do hope you are not unwell, Duchess,' Lily said and the Duchess gave her a gentle smile.

'You dear girl, such concern for others! Just a bit of

dizziness now and then, I fear. The damp of London, perhaps.'

Lily thought she had never seen anyone look quite as healthy as the Duchess. So golden and vibrant in the sunlight. She and her son did seem to share a certain vigour of life which Lily couldn't help but admire, even envy. 'I am terribly sorry to hear it.'

'What a sweet girl you are, Miss Wilkins. Here, do have another tart, the raspberries are grown at Roderick Castle's own greenhouses. The Queen herself will have no others for her table at Osborne. I do hope that, before I see you in America, you will join a small house party I'm organising at Roderick. Soon it will not be *my* home any longer, but I do want to show it off one more time.'

Lily exchanged an alarmed glance with her mother. Stella's smile only faltered a bit, but Lily could see what she was thinking—this was it. The next step to a dukedom. 'We would enjoy that, Duchess, thank you,' Stella said, as Lily tried to resist the urge to pop another tart in her mouth. 'We haven't had the chance yet to see much of the English countryside.'

'There won't be shooting quite yet, of course. My late husband was famous for his shooting parties. But it *is* pretty there, if I do say so myself, and there is always excellent riding to be had in the neighbourhood.' The Duchess swept another examining glance over Lily. 'I do hear you are quite the horsewoman, Miss Wilkins.'

Lily swallowed the last bit of raspberry hard. What had she heard about that rainy afternoon in the park? 'I enjoy it very much.'

'Wonderful! I shall send a letter with the details this week. Now, Miss Wilkins, perhaps you'd like to explore the gardens a bit? There is a cunning little maze at the back of the lawn I had put in, years ago now. Your mother and I shall have a nice little chat. And perhaps a glass of champagne, Mrs Wilkins?'

Lily had the distinct sense she was being sent away, but she didn't mind. She felt rather pinned like a squirming butterfly under the Duchess's study. She took up her parasol and hurried down the stone terrace steps to the lawn, hoping she might glimpse Aidan somewhere among the crowd.

It was indeed a lovely garden, if a bit overgrown and neglected, though the overflowing flowerbeds and tangled trees gave it a certain charm Lily enjoyed very much. She waved at the twins on the croquet lawn, nodded at Lady Heath who sipped champagne with a group near an old tennis court and followed the gravel pathways until she glimpsed the maze the Duchess had mentioned. Its tall hedge walls gave it a shadowed sense of sanctuary.

As she turned a corner, she saw Aidan at last, standing apart from the strolling crowds on the pathways at the edge of the tall iron fence next to the maze. She raised her hand to wave to him—and then saw he was not alone.

A lady stood with him, very near to his side, her face beneath a silk and lace hat tilted up to smile into his. She wore a gown of form-fitting white lace striped with violet ribbons, very sophisticated and daring, and her smile matched it. She swayed closer to him and laid her gloved hand on his sleeve. He didn't move away. The two of them seemed perfectly at ease together, perfectly understanding.

Lily's hand dropped and she dashed behind a large marble statue of Diana with her bow drawn, hoping no one had noticed her. When she peeked again, Aidan and the lady had vanished. Had they gone into the maze... together?

She had dared to foster tentative hopes for the Duke.

But would even the smallest hopes be possible if he cared for someone else?

'Lily, my dear, there you are. How quickly you dashed away! Why are you lurking here behind this poor huntress?'

Lily turned to find Lady Heath smiling at her. 'I—I was just...' she stammered, and glanced towards the maze. Had she imagined Aidan and his lady standing there?

Lady Heath nodded. 'Just admiring Lady Rannock's gown, I'm sure. She is said to be one of the most fashionable of the PBs.'

Lady Rannock? The one who was said to have been engaged to Aidan's brother, until Aidan himself kissed her? Lily felt suddenly cold and she clutched at her parasol as if the flimsy bit of ivory and silk would hold her up. 'PB?'

'Professional Beauties, of course. Like Jennie Churchill and Lily Langtry and Patsy Cornwallis-West. Their photographs are always displayed in shop windows, you know, and they cluster around the Prince of Wales like hothouse flowers. They make up the dashing core of the Marlborough House Set—so much more fun than the Queen's dour court. Lady Rannock's husband is often absent for his health and she spends time with old friends of her family, like the Duchess.' Lady Heath took Lily's arm and firmly led her away, back towards the light and the crowds. 'Such old friendships can be a comfort. Speaking of the Duchess, I saw her in cosy conversation with your mother. They seem quite bosom bows already.'

Grace and poise. Lily shook off her cold misgivings about Aidan and Lady Rannock, the doubts and jealousy she had no right to have, and smiled. 'Mother will be happy to know she's made a new friend. I think she was a little nervous about this party.'

Lady Heath laughed. 'Oh, the Duchess likes to have her due, but she is kind enough at heart. She just takes her family name very seriously.'

'Everyone here seems to.' And yet, when she had been alone in the rain with Aidan, his name and title hadn't seemed to matter at all. It had just disappeared and he was... Aidan.

Would she ever see *that* man again? The man she liked so much?

'Of course. What else do we have but our pride?' Lady Heath gave her a searching glance. 'You may come to feel the same, Lily dear. A sense of a secure place, of a useful duty to fulfil, should not be under-estimated.'

Lily knew she was right. But what about love? What about connection, emotion, affection? She'd seen all that fade between her parents and she didn't want such a life for herself. Duty and work were important, but couldn't love be important, as well?

She glanced back at the maze and wondered if Aidan had been truly in love with Lady Rannock.

'Marriage and love needn't preclude each other,' Lady Heath said, as if she sensed Lily's thoughts. 'But neither must they rely on each other. Marriage for a woman is much too important an endeavour to trust it to such a fickle thing as a heart.'

Had that been the way of Lady Heath's own marriage? Lily felt terribly sad to think so, for Lady Heath, in spite of her matchmaking, had been kind to her. And she feared that her words might be right anyway. The world was a dangerous place. Marriage could mean safety and security. But also sadness. Look at her own parents.

They came out of a clearing to the edge of the terrace

again, and Lily saw Lord James Grantley standing near the marble urns of red flowers. She felt a sudden surge of gladness to see a familiar face. He was on the list in her notebook. Could he still be? She walked towards him as Lady Heath stayed to greet some of her own friends.

'Lord James, what a pleasant surprise to see you here today,' she said. 'We didn't see you at the Crewe ball and I wanted to learn what you had been reading lately.'

'Miss Wilkins!' he said with a smile, bowing over her hand. 'I was also sorry to miss the ball, but I had business to see to at my father's estate. I haven't had a chance to read the volume of metaphysical poets yet, I fear. And I haven't had a chance to see the Society of French Artists exhibit at the Durand-Ruel Gallery. Have you been yet?'

'We plan to go tomorrow, I think. Or I hope.' If there was a country house party at Roderick Castle, Lily feared her mother would insist on a trip to the dressmaker instead. 'I am quite longing to see them for myself; they sound so wild and strange.'

As they chatted about the new French paintings, Rose came up to Lily with a sigh. 'Oh, Lily, I am quite tired of croquet now! But Vi still insists on playing.'

Lily laughed and wrapped her arm around Rose's shoulders. 'You poor thing! Lord James, this is my sister, Miss Rose Wilkins. Rose, Lord James was just telling me about the Durand-Ruel exhibition. I do think your *mademoiselle* should take you and Violet to see them.'

'Oh, she already has!' Rose enthused, perking up quite a bit. She always preferred art to sport. 'Tell me, Lord James, what did you think of the use of thick, bright colours? So very *alive*, I thought, so full of passion and summer feeling!'

Lily, sensing that she was somehow no longer needed as Lord James and Rose smiled at each other, backed away and strolled slowly around the edge of the garden maze she'd noticed earlier, studying its dense hedge walls. It really was quite lovely, not like something in the centre of London at all, smelling of summer clover. The sounds of the party were muffled there. She could almost imagine herself completely alone.

But when she came around the corner, she found she was *not* alone. Aidan, the Duke, stood in the shade of the hedge wall, one leg crossed lazily against the other, smoking a cheroot. He looked elegantly non-English, in a pale linen jacket, a straw hat dangling in his other hand. There was no lady hovering nearby.

Lily laughed, secretly glad to find him alone. 'Are you hiding away, too?'

He hastily stood up straight and put out his cheroot. As he smoothed his hair and put his hat back on, he looked so adorably like a schoolboy caught out in some mischief that she had to laugh even more.

He grinned at her. 'Just don't tell my mother.'

'I won't, if you won't tell *my* mother,' she confided. 'She does hate it when I run away from parties. I just needed a little moment alone.'

He nodded sympathetically. 'I understand the feeling.'

Lily thought of how once he had roamed the world, free, and now he was stuck here. 'I'm sure you do, Duke. It must be so different from your life before.'

'I admit I miss the freedom of it all.'

She sighed. 'And I would love to *have* some freedom. But I have this moment and I must say I'm quite enjoying it. Your garden is so lovely.' She waved her furled parasol at the maze behind them. 'Your mother says your grandfather put in this maze. It looks quite Elizabethan. We don't have anything like it in New York.'

'Yes. He built it for his wife, who quite loved her own

romantic version of history. They say no one has ever really made it to the centre.' He held out his arm to her with a smile she was sure no lady could resist. 'Shall I show you around it, Miss Wilkins?'

Lily very much feared she was also not one to resist that smile, nor the chance to see the forbidden centre of the maze. But she couldn't help but remember his companion, who had stood so intimately close. 'Won't your guests miss you?'

'Not for a while. My mother always keeps them so entertained.'

'Then I would enjoy that, thank you.' She took his arm with a smile and they made their way into the cool, shaded hush of the maze. They turned corners back on to the pathways they'd just passed, but Lily didn't notice the circuitous way; she was too fascinated by the deep, rich sound of his voice, by that smile, by his tales of the building of the maze, the history of the Lennox House gardens, places he had seen on his travels.

Until they turned another corner—and found the Duchess and Lily's mother standing there, obviously looking for them. Lily stepped back, feeling strangely as if she had been caught out in some naughtiness, even though they had just been talking.

But her mother smiled happily. 'There you are, Lily darling. We were just wondering where you'd vanished to so secretively. Now I can see...'

Chapter Ten

'Well, it's rather pretty, I'll admit,' Stella said, frowning out the carriage window. 'Not quite like *my* old home, of course, but I dare say it will do. What do you think, Lily?'

Lily knew that by 'old home' her mother meant South Carolina—after decades in New York, Stella St. Claire Wilkins still thought no place could compare. But Lily had only ever seen the rolling hills and hazy shimmer of heat of her mother's home when she was very little and she thought the English countryside would 'do' very well indeed.

It was all dark green and soft in the late summer, quiet as if it held its breath for the crisp crack of autumn. The winding road their carriage journeyed along was lined on one side by a tangle of hedgerows, grown thick and brambly over generations, and on the other by a low, grey stone wall that looked over rolling fields. It was all quiet, empty but for a distant flock of white sheep and some farmers with their ploughs.

At the crest of a hill, Lily glimpsed a small cottage, whitewashed with a dark grey slate roof. A woman was hanging washing on a line in the garden, with two children and some chickens flocking around her. That small family, and the farmers in the field, were the first people she'd seen since the train station where they alighted miles back. To her surprise, the Roderick Halt station was only for visitors to the castle, a fanciful little place painted in the green and gold of the ducal livery and trimmed with lacy gingerbread on the eaves of its pitched roof and along its flowerboxes. The footmen in their green livery quickly took charge of their thirty trunks and boxes and saw them into the gleaming green enamelled carriage, with a gold coronet on the doors. It was all so smooth and easy, Lily barely felt the vehicle moving away.

Even Rose and Violet were quiet for once, staring out the windows with wide hazel eyes, mouths open in astonishment as they watched the vast countryside flow around them. Rose ran her gloved fingertip along the plush, if slightly shiny and threadbare, green velvet upholstery.

Lily took a deep breath at her slightly open window and savoured the green loaminess of the fields, the hint of rose that seemed to follow everywhere in England, the low sky the colour of her mother's pale grey pearls that swept overhead, holding everything together.

It all seemed so peaceful, so quiet, so timeless. As if she could finally breathe again after the clamour of London, the constant motion, the constant expectations. No one was watching her here, judging, giggling behind fans, half expecting her to leap into some Parisian cancan dance.

No one but her own mother. She sensed Stella studying her and she leaned back from the window and sat still against the velvet cushions. She folded her gloved hands in the lap of her aubergine travel suit. She wished so much it was Aidan with her, Aidan she could laugh with now, who could explain his home to her. Aidan, alone with her, no parents or pretty ex-flames to distract them. Nothing to give her doubts.

'Yes, I do think it's very pretty here,' she said. It had a history, a peace to it she'd never found at home. Never even dreamed of, except in books. Now here it was before her, a real place, with a real handsome duke waiting for her. At a castle.

'I think it suits you,' her mother said, arranging her fur muff on her arm with an air of satisfaction, as if she had created the countryside herself. 'I was sure it would. As soon as you were born and they laid you in my arms, I knew you were no ordinary child. You, Lily, were an *old* soul and I've worked hard to do right by you, to make sure you're in your proper place.' She took Lily's hand in hers and squeezed them tightly. 'We are all so close to where we need to be, my darlin' girl! Trust me and listen to Lady Heath, and it will all come out splendidly. Don't you agree, girls?'

Rose and Violet murmured in vague agreement, and Lily looked deep into her mother's eyes. They were usually the colour of topaz, but now they were darker, deeper, like the waning of a summer sun. Could she really be... worried? Really be that set on Lily being a duchess?

She thought of Aidan, of his smile, his kiss. When she concentrated only on him, on seeing him again soon, talking to him, touching him, she didn't feel so nervous at all. But when she remembered all the things that went with him, her stomach clenched and those walls seemed to close around her.

She glanced at that cottage in the distance, heard some snatches of song from the woman as her laundry caught on the breeze. The laughter of the children. If only that could be *her*. Her house, hers and Aidan's. He could be a teacher or a writer, penning tales of the faraway lands he'd seen while she tidied their cosy cottage.

But Aidan was a duke. He had large responsibilities. And if she really wanted him, she had to take those on, too. Had to be worthy of it.

'I will do my best, Mother,' she said.

'Your best is—' Stella said, but the twins interrupted her. They slid across the green velvet seat to crowd against the window, practically pressing their noses to the glass.

'Oh, Lily, I think this is it!' Violet gasped. 'It's like something in a fairy story!'

Lily joined them at the window as they rolled through the pale golden stone arch of a gatehouse. To either side was a symmetrical, octagonal little tower, with bay windows outlined by yellow and red flowers tumbling out of stone urns. A gilded statue of Diana with her bow, much like the one in the garden of Lennox House, crowned the archway.

Lily thought it enchanting, but her mother sniffed, 'Did you see those cracked windows? So unsightly.'

Lily ignored her and the four of them watched in silence as the carriage wound its way along the gravel drive. They seemed all alone in an ancient forest, towering oaks and beeches pressing in close to either side, casting a deep, chilly shade. A few pairs of mysterious, shining eyes seemed to peer out of the grey-green underbrush—foxes or grouse, Lily didn't know—but even they soon vanished.

'I didn't realise it would all be this overgrown,' Violet whispered. 'It's like Sleeping Beauty's palace.'

But then they turned another sharp corner, through a gate in a low, stone wall, and the park opened up to a glorious lawn. Pale, springy and green, it rolled gently forward like a gracefully spreading ballgown skirt, dotted with a few of those black-faced sheep and some marble statues and benches, a small classical temple of a folly in the distance next to a glassy blue lake. Even the sky seemed to lift to make room for it all.

One more turn and there was the house itself. Roderick Castle.

'It's actually a castle,' Rose gasped.

'Yes,' Lily murmured and remembered what Aidan had told her. The castle had been in his family for generation upon generation, added to, expanded, left with their distinctive touches.

'I doubt it's seen a scrub brush since 1400,' Stella sniffed, but Lily could tell that even her mother was impressed. Maybe even a bit…awed? Lily certainly was. 'Those windows are absolutely filthy and the flowerbeds a disgrace. And look how far apart the chimneys are! You'd never get a hot meal here.'

Lily knew her mother was right—Stella could size up houses in an instant and Roderick Castle was vast and old and chilly-looking indeed. It looked as if it had been added on to and rebuilt over centuries without much interest in harmony, not like the mock chateaux and Tudor manors in Newport. The central court was elegantly Palladian, pale yellow stone perfectly symmetrical, with a curving double flight of grey marble steps up to the front doors, framed between Doric pillars. To one side was the old, faded red brick of an Elizabethan wing, to the other something more in the new Gothic style of Queen Victoria's Balmoral. But that section did not seem to be quite finished. The windows were blank, the roof half-done.

As two footmen in that green and gold livery helped them alight once the carriage came to a halt, Lily glimpsed a stable block slightly to one side of the Eliza-

bethan wing. Unlike the rest of the house, it seemed quite
immaculately maintained. At the centre of the drive, the
gravel raked into neat lines, a tall marble fountain stood
silent and dry, topped with another Diana, her bow broken. Red and yellow flowers tumbled out of their beds,
past herbal borders, seemingly in no order.

'More cracked windows. See?' Stella clucked. She gestured to the upper stories of the Palladian wing, which
did indeed seem to be criss-crossed with mending wood.

'Isn't that why we're here, Mother?' Lily whispered.

'Of course. I am sure you would be most equal to
being mistress of any house at all, Lily. Aren't you *my*
daughter?'

A tall, silver-haired, quite intimidating man in a well-
cut black coat stepped through the front doors and made
his stately way down the steps.

'Mrs Wilkins? I am Donat, butler here at Roderick
Castle. Welcome to you and your daughters. Her Grace
is waiting in the Yellow Drawing Room.'

Violet and Rose clutched at Lily's hands as they followed their mother up the stone steps and through the
front doors to the largest, grandest entrance hall Lily
could have ever imagined.

It seemed a space designed to over-awe, with pale,
carved stone walls, a blue fresco of a dome soaring overhead with a twining staircase, the gilded Lennox coat of
arms staring down at them.

'My dear Mrs Wilkins! And your lovely daughters. I
am so happy to welcome you to my home. Well, *my* home
for only a little longer,' the Duchess cried with a silvery
laugh. She stood waiting for them next to a white marble
fireplace, elaborately carved with fruits and vines and
fat little cherubs, and crowned by a portrait of herself as

a younger woman, golden curls tumbling over her shoulders, pink roses in her hand to match her looped and lacy pink crinoline. It echoed the pink day dress she wore now, trimmed with silk flowers and creamy lace flounces on the sleeves. The economies of the castle seemed not to extend to her wardrobe.

Lily quickly glanced around the room and saw it quite lived up to its name.

'We are glad to be here, Duchess,' Stella answered. 'You did say it's lovely country nearby and I must agree with you.'

'I am so glad. I like my guests to feel quite at home.' The Duchess gestured to a tea table laid out near a window, open to let in the fresh breezes and scent of late summer roses. 'And what do you think of the castle, Miss Wilkins?'

Lily felt her throat turn dry, as if to choke her. How could she say what she really thought? That when she looked out at the Roderick gardens and woods she could imagine heaven. Belonging. But was it belonging for *her*?

'It's very beautiful, Duchess,' she said, sitting down at the table between her sisters. Not voluble, maybe, but polite. Her mother's social training did prove useful. 'I think I could wander your pretty gardens for hours.'

The Duchess smiled as she poured the tea from a Sèvres pot painted with violets and ivy twists, surely brought from some royal French court itself by a distant Lennox, like the delicate porcelain ornaments lined up on the marble fireplace mantel. 'I am very fond of our grounds, myself. We have a bit of everything here— a lake with a summer house, my mother-in-law's rose gardens, the shady woods. I'm sure Aidan would love to show them to you. He is out visiting the tenant farms at the moment. He's always so busy with his business. I'm glad you're here to distract him.'

Distract him? Lily wasn't sure she could do that. Maybe they needed Lady Rannock for such a job. 'I'm sure he will have many far more pressing duties during a house party than leading a sightseer around.'

The Duchess's green eyes narrowed, but her smile never faltered. She held out a small plate of cucumber sandwiches. 'Not at all. Lady Heath is arriving this evening, along with the bishop, who is here to deliver the homily at our little village church this Sunday. Everyone else is not due until tomorrow. You are our only guests for the moment. My son has not quite lost his adventuring ways, I fear—he can't settle to quiet work in my husband's library. I'm sure showing an honoured guest our gardens would be a great pleasure to him. Now, Mrs Wilkins, do tell me where you found your lovely hat! I'm just coming out of mourning and feel so behind on the latest fashions…'

Lily sipped her tea and studied the portraits arrayed on the yellow silk walls. Ladies draped in pearls and satins, gentlemen in full-bottomed wigs, looking terribly important on rearing horses or with Roderick Castle in the background. Children swathed in lace and frills. Generations upon generations who had looked out of this window at the very same view.

To one side of the fireplace was an image of two golden-haired boys: one, a bit delicate-looking and with terribly serious green eyes, stared out at the viewer, while the other boy was in motion, leaping as if his energy could not be contained. It had to be Aidan and his brother. The brother who had left him with the responsibility of this house and name. The brother who was meant to have been Duke. He looked as if the weight of the world was upon him, even as a child. Was this why Aidan worked so hard now, living up to that serious-eyed brother?

And what did he really think about one more task, about being told to steer some American girl around his family gardens and impress her? And what about Lady Rannock, the beauty both brothers cared about? How it must have affected Aidan's relationship with his brother! That seemed so ineffably sad.

'Ah, I see you are admiring the study of my two dear sons, Miss Wilkins,' the Duchess said quietly. 'It's by Barnard—such a fine likeness. How studious my Edward was! And Aidan, always so much energy. I could barely keep a nanny employed. How I do treasure that portrait.'

'They are certainly both very handsome, Duchess,' Stella said carefully. 'Were they your only children?'

The Duchess sighed and dabbed at her dry eyes with a lacy handkerchief. 'Sadly, yes. The Duke and I longed for a large family, but we were not so blessed. I should so have liked a daughter!'

'Daughters *are* a joy,' Stella said piously and Lily almost laughed into her napkin. Rose nudged her and Violet stared hard out the window.

'Yours certainly are, Mrs Wilkins! So pretty and such manners. One would hardly believe they were Americans at all.' The Duchess studied Lily so closely that she almost squirmed in her seat. 'I shall certainly look forward to a granddaughter one day. And a grandson, of course, a future Duke of Lennox.' The drawing room door opened suddenly and Aidan stepped in. 'Speaking of which…'

Lily instinctively smiled when she saw Aidan and half rose from her chair at the sight of him, so golden and windblown and welcome in that grand room. A quick, stern look from Stella made her sit back down, but she still smiled. He was wearing riding clothes, doeskin

breeches and rough tweeds, his sun-streaked hair falling over his brow. He laughed a little self-consciously,
and ran his fingers through the tangled strands, mussing
them even more. Lily had to practically sit on her hands
to keep from going to him and smoothing them. Feeling the silk of his hair slide over her skin like when they
were alone at the park…

'Really, Aidan—' his mother tsked '—I'm sure I told
you what time our guests were arriving. And here you
are, looking quite like a stable hand! Whatever will dear
Mrs Wilkins think?'

Lily didn't know what her mother would think, but she
knew what *she* thought—or rather, felt. As though she
wanted to run to him and throw her arms around him.
Especially when he looked rather boyishly chagrined.

'Oh, heavens, but I don't mind!' Stella laughed, waving her hand airily. The dusty light from the window
caught the diamonds on her fingers, bright and new in
that old room. 'When darling Coleman and I married,
we hadn't a bean! My own dear family lost all our right-
ful possessions in that dreadful war and Coleman was a
law clerk. We were living in… Oregon, maybe. Or Idaho?
Coleman worked a silver mine. He would come home at
night looking quite like His Grace does. Quite…manly.'

To Lily's amazement, Stella's cheeks turned girlishly
pink and she giggled a bit into her napkin. 'Oh, yes,
those were fine days.' Lily had never imagined her parents were *ever* happy. What had happened? Could such
a change happen to her, in her own marriage, some day?
It was a scary thought.

'I don't remember them,' Violet said a bit sulkily.

'Oh, you and Rose were so tiny. But Lily was so very
pretty, an Indian Paiute chief's wife, who had sadly lost
her own child, wanted to buy her from us. Said Lily had

a sacred old soul hidden in her eyes. I am sure she was right.'

'Mother,' Lily murmured, feeling her cheeks burn. She peeked at Aidan, wondering what he would think of her true childhood, her true life, but he looked rather intrigued.

'Well, then, why didn't you sell her?' Violet said, stuffing a cucumber sandwich into her mouth as Rose nudged her. 'You said you were so poor back then, Mother. You might have had such an exciting life, Lily!'

'My life is quite exciting enough, Violet,' Lily said.

'Sell my darling baby? Certainly not!' Stella's smile turned teasing, a hint of the twinkling Southern belle she'd once been. 'But it was a rather large sum. And Lily *does* have an old soul, one that deserves a special fate.'

Aidan laughed and sat down at the table, tweeds and dust and all, and his mother handed him a cup of tea with a tiny frown. 'It does sound like an exciting time, Mrs Wilkins. Quite like Aidan's own adventures in the last few years! How did you find yourself there, looking for…silver, was it?'

'Oh, I hardly know, Duchess. I was quite young and silly myself! My darling parents had recently passed away and I had gone to stay with my aunt in Charleston. My Coleman was a law clerk then, as I said, and he was working on a case there. We met at a dance. Like the Duke and my Lily, I am sure! It was grand, like something in a novel. I saw him across the room and he was so handsome, so…vigorous. Those dark eyes of his! I was wearing pink, I think, with a wreath of rosebuds in my hair. I danced and danced, and I…'

'Happily ever after?' the Duchess suggested wryly.

Stella laughed. 'Not quite, at least on my part. You

know how it is for us ladies, Duchess. We must be very careful.'

'Oh, yes, indeed,' the Duchess murmured.

'When we wed, I thought he would go back to practice law in the north somewhere. But he was like you, Duke, he craved adventure in his youth. He and his partner heard of a promising silver mine in…'

'Idaho?' Aidan suggested.

'Oh, no. It was Colorado by then. He wanted to try it before he settled down, see if he could make enough money to buy me a diamond for my ring. A house for our babies. I didn't care about diamonds then, of course, I just wanted to be with my Cole. We lived in a tiny little shack in the mountains, with my tiny girls.' Stella reached out to gently touch the loose curl at Lily's temple. 'It was not easy, but then my Cole struck his lode! The Lily Marie mine. And then he moved on to coal mines, railroads, things like that.' She looked sad for a moment, before she veiled herself in her usual smile.

'What happened to the partner?' Violet asked.

'Whatever do you mean, dear?' Stella said, the moment of tenderness vanishing.

'The partner in the mine, Mother.'

'Oh, I don't know. He ran away or was paid off, I think.' Stella waved that bit of her tale away with a flash of those diamonds.

'What an exciting life you have led, Mrs Wilkins,' the Duchess said. 'You do put our dull little existence here to shame, except for Aidan, of course. Our days are all much the same, just as they have been at Roderick for centuries.'

Lily glanced again at the portrait of the two boys and thought of the glamorous Lady Rannock. Love triangles.

It could not have been all that dull. She couldn't begin to compete.

'Oh, not at all, Mama. You were considered quite the dashing beauty in your time, weren't you?' Aidan said, deceptively mild and teasing as he took a slice of seed-cake.

A dull flush touched the Duchess's powdered cheeks and she looked away. 'That hardly matters now, Aidan dear, really. I am a widow now and that was such a long time ago. Now, don't you want to show Miss Wilkins the long gallery? It's so lovely at this time of day and surely the gong to dress for dinner will sound soon.'

'I thought I looked too disreputable,' he said with a grin. A dimple flashed deep in his left cheek, half hidden beneath the golden-tinged stubble of the day, and it was almost unbearably gorgeous and enticing. Lily longed to press her fingertips just there. To lean close, close enough to smell him and the fresh outdoorness that clung to him.

But everyone was watching the two of them, much too closely, and she leaned back in her chair.

'I should like to see the gallery,' she said quietly.

'Wonderful!' the Duchess said with a cat-that-got-the-cream smile. 'Mrs Wilkins, we can have a lovely little chat here before the gong. I am quite aching to hear about what it's like to live in a mine shack. Just like a novel! Donat can have the maids see Miss Rose and Miss Violet to their chamber.'

Violet looked very much as if she wanted to protest, but the Duchess rang a bell by her chair and Donat immediately appeared. Aidan rose and offered Lily his arm and she took it shyly. They had embraced, even kissed, but here in his own home it all felt so different. He was the Duke, as well as Aidan. And either way, he was so tempting, so havoc-making to her good sense.

He led her out of the Yellow Drawing Room, down the marble staircase to the cold blue and white grandeur of the entrance hall. Lily barely dared breathe, with their mothers—Scylla and Charybdis, perhaps—behind them. She was alone with Aidan, at last.

Well, alone with all the footmen and maids stationed around the vast space. At least that slightly frightening butler was busy dealing with the twins. Lily could almost feel sorry for him.

They went through a doorway and found themselves in a small, dark-panelled space, furnished only with two straight-backed old chairs and a tall clock in the corner. 'Ah!' She sighed. 'I think perhaps I can breathe again.'

'Yes, indeed. The tea table interrogation. I have faced it many times myself,' Aidan said with that dimpled grin. He leaned back against a small window, the dusty light shimmering on his hair, and loosened the rough muslin stock at his throat. 'I am sorry it was your first glimpse of Roderick.'

'I did see it from the drive as we arrived. It's quite astonishing.'

'And what did you think?'

Lily closed her eyes and remembered that glimpse as they turned the corner out of the woods. 'Like something from a fairy story. My sister said it was Sleeping Beauty's castle. The mysterious, frightening dark woods—and then suddenly, light! The revelation of the house, like a jewel set in its rolling lawns and gardens.'

'Ah, then you saw Roderick exactly as it was meant to be presented.' He led her out of the antechamber and up another staircase. 'My great-grandfather brought Repton himself to refashion the grounds, and he was, of course, a great proponent of the picturesque. Sweeping views, revelations around every corner, nature forced to conform.

You may have been more impressed years ago, before his plans began to be taken over by neglect.'

'I don't see that it would be hard to restore it. Even make it lovelier! Perhaps add a parterre to the side, with an orangery built on...'

Aidan laughed wryly. 'I love seeing it anew though your eyes, Lily. It used to be my home, but it all feels strange to me. Maybe you can help me see it again. But even simple improvements need money. We have only one ancient gardener now and his grandson, plus a maid for the kitchen garden and a man who looks after the old greenhouse. In my childhood, we had almost a hundred.'

Lily studied the vast space beyond a window they were passing and conjured up from her readings what it *might* be like. Vast gardens overflowing with flowers, a kitchen garden fragrant with herbs, greenhouses filled with pineapples and lemons.

'I see the rose gardens must have been meant to expand over that way,' she said, gesturing. 'But I think a chamomile lawn would be just the thing to improve the sightlines to the folly. And perhaps a grove of beech there, to give some silvery colour? A perfect place to put a table for al fresco luncheons. They say the Prince of Wales enjoys a picnic. Maybe he could be lured to a party there? How funny that would be!'

Aidan stared down at her, his expression unreadable. 'You are quite right. And what of that strange stand of pines over there? Would it need to go?'

Lily tilted her head as she studied the silvery-green trees. 'Roderick Castle is large. It surely needs many Christmas trees, yes? Like the Queen at Windsor.'

'Lily, Lily. Is there anything you don't know?'

Lily laughed nervously, wondering if it was a compliment. 'My mother did insist on a broad education.

And I love to read. History and botany are both always interesting.'

'That must have come after the silver mine.'

Lily frowned, remembering her vague memories of the tiny house, wind whistling through the paper windows. 'Indeed. I don't remember the Paiute chief's wife, or being an old soul. As for my father's partner, after he left…'

'Left?'

'Yes. Violet doesn't know, but the poor man was killed by cattle rustlers. My mother insisted on finding some civilisation after that. We moved to New York and my father diversified into his railroads and his Pennsylvania coal, steel, that sort of thing.'

'Yes,' Aidan said quietly. They both knew 'that sort of thing'. Money. It was what had brought them together now, in this sleeping castle. If she was not the Lily Marie of Colorado, he wouldn't need her. She suddenly felt cold and wrapped her arms around herself.

'The lady was right, I think,' he said.

'The lady?' Lily asked, puzzled.

'The one who called you an old soul. Just think, you might be an Indian princess now instead of being here with me.'

She laughed. 'I don't think it quite works that way. And a duke is almost like a prince, too, I believe?' She suddenly wished she hadn't said that. He might think she wanted to be *his* princess.

And she did. Too much. Just not his 'dollar princess'. His princess of the heart, if such a fanciful thing would even be possible for a man like him.

Aidan frowned and shrugged. 'I suppose a prince has it worse. Look at poor old Bertie. He will have to be in charge of an entire kingdom, once he gets out from under his mother's thumb. I just have an estate.'

'And the people on it? They rely on you, don't they?'

He arched his brow as if in question.

'I do know something of it all,' she said. 'History and how the land and the people work together. How business is run.'

'Oh, yes?'

'Yes. My father wanted a son, you see, and when he saw he would have none he decided I would do. He taught me accounting and my mother taught me charity, and when I knew we were coming to England, I read your history. The Tudors, the Glorious Revolution, the eighteenth century. Not a patch on practical experience, perhaps, and nothing like all those girls I met in London who grew up knowing these things instinctively, in their bones. But a start.'

Aidan laughed, not the wry sound over the tea table with his mother, but one filled with light and golden glory, like champagne bubbles. A real laugh. Lily found she would give anything to hear it again. 'An equestrienne *and* a gardener. What other secrets do you harbour, Miss Lily Wilkins? What plans do you have for England?'

Emboldened, she reached out, ever so lightly, and touched that dimple as she had longed to do. His skin was warm under her touch, slightly rough with his amber-tipped whiskers. For an instant, he leaned his cheek into her palm. 'You don't even know the beginning, Duke.'

His green eyes darkened to the grey of clouds just before a storm and his expression intensified, grew leaner, hungry. He leaned close, so close she could feel his cheek brush hers, tingling, and could smell the leather and sweat and hay and heat. She could barely breathe, but she wanted to fall into him, *only* him, and never be found again. He studied her, too, as if he had never seen anything like her before.

He raised his long, sun-browned fingers and carefully brushed their tips over her cheek, feather-light. She shivered. He leaned closer, even closer, and her eyes fluttered closed. She wanted to taste his kiss again so much she shook from it.

A door slammed somewhere upstairs and he pulled away. Cold, tingling with disappointment, Lily turned from him and pressed her palms against her cheeks.

'My mother will surely not be happy with whoever dared slam a door here,' Aidan said roughly. 'Strictly forbidden at Roderick.'

Lily dared to peek back at him. He was running his hands through his tousled hair, smoothing it. He smiled, but his eyes were still dark. She found she was glad someone *did* dare to do so; they had stopped her from making an utter fool of herself.

They stood together for another long moment, trapped in silence. She could hear the loud, stentorian tick-tock of the old clock in the corner. Time waited for no one, even in a moment she wished could go on for ever.

Then it seemed a curtain dropped over him and his smile turned carefree and teasing. That flashing white grin he had given her as they danced, or as they raced their horses against a rainstorm, had returned. It was surely the English way, she thought—all hidden.

'I did promise you a look at the gallery, Miss Wilkins,' he said. 'Shall we?'

'Of course,' she murmured, and followed him from their secret little room. He didn't take her arm this time, or walk close to her. He might have been a tour guide in truth. They hurried past what he said was the Red Dining Room to the grand White Drawing Room—'Used only by *very important* guests,' he said with a laugh. 'The Queen and Prince Albert played cards here in 1855, I believe!'—and then the pretty pink and green Music Room where Lily longed to try the piano.

She could barely take it all in. The frescoed ceilings, the Van Dyck paintings of past Lennox Dukes, the tapestried furniture and velvet curtains. They went up yet another staircase, pale wood, elaborately carved with rose trellises and confusingly switch-backed. It was all a large job indeed.

At the last turning was a seven-foot-tall portrait of a lady in diaphanous green fabric, looking rather terrified as she ran from an approaching storm, glancing over her shoulder as her dark hair streamed in the wind.

'Mrs Siddons, the great dramatic actress,' Aidan said. 'She was a great friend of my grandmother. I forgot she was even hanging here. How you are introducing me to my own home, Lily, making me see it all anew.'

'Am I, indeed?' She studied the portrait carefully. Lily could sympathise with the look of sheer panic in her eyes.

He opened a door at the top of the stairs and she followed him into what seemed like a different time entirely. One wall was all windows, curtained in heavy tapestry fabric, looking out at the lake and a stone summer house. The other wall was panelled in dark wood, with no less than three grand fireplaces carved with fruit cornucopias and grinning theatre masks. Smoke-darkened portraits of men in ruffs and ladies in embroidered satins hung between them, along with old weapons and battle flags, and even a rusting suit of armour who kept watch.

'This is the Elizabethan gallery,' he said. 'The oldest part of the house.'

Lily was quite enthralled. She dashed from tapestry to tapestry, portrait to portrait, then to the views from the high windows. Through the hazy old glass she saw the gardens, but they seemed transformed, like watercolours. The stone folly shimmered in the distance, the lake beyond like aquamarines.

'We visited Hardwick Hall, but I think this is even more magnificent,' she said. 'I feel like Mary, Queen of Scots!'

'Oh, I do hope not.' Aidan leaned against one of the old wood mantelpieces, his elbow casually perched on a carved rose, smiling at her. 'She was so terribly unhappy. At least she never visited here, so her ghost isn't one of the many cluttering up the place.'

'You have ghosts? How wonderful!' Lily forgot herself for a moment, and twirled—actually *twirled*—down the centre of the long, narrow room.

'All self-respecting old English houses have a ghost or two. They probably wouldn't let us stay here if we didn't let them have free rein.'

Lily collapsed, dizzy, on to a faded velvet chair. 'And who is your ghost?'

'Which one?'

'Which *one*?'

'We have several. The obligatory Grey Lady, who once lost her lover in battle and now wanders the garden on full-moon nights, then vanishes into the lake. A Cavalier soldier who buried his jewels under a tree before fleeing the Roundheads—now he tries to dig them up every October.'

'October? Why?'

Aidan shrugged. 'Who knows the ways of ghosts? There's also a spaniel puppy who bounces his ball down the great staircase…'

'I should love to meet that one. I do love pets and Mother never lets me have them.'

'Dogs have always been welcome at Roderick, fortunately. Though I fear at the other end of our supernatural spectrum, there is an elemental.'

Lily shivered at his ominous tone. 'What is that?'

'Some primeval creature that looks like mud and smells like decay, I believe. One of my old nannies used to say he hung about in the priest hole near the chapel.'

'Are the Lennoxes Catholic?'

'Not since the time of Queen Elizabeth. Too much trouble. Now I suppose we aren't much of anything.'

Lily thought an old chapel sounded wonderfully romantic—though without any elementals. 'I should like to see it very much. But not any ghosts.'

'So you shall. But the gallery is enough sightseeing for one afternoon, I'm sure. I don't want to scare you away. It must be time to dress for dinner soon.'

Lily rose from her chair, running her fingertips over its worn carving, wondering who had sat there over those many years. 'Very well, but you must promise to show me the chapel later. And the Grey Lady's paths. And, well, everything.'

He smiled and nodded, his real smile back again. 'I see you are as besotted with history as my grandfather once was! Yes, very well, everything. I will learn it along with you.'

Lily swallowed and felt that horrid blush in her cheeks again. 'Everything?' she said. She dared to reach out and lightly brush her finger over his sleeve as she walked past him.

'Almost everything,' he said, a bit roughly.

She paused to examine a cluster of silver-framed photographs displayed on a velvet-draped table. The Duchess, in trailing, fur-trimmed pale chiffon at Ascot, on the arm of an older, silk-hatted gentleman. And another, in dark velvet, in an opera box with another man, one with copious whiskers and a merry smile.

'My father,' Aidan said, gesturing to the Ascot image. 'And my stepfather-to-be.'

'The Earl? I see.' Lily trailed her fingertip over the other photos. Prince Bertie in his royal orders, signed to the Duchess. Princess Alexandra, beautiful in low-cut lace and tiara. Princess Louise. The old Queen herself in an open carriage, swathed in widow's veils. Babies in lacy christening gowns, two sturdy toddlers hugging their mother—Aidan and his brother, surely. The Duke and Duchess in velvet and ermine mantles and coronets for some state occasion. Two lanky boys fishing at the Roderick lake, the summer house behind them.

She picked it up to examine it closer, to see the real boys behind the portrait in the Yellow Drawing Room. Both tall and skinny with youth, waves of golden hair flopping in their eyes. But she could see which was which: Edward frowning in serious concentration, Aidan whooping with laughter as he flung his line back. Aidan—always free.

'You were both very handsome lads,' she said.

'My mother always said Edward had the more refined nature, like her own family. She claims she has an artist uncle somewhere on her family tree, though she isn't sure who he was exactly. When we were children, she would talk vaguely of how she might have been a great Shakespearean actress, if she had only the chance. Then she would drape herself over a *chaise* with copious chiffon scarves to wave and call for sherry.'

Lily laughed at the image. 'I find it hard to imagine that.'

Aidan took the photo from her and placed it carefully back on the table, his expression very far away. 'Eddie and I were sometimes recruited to be in her famous *tableaux vivant* at parties. Arabian Nights. Medieval troubadours. Cupids in white draperies. A garden scene from the Petit Trianon, in satin knee breeches dancing a minuet with ladies in flower-draped panniers. Terribly embarrassing for a young boy.'

He showed her another photo, of a group of young adults clad in those antiquated costumes, dancing to a background of pillars and flowers. The girl who held Aidan's hand looked familiar, though younger, her lovely face a bit rounder, her curls paler. One graceful hand held high a wreath of roses, while the other was held tightly in Aidan's. They stared into each other's faces with besotted smiles.

Lady Rannock. So she had known, had adored, Aidan. And had broken apart two brothers. It sounded much too sad to be borne.

Lily glanced away from the image. Aidan put it back down, a crooked, wistful smile on his face as he stared down at the fanciful, happy image. The pretty girl who held his hand. 'I did have such a tantrum about that costume.'

'But you look so adorable,' she said. 'And Lady Rannock looks very beautiful.'

'Melisande always did. Does.' He nudged the frame into place with his fingertip and Lily saw it was next to another image. Lady Rannock standing on the Roderick terrace with Edward. She smiled at the camera, but he looked only at her.

'Do you miss her?' Lily blurted out. 'Lady Rannock. You must have been good friends.'

He frowned. 'Melisande? I just saw her at Lady Crewe's ball.'

'I mean—I did hear—I thought...' Lily faltered, wishing she had not said anything at all. She turned away to face a rusting suit of armour with battle flags draped behind him, tatters of red and blue and gold. She longed to crawl inside and lower the visor. 'I just heard you were once friends.'

'We were, once. Her mother and mine were at school together. When her mother died, mine took Melisande under her wing a bit. Poor Melisande.'

'And did the Duchess try to matchmake, too?'

Aidan gave her a puzzled glance. 'Perhaps with my brother, until Melisande's dowry proved to be much smaller than expected. Edward was quite disappointed.'

By the dowry? Or by Aidan's rumoured attentions to Melisande Rannock? Lily remembered the gossip she'd overheard between her mother and Lady Heath, and wished she had never lingered behind that door. Such pain it must have caused.

Aidan's smile faded. 'You shouldn't listen to London tittle-tattle, Miss Wilkins.'

'Because it's so seldom true?' she whispered.

'Because it is impossible to know the difference. None of us remember only what was real and what is not.' He offered his arm, his smile fading entirely, leaving him looking so serious again. 'Shall we take a shortcut through the gardens before we have to change for dinner?'

She nodded. The ancient room, so enchanting before, had grown stifling. She laid her fingers lightly on his sleeve and let him lead her away. At the doorway, she glanced back and imagined all those Dukes and Duchesses, a long line of them in their ruffs and panniers and pearls, trapped there for ever. She turned sharply away, and followed Aidan down a narrow, twisting back staircase.

Even there Lennox history lurked. At the foot of the stairs was a portrait of his mother, much younger, on horseback, elegant in silk, a veiled hat and black broadcloth, the Elizabethan towers of the house behind her. She looked as if she had always been there and *would* always be there.

'It's a fine likeness of the Duchess,' she murmured.

Aidan tilted his head, as if he had never studied it before. 'Indeed. Perhaps one day you should have your portrait done on horseback, Lily? It would suit you.'

To be hung on the wall as one of the line of Duchesses? Lily didn't know what he really meant, or how she felt about that. But she just nodded and followed him out of a side door just beyond the portrait.

They crossed a gravel courtyard, past a series of old brick outbuildings, and turned towards a long, low red brick stable block. It was quiet at that time of day, the sun sinking low in the sky and work having finished, but she could still smell that comforting, familiar, lovely smell of hay and horses.

'I fear we have few riding horses, or my father's old pride, the Lennox racehorses,' Aidan said, swinging open a wooden door. 'Mostly just farm horses now.'

Lily strolled slowly past the empty boxes, stopping to pat an old plough cob and coo over an adorable Shetland pony.

'Yours, I imagine?' she teased.

Aidan laughed. 'Decades ago, maybe. He does look rather like my old friend Strawberry. He belongs to a tenant's lad, but boards here sometimes.'

Lily smoothed his coarse mane, making the pony snort. She laughed and looked towards a glass case at the end of the aisle. It was filled with tarnished silver bowls and faded green and gold racing silks. Photographs of horses wreathed in roses, all with a beaming, bearded man beside them. In one image, he accepted a trophy from Princess Alexandra—the same man she had seen in the Ascot photo with the Duchess.

'Your father?' she said.

'Yes. He adored racing. Poured all of himself into it.'

Lily looked at a portrait of a gleaming bay, no doubt painted by Abraham Cooper. She wondered if that was where Roderick's roof had gone, those pale, empty squares on the walls, the cracked windows, into race horses.

'Impressive,' she said and turned away to hurry back into the fresh air.

'Don't worry, Miss Wilkins, you'll be able to ride while you're here,' Aidan said. 'Mother's hired a mare from some neighbours. Young and fiery, they say, but I told her you could more than handle it.'

Lily laughed. Worried about the fatted goose breaking her neck, was the Duchess? She remembered the gallop across the park, the freedom of it. 'I can't wait. Roderick does look like a beautiful place for riding.'

'Do you really think so?' he said. He sounded uncharacteristically uncertain, as if he really *wanted* her to like it.

She turned to study him, his hair gleaming streaked gold in the setting sun. 'Yes, very much.'

He nodded slowly, as if musing on something. 'I am very glad, Miss Wilkins, that you're here at Roderick now. I look forward to rediscovering it at your side.'

Chapter Eleven

Aidan ducked deep into his lukewarm bath, letting the water close over his head. The plasterwork flower wreaths high above looked blurry and pale. He wished he was in some jungle river rather than this old tin bath, warm expanses where he could kick free, swim to wherever his fancy took him.

But he was trapped. He sat up in a great geyser of sandalwood-scented bath salts and shoved the heavy, sodden locks of hair back with both hands. If Roderick had an American mistress, there would surely be a state-of-the-art bathroom, running hot and cold water, fluffy towels. He laughed to imagine the changes that might sweep over the ancient castle and its unsuspecting staff.

Not that Lily seemed the sort to swan in and demand change. But she deserved it. She deserved the best. And he wished he could give it to her, more than he had ever wished for anything before.

A footman stepped forward with a pile of towels. The linen had worn thin, but it was still embroidered with the coronet and initials of the Lennoxes. It was surely almost time for dinner and he couldn't be late. Sherry in the Green Room, nine courses in the Red Dining Room, coffee and cards and music after, like clockwork. For all his years away, nothing had changed.

Maybe he could at least persuade Lily to play duets with him. Brighten the evening with her smile.

Lily. He closed his eyes and pictured her as she was in the empty stables, cooing softly as she patted the old pony, her face soft and unguarded for once. He had wondered what she would think of Roderick, of Monty, the rusted suit of armour, the crowds of portraits and photographs and battle flags that constantly watched, constantly whispered of the past. Of constant needs and expectations.

Her eyes, those dark stars, glowed so brightly as she dashed from tapestry to vase to window, full of questions and curiosity. Most rich young American girls would surely recoil from the damp and chill, the old hip baths. But not her. Curious, kind Lily.

Could it work after all? Could he really save Roderick and be happy, too? It seemed too good to be true. Since the terrible events with Melisande, he had given up on romantic happiness altogether. He dared not hope again just yet. Lily hadn't even seen Roderick at its worst yet, seen what life as a duchess really meant. She might still run away, dashing off like the trembling, wide-eyed fairy she seemed.

He shrugged into his brocade dressing gown and smoothed his damp hair back from his face. The sun was sinking low beyond the window, pale pink and lavender and orange, washing over the park and turning the distant summer house to gold. The summer house where once he had given in to his terrible passion and dared to kiss Melisande.

He ruthlessly pushed that memory away. Melisande, and the bad things that had happened after that kiss were gone now. The summer house was just that—a pretty stone folly. The sunset light was so beautiful it made his eyes ache, almost as if he wanted to cry. He'd seen so many beautiful things—vast mountain ranges, white deserts, ancient temples—yet none was quite so lovely as Roderick. There had been so many times he had wanted to see it again. And times he had *never* wanted to see it again. He'd run across the world to get away from it. Now it was in his charge for ever. It was *his* responsibility when it should have been Edward's.

As he stared across the lawns of Roderick, the pale pink and white roses of his grandmother's famous garden, he saw a figure move slowly across the raked, striped gravel pathways. For an instant, he wondered if he had accidentally drunk *cana*, the vile, bitter South American concoction more intoxicating than anything England could offer. But then he blinked and laughed. It was Lily.

He had no idea how she had escaped their mothers and the army of Roderick maids, but she seemed quite alone. She hadn't yet dressed for dinner and wore a pale tea gown that trailed across the roses and caught in flutters on the breeze. Her hair was loose, a cloud of dark curls tumbling over her shoulders. She tilted her head back and laughed at something, her heart-shaped face golden and alight in the sunset, filled with delight. He pressed his fingertips to the cold glass of the window and a desperate longing washed over him, the longing to reach for her, touch her, take her in his arms and make her joy his own.

But they were so far apart, kept that way not just by glass and bricks. He knew too well that Roderick Castle was a stern taskmaster—could he let sweet Lily be closed within it? See her smile smothered, as so many Duchesses before her had been?

As he watched, she gave a little twirl, as she had in

the gallery, her arms spread wide as if to take everything in. Maybe, just maybe, Roderick had met its match in the delicate American fairy girl. Maybe it needed a little laughter and tenderness.

Perhaps he did, too. But did he deserve it? Deserve Lily? After the way he had hurt Edward and run away from his duties? He was not sure.

Someone seemed to call her and she spun around to face a girl in a black dress, a gown of frothy sea-green draped over her arms. The girl in black shook her head and pointed back at the house, as if telling Lily she had to go inside. Lily laughed, but she nodded and followed on meekly enough. At the edge of the rose garden, she glanced back, her expression wistful, and Aidan wondered if she saw him there. He *willed* her to see him there, to wave, to smile, only at him.

She tilted her head back, the pink light glowing on her skin, and finally, finally, she raised her hand to wave. He waved back and she laughed and moved gracefully away.

Aidan laughed, too, feeling lighter than he had in... well, ever. Certainly ever at Roderick.

As he turned away from the gathering night and reached for his hairbrush, he remembered those photographs Lily had examined in the gallery. Bits of his past caught in silver nitrate. Edward.

Melisande. When the three of them had been inseparable.

Some of the golden glow faded from the evening and Aidan tossed his brush back on to the dressing table. The delight of Lily faded under memories of Melisande, dancing with her, kissing her, falling under her spicy perfumed spell. How young he had been.

And the day he realised she would marry Edward if she could, because Edward was the Duke, had shattered all their lives. He still felt as if he had betrayed his brother in some way, as if he owed him something.

She wanted to change things back now; he remembered the touch of her hand at the Crewe ball, the soft, beseeching light in her blue eyes, as if she could erase all the years. But the past could never come back.

Could it?

How foolish he had once been. He couldn't afford to be foolish now. He was the Duke, Roderick was on his shoulders and it needed the right Duchess. It was his duty to do what was right.

He could afford no missteps. Not even with a dark-eyed fairy.

Lily stood very still in front of the full-length looking glass as Doris finished mending the hem of her gown. She hardly dared breathe, let alone move, and it had felt that way ever since she'd stepped foot in that chamber. The Queen's Chamber in the Elizabethan wing, Mrs Bright, the stern housekeeper, called it, with the implication it was a great honour to be lodged there, especially for some young American girl.

And if Lily imagined something called the Queen's Chamber in a novel it would be much like this. A vast bed set high on a dais, draped in sea-green brocade with gold cords, matching the green silk wallpaper dotted with pastoral paintings. More green silk looped around the dressing table, iced with frills of creamy lace, and the fireplace was carved white stone with a deep mantel lined with cavorting porcelain shepherdesses and spaniels. The carpet was green and yellow and pink, looped with pink ribbons, and the tall windows looked out on to the rose garden.

After a lukewarm bath by the fireplace in a copper

hip bath, she'd rung for Doris, but as the maid surely had miles to traverse before she got to the chamber, Lily had grown restless and nervous. It had started to feel as if those ever-present portraits were staring at her, wondering about her, judging her. And there was that beautiful garden below her window, just bursting with late summer roses.

She'd known she would never find her way out there through the thickets of stairs, so she'd taken a page from Violet's book. She dressed in her lightest tea gown, prised open a window, and climbed down the thick ivy that covered the red-brick wall.

It had been so long since she'd done something so naughty and, if she was honest with herself, it felt *delicious*. She smelled the flowers, felt the warm sun on her face and examined the vast chimneys and rooftops and walls of the castle. Her time with Aidan had certainly whetted her interest in the history of the place; she wanted to know about every Duke and Duchess, how every painting and vase and snuffbox came to Roderick, why it was all arranged just as it was. Which Queen had slept in her chamber.

She also wondered what lay *beyond* its walls, in the farms and woods and fields, the pretty cottage she had seen from the carriage, who worked and lived there. Not that she felt brave enough to explore them all just yet. One wall-climb per day was quite enough. And then Doris found her and brought her back inside. Away from dreams and into the real world. She'd tilted her face up to the pink sky, so heavenly gorgeous with those streaks of gold, and then she saw him, Aidan, staring down at her. Did he think she was a terrible hoyden, no fit guest for the Queen's Chamber?'

She'd given him a smile and a wave, but she couldn't

see his reaction beyond the shadowed glass. Now she was in that Queen's Chamber, standing very still as Doris finished the ruffled hem. It was her prettiest new gown, pale green silk trimmed with white lace beaded with tiny pearls and sequins, frothing over the neckline and sleeves. A flock of embroidered butterflies shimmered across the skirt and train and her mother's pearls gleamed at her throat. Doris had piled her hair high and fastened it with more jewelled butterflies.

She remembered all those Duchess portraits, their stern glances and silken gowns, their lack of flashing jewels when they weren't in their official robes. Next to them, she felt rather overstuffed, over-bright, too trying.

'Are you sure I look all right to dine at a ducal table, Doris?' she asked.

Doris put the final touch on the hem and stood back to examine her work with a smile of satisfaction. 'I should think so, Miss Lily. You put all those dusty, squinting old Duchesses to shame!'

Lily laughed. Some of the portraits might be just the tiniest bit squinty. But the Duchess certainly was not. Nor was the beautiful Lady Rannock. They were all dash and glamour, perfectly at ease in grand surroundings.

Lily bit her lip when she thought of Melisande Rannock in that smiling photograph in the gallery and glorious in satin and diamonds at Lady Crewe's ball. How could she ever compare to a woman like that, really?

But Melisande Rannock was not here now, Lily reminded herself. *She* was. In the Queen's Chamber. It was she that Roderick Castle needed.

Yet did she want it to need her? Did she even know how to begin?

She had been so sure she would marry someone like Lord James Grantley. Kind, easygoing, someone who did not make her stomach flutter just to be around him. But now she was here, in an entirely different world. With Aidan, whose kisses made her toes curl, in his grand home, filled with glorious history. Which way should she turn next?

The final gong sounded and Lily smoothed her skirt one more time. The butterflies on the silk seemed to flutter inside her, too, making her nervous. Was the gown truly right? Or was it too…frivolous?

It was too late to change, though. Doris held out her gloves and her feathered fan.

'You'll do very well, Miss Lily,' Doris said with a kind smile. 'This house has never seen anyone so lovely and sweet, I'm sure! The footmen downstairs were telling everyone how kind you were.'

'Really, Doris? How nice of them.' Lily doubted the Duchess's maid would ever speak that way to *her*, like a friend, but Doris's kind words steadied her. She always had Doris and the twins behind her, no matter what.

She drew on her tight-fitting kid gloves and made her way out of the room towards one of the many staircases. She passed several marble statues in their niches, gods and goddesses who seemed to watch her pass, Chinese porcelain vases on marble plinths, footmen who seemed to only look over her head.

Past the grand hall, all pale shadows in the gathering night, two intricately carved Jacobean doors were swung soundlessly open by more green-liveried footman and she moved into the White Drawing Room, the one Aidan said was reserved only for very important guests. True to its name, the walls were plastered pure snow-white, with raised details of palm fronds, swags of ribbon and cherubs. More portraits of former Dukes and Duchesses stared down at the company with faintly disapproving stares. A particular grand image of a duke on rearing horseback, his full-bottom curled wig and velvet jacket vivid, hung above a red marble fireplace. The chairs and sofas were crimson cut velvet, matching the curtains at the tall windows, the doors that led on to a terrace.

It seemed she was the last one to arrive, for her mother and the twins, the Duchess, Lady Heath and an elderly gentleman in purple bishop's attire, along with Aidan, were gathered near the vast fireplace, glasses of sherry in hand, the painted eyes of the giant Van Dyck family portrait behind them watching. Aidan was telling them some tale that made them all laugh, gales of merriment like an oasis in that vast, cold room.

Lily glanced over her shoulder, unsure what to do. Stride forward? Wait to be invited near? The doors had closed behind her, blocking off escape. She stood very still in her butterflies and lace, trying not to tremble.

'Miss Lily Wilkins, Your Grace,' Donat the butler said, making Lily gasp. She hadn't even seen him there in the deep shadows of the room.

'Miss Wilkins!' the Duchess called with a smile. 'How charming you look. I so envy you American girls and your unmistakable style. It comes out whatever you wear. Remember when we were girls, Eleanor? White dimity with plaid sashes, so boring.'

'And black velvet in the winter,' Lady Heath said with a laugh. Her own gown was also plaid now, dark purple edged in green velvet, her only ornament a green velvet ribbon around her neck. Next to her, Lily's mother's blue and fuchsia brocade glared. But Lily had hoped that in taking 'English' style advice from Lady Heath, she would not stand out so very much. It seemed she would look 'American' no matter what. 'How those lace collars itched!'

'Do have a sherry and join us. You and Lady Heath are already great friends, I know, and this is Bishop Talbot, who christened Aidan and Edward so long ago,' the Duchess said, gesturing to a footman with a silver tray bearing small crystal glasses. 'Aidan was just telling us such a tale of some snowbound Canadian cabin, with only bear meat to eat. I am not quite sure I believe him.'

Aidan gave one of his crooked smiles to Lily, which emboldened her to join them at last, standing near him. She took one of the sherry glasses and tried not to gulp it down.

'I do assure you, Mama, it is all true,' he said. 'Bears and all. It tastes quite like pheasant.'

The Duchess laughed and the sapphire stars in her hair, which Lily recognised from a portrait of a Restoration-era Duchess in the corridor, glittered in the firelight. 'How extraordinary. And to think my own son was there! Is it like that where you once lived, Mrs Wilkins?'

Lily's mother frowned. 'Perhaps long ago, Duchess. But certainly not now. We live quite comfortably.' She glanced pointedly at a spot of damp on one of the ornate plasterwork rosettes of the ceiling.

'Dinner is served, Your Grace,' the butler announced.

'Thank you, Donat. Aidan, dear, will you take Miss Wilkins in? And I am sure you, Bishop Talbot, can escort Mrs Wilkins? I am afraid our numbers are terribly off, but we are just an informal family party tonight, are we not? So much more fun.'

Lily strolled to the edge of the terrace, as far as she dared into the night darkness. The tall windows of the White Drawing room were open and she could hear the chatter of her mother and Lady Heath and the Duchess over new fashions in hats, the clink of delicate coffee cups. She knew she would have to go back there very soon, to join them and smile and nod, play cards with the twins, but not just yet. Now she had a few precious moments alone.

She draped the long train of her gown over her arm and climbed up to perch on the wide stone balustrade. It was a warm evening, a gentle breeze brushing around her that smelled of grass and roses from the garden. It smelled a bit, in fact, like Aidan himself.

Lily hadn't realised before, in London, how much he belonged to this place. She'd never felt that she *belonged* anywhere. Not in New York or Newport. Only with her sisters. What would it be like to have a home, a *real* home, a family to call her own?

She looked up at the sky, so close that night, like a black velvet ball gown sprinkled with diamond stars, a golden moon shimmering on the stones of the house. Whimsically, she reached up her hand as if she could snatch it down.

'Glorious, isn't it?' someone said, a wonderfully familiar, whisky-rough voice. Startled, Lily almost tumbled off the balustrade. Aidan's arm came around her waist, catching her, leaving her breathless. She caught his shoulders, feeling the powerful strength of him under his fashionably cut coat.

He stared at her, his eyes shining in the night, that wonderful crooked smile on his lips.

'I'm sorry I startled you,' he said, that smile even in his voice.

'I thought you were in the dining room with your port and your sporting chat,' she managed to whisper.

'And listen to the bishop list all sixty candidates he considered for the living at Roderick village's church, before he settled on Mr Bybee? No, thank you,' he said with a laugh. 'He can tell my mother about it all. But I wasn't quite ready for the drawing room, either.'

'I also needed a quiet moment. I told my mother I needed to mend my hem,' Lily said. His arms tightened around her waist and he swung her down from the balustrade, as easily as if she were feather. Before he set her down, he twirled her around and around until she laughed helplessly, dizzily. It was as she always felt with Aidan: giddy, free, outside of herself. She even forgot the weight of Roderick Castle bearing down on them and there was only him.

'That's more like it. I love to hear your laugh,' he said, lowering her satin shoes to the flagstone terrace. He still held her close as the world slowly grew steadier, the stars still blurry overhead. 'I was afraid Roderick had stolen your beautiful smile.'

Lily shook her head, and stepped back to lean against the balustrade before she could do something foolish like kiss him. 'It's a beautiful night. I've never seen a moon quite so jewel-like before.'

'Ordered up just for you. Only the best for guests at Roderick Castle.' He leaned on the stone balustrade beside her, so close she could feel the warmth of him wrap around her. 'I wish I could snatch down the stars and put them in your hair.'

Lily laughed at his whimsical words. 'They could never rival your mother's tiara!'

He shook his head. 'It would be a thousand times lovelier than any tiara. And the only thing that could be worthy of you, Lily.'

She was quiet with him for a long moment, shivering at the thought that maybe his words could be true. Maybe he did care about her, as she longed to be cared for. As she cared for him. Dared she hope? 'What were the stars like in your deserts?'

He was also silent for a moment, as if deep in thought and memory. He took out a slim silver case and opened it to remove a dark cheroot, the kind she had sometimes seen the sailors in Newport smoke. 'Do you mind?' he asked and she shook her head.

He lit the tip, a brief flare of orange in the night, and exhaled a silvery plume.

'They were like nothing I could ever have imagined,' he said at last, staring out at the garden. 'So much vast emptiness, shimmering sands like jewels under the moon. And the silence. Deeper than anything I've known.'

'I do envy you your adventures, Aidan.'

'But you must have seen such things, too,' he said. 'In Idaho, was it? Or Colorado?'

Lily laughed. 'Oh, my mother and her tales! I was only young then, before my father made his fortune. I remember so little. I wish I did remember more. But I'm surprised my mother mentioned those years at all and to a duchess no less. She never talks about it. For her, there is only her old South Carolina family and when she came to New York. And ours to Europe. It whetted her appetite to find a life for my sisters and me here.'

'And what about you? How do you see your life?'

Lily glanced back at the house, so grand and silent in the moonlight, so secretive about all it must have seen. 'I never was allowed to make my own plans. It's all been laid out before me.'

'So was my life, when I was a boy.' He took another long drag on his cheroot, watching the glowing end with a frown. 'I suppose that's why I ran away. To see if I could find Aidan out there in the wide world.'

Lily wished she could find him, too, see him clearly. Know him. 'And did you?'

'I think so. I realised I could rely on my own strength when I needed to. That I wasn't just the spare. But there's something in Roderick, some invisible cord, that I suppose I always knew would pull me back eventually.'

'I can see why.'

He looked at her closely, his eyes narrowed. 'Do you?'

'Oh, yes. The history in every corner, the ties to your own family in every portrait. It's beautiful, built up by so many people over so many years. All the stories in every chair and vase. Not like my home. That place is no older than me and our paintings and porcelains come from other families.' She suddenly realised what she had said, the bare patches on Roderick's walls, the empty niches. 'I don't mean…'

'No, no, Lily. It's not your fault my father was profligate and yours prudent.' He ground out his cheroot in the flower urn beside him. 'I'm glad you like Roderick.'

'I do,' she said. 'Very much.'

He gave her his beautiful smile, something teasing at its edges. 'Would you like to see something?'

Lily glanced back at the windows where she could see figures moving and shifting behind the wavy old glass. 'Should we not go back?' But she did not want to. She wanted to stay just like this, alone with him.

'They won't miss us for a few more minutes. It's one of my favourite spots here.'

'Then of course I want to see it,' she said. She felt very daring as she took his hand.

They made their way down the steps to the lawn that rolled away from the house to the rose garden and the woods beyond. Somehow they didn't seem as ominous as they had before, even in the darkness, but like something magical and enchanted. Aidan held her hand to lead her over the grass and they dashed away together, laughing like truant schoolchildren.

Lily's heeled shoes caught in a hole and she fell against him, still laughing. 'Aidan, I can't keep up!'

His arms came close around her and held her steady. 'It's just up there.'

Their arms still around each other, they climbed a low hill to the summer house, that fanciful octagonal stone folly. A statue of Diana, her bow tipped with gilding in the moonlight, stared down at them from the peak of the roof. To Lily's astonishment, it was lit up, strung with red and blue lanterns that cast shifting, stained-glass patterns over the classical columns, the domed roof and Diana's statue. The lake beyond was striped with moonlight on its rippling waves.

'It's wonderful.' She sighed. She hurried up the sloping ramp to the sheltered walkway that ran all around the little structure. She twirled in a patch of blue light.

'Is it always lit up like this?' she asked.

'Only when my mother has a party. She likes guests to look out the drawing room windows and be awestruck,' Aidan said wryly.

'I can see why. It's like a fairyland! What do you use this place for? Parties?'

'Nothing, really, not any more. My great-grandfather built it for my great-grandmother. They went on a tour of Italy and I think this reminded them of the ruined temples they saw there. My grandparents liked to have card parties inside with their closest friends. Now it's just—here.'

'Is there a door, then?' Lily cried. She dashed around the walls until she found the door, peeling, grey-painted panels crowned with a fanciful fresco of ancient gods, but the latch didn't turn in her hand.

'I think Donat might have the key,' Aidan said.

'Oh, I daren't ask him,' Lily said, thinking of that stern old butler. She left the door and went to gaze out over the lake, so very conscious of Aidan close to her, wrapped up alone with her in the night. 'Is that where you and your brother fished? In that photograph?' She pointed to a small wooden pier that extended out over the water.

'Yes, sometimes. The lake is stocked with trout. Edward always caught far more than I did; I haven't the patience. I liked boating out there, though, and swimming.'

'Yes, I can imagine that.' And she could. His hair, sleek and dark gold in the water, his strong, bare arms slicing through the waves. She remembered the classical statues they had seen in the museums in Paris, all lean muscles and elegant lines, and she was sure he looked just like that.

She shivered to imagine Aidan actually *naked*.

'Are you cold?' he asked, concern in his voice.

'Oh, no,' she said, but he slipped out of his evening coat and wrapped it around her shoulders. It felt like being surrounded by his heat, his scent, and she drew it closer.

He cleared his throat, as if he was somehow affected by their nearness, as well. 'Do you swim?'

'Not well, though I know how. My mother wouldn't let us near Bailey's Beach in Newport or on Papa's yacht without it! I'm better at rowing.'

'Rowing?'

She laughed. 'You needn't sound so doubtful. It's another thing we must know on my father's yacht. It's not a grand ship, like Mr Astor's or Mr Jerome's, just something to amuse guests out on the water. And he taught my sisters and me to row dinghies when we were children.

It was such fun! Papa loves the water.' She felt suddenly wistful for those bright days on the waves.

'Does your mother love it, too?'

Lily hesitated. Even she had heard the rumours—when his family was gone, Coleman Wilkins used the yacht to entertain actresses. All her old doubts about marriage seemed to hover just there, under the surface, waiting for her.

'Not really, no. She gets seasick. I haven't been rowing in a long time.'

'Then we must go.'

'Us? Row?' she said, a spark of anticipation snuffing out doubts.

'We'll make a party of it. We have a few more summer days yet. I'll row you far across the waters, Lily Wilkins.'

She laughed in delight. 'You know, I think I still haven't had my prize after our horse race in the park.'

'No? How remiss of me.'

He stared down at her and suddenly the air between them seemed to change, growing charged and sparkling. She could hardly breathe, especially when he reached for her and drew her closer, his touch so warm through the thin silk of her gown. All her senses tilted and whirled, and all she knew in that moment was him.

As if in a hazy dream, far away, yet more immediate and real than anything she'd ever known before, his head tilted to hers and he kissed her.

The brush of his lips was so soft at first, like warm velvet, pressing softly once, twice, as if he were asking her, as if he feared she might run away. But she could not have moved away from him then for anything. As she moved to meet him, to hold on to him, his kiss deepened. It grew so hot, so urgent, so full of hunger.

Something deep in her very core responded to that

urgency, to the rough excitement that grew and grew until she was sure she would burst from it. She moaned, parting her lips to the shocking feel of his tongue seeking entrance, sliding over hers. There was only him and that one perfect moment...

'Aidan? Miss Wilkins? Are you out there?' someone called, their voice carried on the green garden breeze. The Duchess. 'We need your talents on the piano, my dears.'

Aidan drew back a bit and Lily saw him smile down at her in the moonlight, that wonderful crooked smile of his.

'Don't you wish you were back in the jungle?' she whispered. 'Or the desert?'

He laughed and raked his hand through his hair, disarranging it even more. 'But then I couldn't play duets at the piano with *you*, Lily Wilkins, and that would be a shame indeed. Would you ride with me tomorrow morning? I can show you over the home farm before the other guests arrive.'

Lily nodded. Everything seemed to be coming together, beyond even her wildest dreams of romance and excitement. Were her doubts so silly, then? She hardly dared breathe for fear it would all blow away. 'I would like that.'

They made their way back across the lawn, properly arm in arm now rather than hand in hand. The Duchess waited on the terrace, her smile firmly in place, her tiara shining.

'Miss Wilkins wanted to see the lights on the folly,' Aidan said.

'It is quite enchanting, Duchess,' Lily said.

'I'm glad you like it, Miss Wilkins,' the Duchess said, still smiling. 'Roderick is quite special, I think, and I hope you do agree.'

Lily glanced up at Aidan. His own smile had faded, leaving him looking tense and austere in the light from the windows. But the magic of the folly lingered. 'Oh, yes, Duchess. I do quite agree.'

Chapter Twelve

Lily hummed a little tune to herself as she made her way down Roderick's grand staircase early the next morning. She realised with a laugh that it was *Alabama Blossoms*, a sentimental American favourite she had played last night with Aidan at the piano. The house was quiet at that hour, almost everyone else still being abed; a few maids hurried past with their buckets and polish. Lily had wanted to dress in her riding habit and meet Aidan at the stable before her mother could see her and question her.

She swung the hat in her hand, its tulle veil swirling. In the morning light, even the pale, chilly entrance hall didn't look quite so forbidding. She felt almost as though she could run across the gleaming floor, dance, spin.

To her surprise, the door to a small chamber just beyond the dining room stood open and the Duchess waited there. So, Lily wasn't as alone as she thought. Perhaps no one was ever *really* alone in a house like Roderick.

'Miss Wilkins,' the Duchess said with a smile. 'Won't you join me for some tea and toast?'

'I…' Lily glanced at the front door, flanked by those ever-present green-liveried footmen.

'You're meeting my son for a ride, I know. He's just

have their heads and raced over the fields. The wind rushed past them, smelling of freedom.

Eventually Aidan led her down a path so narrow they had to leave the horses. It was lined with thick hedges and eventually they arrived at a two-storey farmhouse, all tidy whitewash and grey slate roof, with a neat little vegetable garden enclosed by a low stone wall. Chickens pecked around the yard, with roses growing over the door, like something in a painting of 'old England' Lily had seen. She could sense someone watching from behind the thick old windows.

'Perhaps I should wait here for you, if you have business,' she said uncertainly.

'It's far too warm out here, Lily! Besides, the Halls are the kindest of people. Their family has farmed at Roderick for decades. I know they love company.'

'I'm not—' But she could make no more protests, as the door flew open. A man stood there, very tall with a farmer's broad shoulders and ruddy cheeks, a little girl with a long, blonde braid holding his hand. The man smiled and waved, and the girl jumped up and down. The warmth of their greeting seemed to spill right out of the pretty farmhouse and wrapped around Lily in a bright welcome that made her smile.

'Your Grace!' Mr Hall said. 'We didn't expect you today.'

'The agent said you had a problem with your chimney,' Aidan said, drawing Lily forward with him across the yard. 'And my mother mentioned your mother was ailing. I do hope she's recovering.'

'Aye, thanks to the doctor Her Grace sent.' He gave Lily a curious, though friendly, glance and she smiled back, feeling shy.

'Your Grace, Your Grace!' the little girl trilled and

gone to fetch the horses and shouldn't be back for a half-hour or so. You'll need some sustenance for a day riding over the farms. I know I always did.'

'Yes. Of course,' Lily answered slowly. 'Thank you, Duchess.'

To Lily's surprise, she found herself in a very pretty room, tiny, round and papered in yellow and white flowers that matched the chintz chair cushions and curtains. The open windows looked out on to the rose garden and the only furniture was a round table and a small white and gilt French sideboard. The yellow tablecloth was covered with toast racks and teapots, a stack of ledgers and lists piled next to the Duchess's place.

'I do like to make an early start to the day when guests are expected,' the Duchess said, gesturing to Lily to sit across from her and pouring tea from yellow-flowered china. 'So many things to consider! Menus and room assignments, the flowers…'

'Yes, of course,' Lily answered, remembering Lady Heath's leather seating chart and dog-eared copy of *Debrett's*. What would a dinner at a ducal house entail? Could she ever do one properly herself, ever remember all those vital details?

That seemed to be what the Duchess wanted to discuss, too. 'I suppose your mother's houses are quite large, as well? One does hear of such grand and imaginative parties in Newport! Circus balls and vegetable parties, whatever they might be. And I suppose you had a governess?'

'Yes, an English one.' Lily's mind was spinning at the quick changes in topic and she took a nibble of toast as she remembered her strict governess, Miss Johnson 'My sisters have a French *mademoiselle* now, helping give them a final polish.'

'And what did she teach you? It seems ages since I heard anything of governesses, as I only had sons. My own governess when I was a girl just liked to play cards all day and go for walks to catch a glimpse of her footman suitor! I'm surprised I learned anything at all.'

Lily laughed. 'Miss Johnson sternly disapproved of cards.' She told of French and Italian lessons, dancing at Monsieur Lalliet's school, music, sketching. Her gaze wandered to the portrait on the wall behind the Duchess, a tall, golden-haired man staring down at her with piercing dark eyes.

'I see you are admiring Eddie, my late husband,' the Duchess said lightly. 'He was handsome, wasn't he?'

'Yes, very much.'

'Aidan favours him in this, I think, though not much in temperament. Aidan is not like most men in his position.'

Lily understood that. She didn't think Aidan was like any other man at all. 'Is he not?'

'He always had such a questing spirit, even as a child. He takes after my own family in that way. So restless, so curious! I wasn't surprised when he was gone for so long, adventuring over far continents. But I admit I have fears for him now.'

'Fears for him?' Lily said, alarmed.

'Being Duke of Lennox is no easy path, even for those born to it. But the key to a well-run estate is truly the Duchess. I myself found it a challenge at times, but also a great fulfilment. A good duchess makes all the difference to so very many people. My Aidan needs such assistance. I'm sure you understand, Miss Wilkins, being such a clever young lady yourself.'

Lily wasn't at all sure she did understand. Was the Duchess giving her some kind of warning? 'Yes, I suppose I do.'

The Duchess smiled. 'I knew you would. Now, my dear, perhaps you could glance at this menu and tell me what you think? Mrs Porter is an excellent cook, she's been here at Roderick for years, but I do wonder if she's sometimes a bit old-fashioned. Should we try a salmon mousse here instead of the chicken tart for a savoury?'

Menus were something Lily did understand, thanks to her mother, and after going over the dinner and tea lists with the Duchess and suggesting a few small changes, she left for the stables, feeling as if she had been given some sort of test. Had she passed? Roderick Castle seemed more and more like a lovely but foreign place.

Her doubts faded as she saw Aidan in the stable yard. He was chatting with a groom as they examined two horses, his head thrown back on a laugh. Here he seemed like the Aidan she knew in the park, free and easy, the load of the castle a bit lighter on his shoulders.

'I'm sorry I'm late,' she said, hurrying to his side. He smiled down at her and shook a tumbled lock of hair back from his brow. 'I was caught for breakfast with your mother.'

'Oh, no, Miss Wilkins! I would say you certainly deserve a good gallop after my mother first thing in the morning,' he said lightly.

Lily gently patted the mare's nose and she snorted.

'She's a fast one, miss,' the groom warned.

'We needn't worry about Miss Wilkins, Charlie, she rides like an Amazonian,' Aidan said.

Lily smiled at the compliment, her cheeks warm. 'I think she's quite lovely. And, yes, I am dying for a good gallop.'

They quickly mounted up and rode out into the fine day. Once past the gates of the castle, they let their horses

skipped down the pathway to tug at Aidan's coattail. 'I have a new dolly.'

Aidan laughed, and swung her up in his arms, twirling her around and around until she shrieked with giggles. 'Do you indeed, Meg? Is she as pretty as you?'

She peeked over his shoulder. 'Maybe as pretty as this lady. Who is she?'

'Meg,' he father admonished, but Lily laughed. She was utterly delighted by this house, by Meg Hall, by this light-hearted side of Aidan.

Aidan gave her another twirl. 'This is Miss Lily Wilkins, all the way from America. Miss Wilkins, this is Miss Margaret Hall.'

Lily gave a curtsy. 'How do you do, Miss Hall.'

Meg studied her carefully. 'You *are* very pretty.'

'Indeed she is.' Aidan smiled at Lily over Meg's tow-head. Lily blushed and laughed.

'Meg, do let His Grace and Miss Wilkins come inside now,' her father said.

Aidan put Meg down and the girl led him by the hand to her father. 'And this, Miss Wilkins, is Robert Hall. He and his family have been farming here for as long as I can remember and are old friends.'

Mr Hall bowed a bit shyly and ushered them inside. 'You're most welcome indeed, Miss Wilkins. We'd love to meet more friends of His Grace now that he's home at last! I only wish we had a grander reception to offer you. My wife has gone to visit her sister, she'll be that sorry to miss you. Only my ma is here.'

'I'll be very pleased to meet her, Mr Hall. And your home is lovely.' She glanced around the cosy entrance hall, the neatly swept floor with its bright rag rugs, bundles of dried herbs hanging from the old, dark wood rafters to scent the air. It was indeed so welcoming, so cosy—so unlike the pale stone of Roderick.

'Oh, do offer the lady some tea, Robert,' a querulous old voice called from beyond a half-open door. 'It's too hot outside. Show the manners I taught you.'

Mr Hall blushed. 'That's my mother in the sitting room, if you'd care to go through.'

Lily laughed. She thought Mrs Hall sounded rather like her own mother. 'Some tea would be lovely.'

'There are cakes, too,' Meg said. 'I made them myself. With my ma helping a little.'

Lily smiled down at her. 'Then I am sure they will be quite delicious.'

'Meggie, why don't you take Miss Wilkins in to your grandma, while I show His Grace the chimney?' her father said.

Meg took Lily's hand, quite unselfconscious, and drew her towards the open door. Lily glanced back to see Aidan already walking away with Mr Hall, the two of them talking in low, serious tones. She was alone, but for once she didn't feel shy at all. Not with Meg's little hand in hers and the pretty, shabby, blue and yellow sitting room before her, filled with garden flowers and two purring cats in the window seat.

Old Mrs Hall sat in an armchair with another cat on her lap, looking just how Lily would have imagined a slightly older Stella Wilkins, if Coleman Wilkins hadn't struck a mine. Her greying hair was twisted atop her head in elaborate braids, while a lace-edged shawl was draped over her erect shoulders. Bright blue eyes set in a lined face studied Lily closely.

'Look, Gran, the Duke brought a lady to visit us,' Meg piped up. 'Her name is Miss Wilkins and she's all the way from America!'

'Is she now? A fine lady come to Roderick?' old Mrs Hall said, those sharp eyes sweeping over every inch of Lily's windblown hair and dusty habit. Lily self-consciously smoothed her skirt. 'It's about time he brought a lady around. Roderick needs a new duchess.'

Lily choked on a laugh. 'I'm afraid I'm only a guest at the castle, Mrs Hall. Not really Duchess material.'

'No? Well, that's a disappointment. I suppose you had better sit down, anyway. Meggie, dear, will you fetch the tea? Use the good china, with the violets.'

As Meg ran away on her errand, Lily sat down carefully on the stool next to Mrs Hall's chair. Despite the warm day outside, the farmhouse's thick walls kept the chamber cool. 'It's very kind of you to welcome me at such short notice, Mrs Hall.'

'We don't get many guests, not since Her Grace went away to get herself engaged again. At her age! I was never so happy as when I found myself on my own at last.' Mrs Hall harrumphed. 'That's why the castle needs a new mistress. Are you sure you wouldn't want to take it on?'

Lily had never really had anyone speak to her so bluntly before and she found she rather liked it, even though she had no answers at all. 'I'm not sure. They don't teach us to be duchesses in America.'

'Nothing to it, I would say, if you're a lady with money. Are you?'

'My father has money. I don't.'

Mrs Hall laughed. 'It's the same thing. And I dare say His Grace wasn't raised to be a duke, either. Not like his brother.'

'He's not much like his brother, then?'

'Not half, Miss Wilkins, not that it's such a bad thing. His Grace, the late Duke, was a pale lad, not much for getting out and about and getting his hands dirty. Though he was kind enough.' Her eyes narrowed. 'He didn't seem to be getting along with finding a duchess, either. Not anyone suitable, anyway.'

Lily swallowed hard, remembering how both brothers had admired Lady Rannock. 'Did he not?'

'Eh, he was young. But His Grace, the current Duke, he's lived in the world. He needs someone to help him in his new life. Every grand house needs a mistress. But the right sort.'

'The right sort?'

'Someone calm and kind, a good, practical head on her shoulders. The Duke's mother is good enough, but always running off to London! And someone rich, of course. Roderick's not as grand as it used to be.' She studied Lily closer. 'You seem quiet and kind. I like you.'

Lily laughed. 'Thank you. I rather like you, too. But I'm not sure about duchessing.'

Meg brought the tea, carefully balancing the tray on her little hands. She was the perfect young lady as she poured and served, and soon they were all laughing at Mrs Hall's tales of wild parties in the youth of Aidan's father.

'You all seem very merry,' Robert Hall said when the men joined them. Aidan swung Meg into the air again, making her giggle.

'Oh, yes,' Lily said, slicing more cake for them. 'Mrs Hall was just telling me about the wild parties your parents once had at the castle! Who could have imagined it?'

'Nothing to do with me, I promise,' Aidan said with a roguish smile, stuffing a bite of cake into his mouth.

It was growing late in the afternoon by the time they left the farmhouse, Lily feeling a warm glow from the merry time as the Halls waved them off. The horses were freshly rested and ready for another gallop back to the castle and Lily and Aidan raced back over the fields and meadows.

They stopped by the lake and folly, drawing in to catch their breath and take in the beautiful view.

Lily turned to Aidan, laughing, about to say something about the beautiful lights last night and the magic of the place, but something in his expression stopped her words. He seemed to freeze in place.

She glanced back at the folly and saw the flash of something crimson against the pale stone. She shielded her eyes from the bright sunlight off the water and saw it was a lady in a red-and-black-striped walking gown, her red-plumed hat set at a jaunty angle on elaborate curls of golden hair.

It was Lady Rannock, Aidan's old love. For just a moment, Lily thought she also saw a man in the shadows; he was tall, too tall to be Lord Rannock. She thought he wore a dark jacket, but when she blinked he was gone and Lady Rannock was alone.

Lily looked up at Aidan, who still stared at Lady Rannock, frozen in place. She had seen them and waved merrily; Lily refused to give in and run away. They dismounted and she followed Aidan towards the folly as Lady Rannock came down the ramp, her ruffled skirts trailing behind her. She looked so elegant, so tall and fashionable and dashing, that Lily felt quite dusty beside her, like an urchin beside a queen.

Lady Rannock's gaze, icy blue in her classical oval face, swept over Lily in one quick flash before she dismissed her and turned to Aidan. Her smile widened and she held out her hand.

'Aidan, my dear Duke! So glorious to see you at Roderick again, it is quite like old times,' she said, a purr in her voice. 'And—Miss Wilkins, is it? Didn't I see you at Lady Crewe's ball?'

'You may have, Lady Rannock,' Lily said. 'The Duchess did say you and Lord Rannock were expected today. I hope he's well?'

Her smile quirked at the corners. 'Quite. But I fear Gerald does get so tired when we travel. He hasn't got your intrepid spirit, Aidan. I thought I would explore a bit while he rested.' She stepped closer to Aidan and laid her hand, bare of gloves, on his sleeve. He didn't move away, his expression taut as he looked down at her.

Lady Rannock's smile turned sultry, her eyes narrowed. 'I well remember this lovely little folly, don't you? The night of that ball…'

'I remember,' Aidan said tightly.

Lily suddenly felt terribly embarrassed to be there, to be watching such a personal moment. Her own magical evening in that folly suddenly seemed cheap. It was clear the place meant something to Lady Rannock…and to Aidan.

'Excuse me,' she murmured, though she was sure neither of them noticed as she backed away. She hurried to fetch her horse, scrambling awkwardly on her own into the saddle. She couldn't face the embarrassment of running away, but she urged her horse to a quick walk back towards the house.

'Miss Wilkins,' she thought she heard Aidan call, but she dared not look back to see him with Lady Rannock. The perfect, golden day had turned grey and shadowed, even though the sun still glowed overhead and Roderick was as beautiful as ever. For one moment, she'd imagined she might be able to belong there. But Lady Rannock already *did* belong; her every easy movement, her confident smile, showed her to be a part of this world. Aidan's world.

Once he had cared for Lady Rannock. He had kissed her. Maybe even in that very summer house! Now that his brother was gone, maybe Aidan could give full run to his old emotions, since Gerald Rannock did not have Aidan's…intrepid spirit.

Lily guided her horse back to the stable yard, feeling so numb, so silly, so tired. A groom dashed out immediately to help her alight and she saw that, far from being empty as the yard had been when they rode out that morning, it was now crowded with carriages. The party was beginning and she couldn't hide away alone.

'Thank you,' Lily said, swaying a bit as her boots met the cobblestones. 'Tell me—Charlie, is it?'

'Yes, miss.'

'Is there a side door where I could slip into the house? I do feel rather windblown at the moment and it does look busy here.'

'Everyone did seem to arrive from the station at once, miss,' the groom said. 'If you go round to the rose garden, I think you could slip in through Her Grace's breakfast room.'

Lily remembered sitting with the Duchess in that room that morning, when she had spoken of the importance of 'the right Duchess'. It seemed a year ago. 'Thank you, Charlie.'

She draped her train over her arm and hurried around to the rose garden. She glimpsed a couple strolling there, arm in arm, shaded by the lady's lacy parasol, laughing with their heads bent close. To her shock she saw it was Rose and Lord James Grantley. They looked terribly comfortable and happy in each other's company.

Once, Lily had imagined she could make a life with

Lord James, or someone like him. How far away that seemed now! And how silly when looking at him with Rose now. It seemed she could only gain a different sort of intimacy, but how could she do that if Aidan still loved Lady Rannock?

She shook her head, feeling so muddled and confused. She slipped through the tall windows into the breakfast room, empty and shadowed now. The old Duke seemed to watch her from his portrait, judging her with his dark eyes, but she turned away from him. She hoped to slip up the stairs to her chamber and ring Doris for a bath before anyone else saw her. A burst of laughter from the hall stopped her.

'Oh, Miss Wilkins!' the Duchess called. She wore a tea gown of pale green satin and lace and looked bright and light. She tugged a man forward and he smiled, his handsome face silver-bearded and beaming. 'Do come and meet my fiancé, Lord Shelton. Shellie, darling, this is Miss Wilkins, the pretty American girl I was telling you about.'

He bowed and took Lily's hand, his kiss brushing her gloved knuckles as his beaming smile widened. *What an old roué*, she thought. She couldn't help but like him.

'How do you do, Lord Shelton,' she said with a smile, very glad now of Miss Johnson's lessons. She could appear calm and cool even with disappointment washing over her like a cold wave. 'Do forgive my dusty appearance.'

'You must have just returned from your ride,' the Duchess said, glancing over Lily's shoulder. 'Is Aidan not with you?'

'He met Lady Rannock in the garden and I went on ahead,' Lily said.

The Duchess frowned. 'Such an old friend, dear

Melisande,' she said shortly. 'I will have to go find them. Shellie, do you fancy a little stroll?'

'With you, my darling, always. I would stroll to the ends of the earth,' he said loftily, making Lily laugh. How lucky the Duchess was and Rose, too. If only she could borrow some of that fortune. 'And I need to find my cousin, Lord Clarenden, while I'm at it. He does tend to vanish and I know he's quite an admirer of Lady Rannock—he won't want to miss greeting her.'

Lily nodded and fleetingly wondered if Lord Clarenden was the tall man who had been with Lady Rannock in the garden.

'Your mother is in her chamber, Miss Wilkins, and I believe your sisters are out in the gardens,' the Duchess said. 'Shall we see you at tea? We'll be quite an informal group today.'

'Yes, of course, Duchess. Lord Shelton.'

She ran up the stairs to her own chamber, as if escaping something nipping at her heels. Doris wasn't there yet, but Lily impatiently tossed her hat down and tore at the buttons on her sleeves, desperate to be free of her habit, free of the feelings she didn't understand. What did she really want? And how could she find it now?

Aidan looped his cravat carefully around his throat, staring into his dressing room mirror as his valet brushed the shoulders of the finely tailored black wool coat and smoothed the cream brocade waistcoat. It was all so different from the evenings of his old life, sitting by a fire in old dungarees and a loose linen coat, drinking cheap whisky and listening to the howl of hyenas in the darkness beyond.

Roderick was his home, yet it didn't feel like it. It had only begun to feel like it as he rode over the fields with

Lily beside him, seeing it all through her eyes. As he sat with her in a farmer's parlour, hearing her easy chatter, her laughter, she had made everything look new, full of possibility. She had showed him his home anew.

Then he glimpsed Melisande and the past drifted over the now once more, like the slide of an eclipse over the sun. The past never seemed to leave him alone. Poor Eddie.

Aidan's fingers stilled on the folds of his cravat. Once, when he was young and full of passion for everything in life, Melisande had seemed like a goddess to him. Just touching her hand filled him with fire. He'd thought she felt the same until he had learned that Edward also loved her. Edward was the Duke and she would go with *him*. It hadn't worked out that way, of course. Edward had died, Melisande had married Rannock and Aidan had sailed for South America. It had all been left behind.

Or so he had thought. Today, when Melisande had touched his arm and smiled up at him with that same tilt of her golden head, the years had vanished for an instant. He was the same passion-struck young man who had kissed Melisande in the folly, beneath the Diana statue's watchful, disapproving gaze.

'…such a very special place,' Melisande had whispered, going up on tiptoe to place her lips near his ear. 'I've never forgotten it, have you?'

Aidan hadn't forgotten, though he had tried. It was the great regret of his life, yet Melisande's beauty was still there.

He had glanced back, but Lily was gone, that cold, wide-eyed look of realisation gone with her. He couldn't bear to have her think ill of him, to think he still lived in old romances. He would have to find her tonight to explain. But how?

'I'm in the Chinese Room, Aidan,' Melisande had murmured when they parted at the terrace. 'Just down the corridor.' And with one more smile, one more touch, she had swayed away in her red-and-black gown.

Only then did he see his mother and Lord Shelton at a table at the far end of the terrace—with Mrs Wilkins. *'We went to look for you in the garden, darling, but must have missed you,'* his mother had said with a slight frown. *'So we came back for tea. Care for some?'*

'All ready now, I think, Your Grace,' his valet said, tearing Aidan away from the memory. He handed Aidan a small box with a cameo-headed tiepin and Aidan fastened the somewhat twisted folds of his cravat. He feared he was a disappointing duke.

'Yes, thank you,' he said. All dressed, he left his chamber and made his way down the corridor to the main staircase. He passed the door to the Chinese Room with its tiny name card in the gold slot: *Lady Rannock*. It was quiet there and he didn't pause.

At first, he thought the White Drawing Room was empty. He was the first to arrive, but then he heard a rustle near the window. He saw his mother there, wearing her mauve satin gown and the Lennox diamonds, re-arranging a group of snuffboxes on a table.

'What do you think, Aidan dear?' she said, not even looking at him. 'I do believe the Peter the Great box should be in the centre since it is the most impressive. I promised to show Mrs Wilkins the collection before dinner.'

He went to his mother's side, the golden light of evening casting a glow over the gilt and pearls of the boxes. He was amazed they were still there, not sold on like many of the paintings and sculptures. 'You and Mrs

Wilkins seem to have become great friends, Mama. I'm surprised.'

'Why would you be surprised? She and I understand each other.' She moved two of the boxes and pursed her lips as she studied the effect. 'She also grew up in a world that understands family, tradition and duty. I'm sure she passed that on to her daughters.'

Aidan thought of Lily laughing easily with the farm family and how her face glowed as her fingers flew over the piano. 'Her daughters are certainly extraordinary.'

'Oh, that one twin is quite a hoyden. I'm sure I saw her climbing a tree today. But the eldest Miss Wilkins… one would scarcely believe she was American. So quiet and sensible. Pretty, too.'

'And rich?'

'Of course. It's so crass to have to say it, but we both know that is essential.' She twitched at the scarlet velvet curtain, covering a long crack in the decorated plaster wall. 'This is so important, Aidan. And you do seem to like her.'

'Yes. I like her.' Too much.

'Then we must do nothing to jeopardise the happy conclusion of this…this…'

'Deal?' he said shortly.

She pursed her lips. 'This match. I saw you with Melisande Rannock today.'

'You did invite her to this party.'

'Perhaps that was a mistake. I still remember such tender feelings of friendship for her mother and life must be so dull for Melisande in Scotland. I thought all that old nonsense was long past.'

'And so it is.' It had to be.

His mother studied him carefully. 'I do hope so. I

would so love to see you safely settled before I marry Shelton.'

'What makes you think Miss Wilkins would have me?'

She laughed. 'She will—*if* you continue to play your cards right. Did you not learn poker in some dusty saloon in your travels?' Donat came into the drawing room then, followed by the footmen with their silver trays of sherry. 'Ah, the aperitifs! Excellent, Donat. Everyone should be down soon. And do straighten your cravat, Aidan dear. We were talking about having a picnic at the lake tomorrow. You can take dear Miss Wilkins rowing! Won't that be lovely? And Mrs Wilkins was just telling me today that she had a telegram from her husband, the delightful millionaire. He should be here just in time for any… happy announcements.'

Chapter Thirteen

'Oh, Lily! How exciting! A picnic!' Violet cried, as the twins burst into the Queen's Chamber as Lily finished dressing. 'No more being stuck in this enormous edifice. I'm sure I can take some lovely photos of the lake.'

'I rather like it here,' Rose said. The two of them perched on the edge of Lily's bed, watching as Doris finished fastening the pearl buttons at the back of Lily's pink muslin dress. 'There's so much to look at everywhere! All the paintings and flowers, the books in the library...'

'That's just because you like wandering around with Lord James,' Violet teased.

Rose blushed the colour of her name and Lily gave her a wistful smile.

'Better than climbing trees, Vi,' Rose said. 'We're not ten years old any more.'

'I was trying to see the summer house,' Violet said, kicking up her heels under the lace hem of her white skirt. 'The gardens *are* very pretty, I admit, and we get to see the lake today. What do you think of it all, Lily?'

Lily remembered the fields flying past under her horse's hooves, the gleam of the house in the distance.

The moonlit folly. 'I don't think anyone could help but be impressed by it all.'

'But would you want to live here?' Violet asked.

'I would miss you all so much,' Lily murmured. She didn't know how to answer otherwise. She *could* see living here—with Aidan, if he wanted her there just as much. If he didn't still carry a torch for Melisande.

'We could come stay with you,' Rose said eagerly. 'England is so much nicer than New York.'

Lily glanced at them, until Doris shooed her back around to straighten the lace collar. 'Would you really rather stay in England?' That would be the perfect outcome to her plan to take care of her sisters. Bring them into her own home, give them such freedom. Freedom she had never known.

'Of course,' Rose said. 'It's so peaceful here, so pretty.'

'I dare say it doesn't matter to me,' Violet said. 'I'm determined to learn to ride a bicycle now and I can do that anywhere, as well as take my photographs.'

Doris pinned Lily's straw boater to her upswept hair and handed her a parasol.

'Well, it's all just daydreams anyway,' Lily said. 'We leave Roderick Castle on Monday. The Season is almost over.'

'It's surely only a matter of time, Lily,' Violet said, jumping off the bed and plopping her own hat on her head. 'Roderick Castle will be your home very soon, if you want it.'

Lily sat back on the blanket spread under the shade of Roderick's ancient, towering trees and sighed happily. A picnic really had been a good idea. It looked like a painting, all greens and blues and golds, dappled under the midday sun. The lake rippled in the light breeze and the remains of their feast were scattered around them: cucumber sandwiches and fruit pies, fresh bread and empty bottles of wine, all ravenously consumed in the fresh air. Everyone seemed quiet and lazy now with the sun and the drink.

Her mother watched the twins and Lord James as they played spillikins, Violet laughing noisily. The Duchess and Lord Shelton flirted, while Lord Rannock snored after having drunkenly dozed off. Lady Rannock, her golden hair shining under her white parasol, looked rather bored, whispering sometimes with Lord Clarendon. Aidan, too, seemed asleep as he lay in the shade, his hat over his eyes.

'Come, Miss Wilkins, row with me,' Aidan said, sitting up suddenly from his picnic blanket. He'd looked the picture of indolent languor only a moment before, but now he fairly seemed to vibrate with energy. His green eyes glowed under the straw brim of his hat. 'You did promise me a race.'

Lily glanced at the dock. 'There's only one boat there.'

'Then we'll take turns rowing,' he said. He leaped to his feet and held out his hand to her.

Lady Rannock gave a taut laugh. 'Surely it's too hot to be out of the shade.' Lord Clarendon gave her a lazy smile and waved a fan towards her.

'Oh, nothing like that would ever stop Aidan,' the Duchess said, popping a grape into Lord Shelton's mouth. 'He could never sit still, even as a child.'

Lily took Aidan's hand and everything else faded away. There was only their touch, only his smile.

'Thank you, I'd love to go out on the water,' she said. He led her down to the jetty and helped her on to the narrow wooden seat. She smoothed her pink skirts around her as he unmoored the boat and leaped lightly on to the seat across from her. He pulled effortlessly on the oars, long, smooth strokes that carried them far out on to the sun-dappled water. His lean, powerful shoulders strained against the thin muslin of his shirt, making those butter-flies flutter in her stomach again.

To try to calm those stormy feelings Aidan always stirred in her, she looked back to the shore. Everyone had returned to their lazing, except for her mother. Lily could see her satisfied smile even from across the water. And Lady Rannock, who had risen to her feet and stared after them, was as still as a statue.

Well, Aidan was with *her* now, Lily told herself. That was all that mattered. She wouldn't let the past, or her doubts of the present, ruin her bright day. She turned back to Aidan and smiled only at him, taking off her hat to let the cool breezes off the water brush her cheeks.

'It really is lovely out here,' she said, studying the idyllic scene of the folly onshore, sunlight glittering on its domed roof, Diana pointing her arrow at them.

'I'm sure it's nothing like the sea in Newport,' he answered.

'Not really. The waters there are grey so often and crowded with boats. I do miss swimming from the beach, but I think I like this better. It's so peaceful.'

'Some of the places I've seen feel so remote you would think there couldn't possibly be another person left in the world. There's only silence and the whir of one's own thoughts.'

'I'm not sure I would enjoy that,' Lily admitted. 'I do like being alone, with nature or a book, but to *only* have my thoughts for company...'

He smiled his delicious crooked smile. 'What would you think about, then, Lily?'

'I'm not sure,' she said. 'Books I've read? Places I've

been? Though nowhere as exotic as what you've seen. What did you think about when you were all alone? Roderick Castle?'

'Sometimes. I ran as far away as I could, but Roderick gets into your blood, I suppose. And I thought about a nice Victoria sponge with raspberry jam. And, yes, things I had read, philosophy and history. I went looking for myself out there.'

'I would be grateful for such a chance, too. Sometimes I think I don't know myself at all. I've always been told what to do. What would I *choose* to do?'

He tilted his head to study her closely, making her squirm and turn away. 'I think I know you, Lily. Or at least, I think I'm beginning to.'

She was intrigued and half scared. Maybe he really had seen things she would rather keep hidden. Lily leaned back in her seat, letting her fingertips trail in the water. 'Do you, Aidan?'

He drew the oars in, leaving them floating alone in the middle of the lake. He leaned his sun-golden forearms on them, studying her. 'I think you are kind and considerate. I think you get to know people, you listen to them, you care about them. Like my farm tenants. You're nothing like they say rich American girls are.'

Lily laughed, discomfited. Her…kind hearted? She fanned her warm cheeks with her wide-brimmed hat. 'I'm sure I do what anyone else would. Your mother, for instance. She seems to care very much for the estate.' And she had said a good duchess was essential.

'My mother has always done her duty, I'll say that for her. But what she cares about is the Lennox title, not seeing it tarnished by gossip about neglect or impropriety. You care about real people.'

'And what do they say rich American girls are like?'

He laughed, throwing his head back so his hair shimmered in the sun. 'That they're bold and brash, full of confidence.'

Lily thought of some of her friends back in New York, of ladies like Jennie Jerome. They *were* confident, sure of their beauty and their brains, sure of their place in the world. She'd always envied them. 'I wish I was bold and brash. But I think I've lived too much in books, too much in my own head. I doubt I'm the kind of American girl your Prince of Wales likes.'

Aidan's grin widened. 'I doubt Bertie and I have much in common, except for bossy mothers. You are exactly the kind of American girl *I* like.'

Lily laughed and reached down into the water to splash some of it towards him. 'And you are nothing like a stuffy old English duke in a book. So we've both learned a lesson.'

Aidan splashed her back, and soon they were tossing handfuls of water and laughing helplessly like a pair of naughty children. Lily tripped over the oars and landed in his lap, holding on to him as they both gasped for breath through their laughter.

He hugged her close and Lily rested her head on his shoulder to inhale his scent of sunshine and lemons in that one golden moment. She was sure she would remember it always and take it out like a jewel from its box on grey days.

'Oh, yes,' he murmured against her hair. 'I have learned a valuable lesson indeed.'

Chapter Fourteen

'What shall we do this evening? Piquet? Charades?' the Duchess said as the men joined the ladies in the Yellow Drawing Room after dinner.

'Perhaps some music?' Lady Heath suggested. 'Your duet with Miss Wilkins was so charming, Duke.'

Lily peeked shyly at Aidan over the gilded edge of her coffee cup. There had been no time to talk more when they had returned to the jetty after the picnic. They had been rushed back to the castle to dress for dinner, but she still felt the glow of their time on the lake.

'Oh, no, we always have music and charades,' Lady Rannock said languidly, from her *chaise* by the window. She waved her painted silk fan. 'What about hide-and-seek? Roderick is perfect for such things. Remember when we were younger, Aidan? The attics had such lovely hidey-holes.'

Lily couldn't help but hear from her tone that something extraordinary must have happened in those 'hidey-holes' once. She turned away, not daring to look at Aidan to see what his memories might be.

He gave Lily a long glance. 'The attics are indeed a fine spot for it.'

'Is that not a children's game?' Stella said doubtfully.

'I don't think feeling young again for an hour could be a bad thing,' said the Duchess.

'Well, I shall stay here and chat with the Bishop,' Stella said. 'You were telling me about the history of the Roderick chapel, I think, Bishop? Fascinating.'

Lady Rannock clapped her hands. 'Lovely! Now, who shall hide and who seek? Clarendon?'

'Of course,' he said with a grin. 'Nothing more amusing, eh?'

'The ladies shall hide and the gentlemen seek, of course. Is that not the way of life?' Lord Shelton said. 'Agnes, my dear, shall you be timekeeper?'

The Duchess laughed. 'Of course! Very well, ladies. Get ready, get set and…hide!'

Lily was caught in the middle of the crowd running out of the drawing room, carried with them into the hallway and up the stairs as they heard the Duchess counting off behind them. 'One, two, three…'

Everyone vanished into the shadows, leaving only floating giggles behind them. She wasn't sure where to go, but the counting went on. 'Nineteen, twenty…'

She dashed up the second flight of stairs and turned down the first empty corridor she found, in a part of the castle she hadn't seen before. It was only lit by flickering lamps at either end of the narrow space and she could hear giggles nearby, as well as the snap of doors closing. She found another narrow flight of servants' stairs behind a baize door and ducked inside. It was a small attic space, muslin-covered furniture hulking in the shadows, and she was able to take a deep breath. Hadn't Aidan said the attics were the best place to hide? Maybe it was a hint.

She wasn't alone there for long. The door opened and

a tall figure slipped inside, outlined by the lamplight outside.

Aidan. It had to be. No one felt like him, smelled like him.

'Lily?' he said, his voice so quiet, as rich and comforting as a velvet blanket on a cold night. 'Are you all right? This silly game…'

'I'm fine, I just couldn't quite breathe,' she said. 'I haven't played hide-and-seek since I was a child! Then I would usually just read in a corner and let Violet win.'

'I'm not so fond of it myself,' he said, stepping closer. 'Except that now I can be alone with you.'

'Yes,' she whispered, swaying towards him, drawn by his quiet strength as she always was.

His arms came out to catch her, drawing her close, and she leaned her forehead against his chest, the soft, fine wool of his evening coat warm on her cheek. She closed her eyes and concentrated on the sound of his heartbeat, so steady, so wonderful.

Outside the door of their sanctuary, they heard running footsteps, a lady's giggle, a man shrieking, 'I can find you, my beauty, no sense in hiding from me!' Lily burst into helpless giggles and Aidan laughed, too, the two of them leaning on each other.

Their laughter faded and, in the long, tense moment of silence, Lily stared up at Aidan in the striped shadows of moonlight from the high windows. He also stared down at her, his eyes glowing, his lips tight.

He reached out and took her hand, balancing it delicately on his palm as if she was a precious piece of porcelain. She couldn't breathe.

'Lily,' he said, so quietly. 'Do you think you could come to love…all of this? Could you be happy at Roderick?'

'I…' *Don't think* she told herself as everything seemed to whirl around her. *Just feel. This is really happening now.* 'If I could only make *you* happy, Aidan, then I could do anything at all.'

He kissed her, his arms coming around her so tightly, drawing her so close there was nothing between them. There was only them. His lips met hers, so sweet, so perfect.

'I think I didn't go about this right, Lily,' he said, his voice hoarse, but touched with laughter that made her laugh, too. She'd never felt so wonderfully giddy.

He knelt down on the dusty attic floor, still holding her hand.

'Lily Wilkins, would you do me the honour of becoming my wife?'

Lily stared down at him, the sharp angles of his beautiful face as he stared up at her. She'd half imagined this moment already, but the reality of it was nearly overwhelming. It felt so fast, grabbing her and sweeping her out to sea. But she wanted it so very much. Aidan and all he stood for—freedom *and* security.

He had said nothing of love, but surely the power of that kiss meant something? Love was waiting just beyond.

She tugged on his hand and pulled him back to her. 'Yes,' she said, holding on to him. 'Yes.'

Aidan laughed and Lily was suddenly very sure she was making the right decision. He would love her one day. His adventures, Lady Rannock—they were all in the past. Surely she was right about that?

'We should tell my mother,' she said. 'And let my father know.'

'Will he give me his consent, do you think?'

Lily thought of her father, of his own questing spirit

that would surely answer Aidan's. 'I dare say you'll get along well.'

He stood back and offered her his arm, a strangely formal gesture. They made their way down the narrow, winding back staircase, through the green baize door to the main part of the castle. As Aidan led her towards the drawing room, under the dome of the chilly hall, it struck her that this would be *her* house, hers and Aidan's. She couldn't quite absorb it all.

Everyone else seemed to have returned to the drawing room before them. Lady Heath was talking with the Bishop, while Lady Rannock fiddled with the piano keys and her husband drank by the window, his face red. The Duchess and Lord Shelton whispered together.

'There you are,' the Duchess said. 'We were just wondering if we should send Donat to find you. We've had a surprise arrival.'

She gestured towards the fireplace and Lily turned to see her mother standing there—with her father, still in travelling tweeds, his greying hair windblown. The twins clung to him on either side, in their dressing gowns, which was no doubt a terrible American informality in a castle.

'Lily Marie, how pretty you look,' he said, hugging her close as she ran to greet him. 'England suits you, I think.'

'Papa!' Lily gasped. She thought she would surely burst with happiness.

'Such a surprise,' Stella said wryly. 'Luckily the stationmaster was still there when the last train of the night arrived and brought Coleman to Roderick.'

'Papa, I'd like you to meet the Duke of Lennox,' Lily said, drawing Aidan forward.

Aidan offered his hand and her father shook it. Coleman looked affable, as always, but also…wary? Did he think Aidan was after his American fortune? 'How do you do, Mr Wilkins? I am happy to meet you indeed.'

'And I you, Duke,' her father said. 'A real-life duke—imagine that. Your house, what I could see of it in the dark, is extraordinary.'

'I do hope you think so, Papa,' Lily said quietly. 'Because, well, you see…' She glanced up at Aidan.

'I am sorry for the last-minute news just as you've arrived at Roderick, Mr Wilkins,' Aidan said. 'But I have just asked Lily to marry me and she has accepted. With your permission, of course.'

There was a sudden sharp gasp and Lily glanced back to see Lady Rannock press her hand to her lips. Lady's Rannock's husband took another deep drink, while Lord Clarendon reached for her hand.

'Oh, my dear,' her mother cried in delight. She and the twins hugged her, laughing, half-crying. Lily wondered if the old drawing room had ever seen such displays of emotion.

'Aidan, how perfectly romantic,' the Duchess said. 'I didn't know you had it in you.'

Lily looked at her father. He still smiled, but his expression was bemused. 'Well, if it makes my Lily happy, Duke. I can never refuse my girls anything. Shall we discuss it tomorrow?'

'Of course,' Aidan answered.

'Yes, nothing so solemn tonight,' the Duchess said. 'We must have champagne! Donat, do we have any of the Dom Perignon left?'

'Aidan, how very splendid,' Lady Rannock said hoarsely. She came to Aidan and kissed his cheek, smiling up into his eyes. 'I hope you shall be just as happy in your married life as I have been.'

Aidan nodded, but he couldn't answer her as the

twins smothered him in a hug. The rest of the evening passed in a whirl of champagne and congratulations, until she could remember nothing else. The past—and the future—seemed very far away.

Chapter Fifteen

'What about this necklace tonight, Miss Lily?' Doris said, holding up a new chain of diamonds and sapphires that Lily's mother had given her. *Just an early wedding gift*, Stella had said with tears in her eyes as she handed Lily the jewel case. It was the first gift Coleman had given her when his mine came in and Lily remembered playing with it as a child.

'Oh, yes, it will go well with the gown,' Lily said. 'And it is a special night.'

'Your engagement party, Miss Lily!' Doris said. She fastened the necklace for her mistress and found a pair of pearl drop earrings in the jewel box before she went to take the blue satin and white chiffon gown from the armoire. She looked a bit wistful as she smoothed the ruffled sleeves. 'You'll probably need an English maid now, or a French *mamselle* like the Duchess has.'

'Certainly not! I need *you*, Doris, or I'd be lost here in this vast house. This new life, on my own,' Lily cried. Her mother was already talking about going back to New York with the twins after the wedding. Surely Mrs Astor would *have* to receive them now. Lily couldn't yet quite imagine being completely on her own at Roderick.

Well, not completely. She would have Aidan. Her husband. Though she had seen little of him in the last few days, with all the wedding preparations rolling down upon them. She just had to hold on to the memory of his proposal in the attic, when it was just the two of them.

'But perhaps I'm being too selfish,' Lily said. 'Perhaps you want to go back to New York?'

'I'll admit, Miss Lily, I like the idea of being maid to a duchess,' Doris said. 'You should see how grand it is downstairs! Two dining rooms, everyone sitting in precedence. A lovely housekeeper's sitting room, where I've been invited to tea.'

'I should go down and see it all,' Lily said, suddenly struck that this would be her job now. She would be mistress of Roderick and she wasn't even sure where to start. 'Perhaps you could tell me if you see anything that needs to be done? Organised? I want to do so well here.'

'And so you will, Miss Lily. You always do. But I've never seen a place as well run as that Donat's domain, even though it's not nearly as comfortable as the Newport house. No central heating and tiny rooms.'

'I'm sure a new roof and hot water pipes will be the first things to go in here,' she answered, though really she was not sure. How would the money work? What was the first priority? She'd been taught how to run a fine American home, but what about an ancient English castle?

'You'll make it all perfect, I'm sure. Now, it's time we got you dressed. Everyone will be here soon, miss!'

'Of course.' Lily let Doris fasten her into the gown, thinking of the party ahead of her. The Duchess had arranged it all very quickly, declaring that Lily must meet all the neighbours. An orchestra for the dancing had arrived from London and the Roderick gardens emptied of flowers. White tents were set up on the lawn for tenants and servants to celebrate. From her window, Lily could see the lights glowing, the Chinese lanterns strung in the trees like fireflies, and hear the music and the laughter.

Once she was dressed, she made her way through the Elizabethan gallery, stopping to say hello to the glaring suit of armour, and down the stairs, twined with ivy and jasmine. Aidan was down there in the hall, talking to a couple she hadn't yet met. He looked up and saw her, a smile spreading like sunlight over his lips. She almost ran down the stairs to take his hand, reassured that all would be well after all.

'Lily, do come and meet Sir David and Lady Orwell,' he said, pressing a quick kiss to her palm. 'They live not far away at Orwell Grange and David is a fellow adventurer. They've just returned from Egypt.'

'How very grand that sounds,' Lily said, giving them a smile. They did look friendly, young and good-looking, Lady Orwell in a very stylish gown of eau de Nil silk and tulle that went well with her red hair. She reminded Lily of the twins. 'I've always wanted to visit Egypt. The pyramids, the temples… I'm so glad to meet friends of my future husband, Sir David, Lady Orwell.'

'Do call me Cora. I'm sure we will be great friends,' Lady Orwell said. 'And Egypt is full of sand and mosquitoes—don't be fooled by romantic rumours to the contrary!'

'But surely everyone should see it at least once, my dear,' her husband declared. 'You should take her there on honeymoon, Aidan. I'm sure Miss Wilkins wouldn't care for your beloved jungles so much.'

'We're just going to Brighton for a few days,' Lily said.

'Too much to do here to go away for long,' Aidan said, though Lily thought he sounded rather wistful. Did he long to get away, *really* away, again?

'Brighton? It's not at all fashionable now,' Lady Orwell said.

'There's the new Grand Hotel, which I read was quite lovely,' Lily said. 'I would love a glimpse of the English seaside.'

After a few moments chatting more about travel, Aidan led her to where her parents and the Duchess waited in a receiving line as guests came up the front steps and through the open doors. Her mother blazed like a Christmas tree in a silver brocade gown and loops of diamonds and pearls, while the Duchess was elegant in mauve satin and sapphires. She caught a glimpse of Lady Rannock waiting near the drawing room door, sipping champagne as she studied the crowd with narrowed eyes, her unadorned gold satin gown a splash of austere, liquid elegance amid all the sparkling jewels. Lord Clarendon whispered in her ear and she nodded languidly.

But Lily didn't have long to study her, for she had to meet dozens of people in a row, struggling to remember their names, to smile and nod. And tried not to worry that the waters were climbing above her head.

'Lily, this is Lady Paul, a cousin of mine,' the Duchess said, without much enthusiasm.

Lily turned to the next person in line, a smile aching on her cheeks, to find an ancient lady in rusty grey silk peering at her closely through a lorgnette. 'How do you do, Lady Paul.'

'So this is the American chit Aidan picked. You always were an eccentric one, my boy, but she's pretty enough,' Lady Paul creaked. 'What do you think of Roderick so far, girl?'

Lily bit her lip to keep from laughing. 'It is very beautiful.'

'Yes, and in rather a mess. But I dare say you'll sort

it out. You look capable enough.' She flicked one gloved finger at Lily's diamond and sapphire necklace.

Lily felt Aidan shake next to her, as if he, too, wanted to burst into laughter. 'I shall do my best,' she said.

'Of course, the first thing you'll have to do is set up your nursery. You Americans do seem good at providing sons,' Lady Paul said confidently. 'At least two of them, mind you.'

'Thank you, Cousin,' the Duchess said firmly. 'I know Lady Heath is quite longing to meet you again. Eleanor, darling?' She passed Lady Paul to Lady Heath and turned back to Lily. 'Now, Miss Wilkins, you must meet Mr Bybee, vicar of our little village.'

Lily's cheeks were burning at Lady Paul's words, croaked loud enough for everyone to hear. She turned gratefully to meet the kindly-faced vicar, who wanted only to speak of committees the future Duchess might like to take on. Charitable duties she could control—having sons she could not. What if she had only daughters, like her mother? Would she be worthless to Aidan then?

One more worry. She wished it could just be Aidan and her, alone in the moonlight again. When it was just the two of them, everything seemed so much easier.

As the vicar moved on, she glanced up at Aidan, who seemed to sense some of her anxiety. He smiled and took her hand in his.

'Do excuse us, Mama, but I feel the need for a dance with my fiancée,' he said.

The Duchess looked towards the door, but it was empty of newcomers. 'Of course, darling. Mr Wilkins and I shall come in and make the announcement in a moment. Mr Wilkins, do tell me more about your yacht, it sounds like such fun...'

Aidan swept Lily into the White Drawing Room,

transformed into a lily-draped ballroom for the party, and onto the dance floor. The orchestra had just launched into a lilting waltz and she laughed as he spun her around and around. It felt just like the night they met, before she knew who he really was.

'I wish it could always be like this,' she said, as she leaned into him, holding on tight in a spinning world.

He flashed his adorable crooked smile. 'What, being harangued by elderly relatives and vicars?'

Lily laughed. 'Well—perhaps not that. Though this vicar hardly harangued, he just tried to get me to join the flower-arranging society. No, I meant *this*. Dancing with you, for ever and ever.'

'As long as I don't tread on your toes? I didn't have much practice waltzing on my travels.'

'You're a very good dancer. You're good at everything.' And so he was, she realised. Good at riding and dancing, kissing, talking to people. Good at just being himself.

'I'm not so grand at being a duke,' he said.

'You may be new at it, but I dare say you'll soon be the best Duke of Lennox the family has ever seen.'

'Only because I have the best Duchess.'

The music came to a flourishing end and Lily heard the burst of applause that reminded her they really weren't alone. She glanced around, startled to see that the dancers around them had cleared a path, leaving them dancing alone on the parquet floor, and she hadn't even noticed. It really was just Aidan and her.

Her father and the Duchess, cosily arm in arm, climbed onto the dais in front of the orchestra and Lily knew this was it. The moment of no going back. She held tighter to Aidan's hand and he squeezed her fingers. When she peeked up at him, though, he looked somehow doubtful.

'My dear friends,' the Duchess said, a bright smile fixed on her face as she lifted a glass of champagne. 'Mr Coleman Wilkins and I are so pleased to make this official announcement tonight...'

Lily left the ladies' withdrawing room, feeling the ache of tiredness in her shoulders. Her feet were sore from dancing with everyone and the hour grew late, but there was still music and laughter from the party. She was supposed to go out to the tents with Aidan and greet the tenants, but she craved a moment of silence.

She noticed the door of the library was open and slipped gratefully inside. She hadn't had the chance to spend much time there yet, among all the lovely books, but she was sure it would often be a refuge.

It was quite unlike the rest of the house and Aidan had said his grandparents had redecorated it in the Gothic style so beloved of the Queen when she was young. It was a fantastical, medieval-looking space, with a soaring, carved beam ceiling and wine-red velvet upholstery on the fringed chairs and hassocks. More dark red covered the tall windows and even draped along the tops of the floor-to-ceiling shelves which were full of enticing leather-covered books. She sat down on one of the window seats and drew the curtain to close herself into the wonderful little alcove.

Lily looked out the bow window, to the quiet stretch of garden beyond. It wasn't the lawn with the brightly lit tents, but a knot garden in the old style, intricate patterns of herbs and flowers laid out around white gravel paths gleaming in the moonlight. It was not quite empty, though. She glimpsed the gleam of that moon on Lady Rannock's gold satin gown, the train trailing over the green borders. She was strolling slowly in the distance, her arm looped through that of a tall man in black evening dress. But Lily couldn't see who it was.

Could it be Aidan? She remembered the two of them at the summer house and all the memories that seemed to fairly vibrate between them. She instinctively ducked behind the curtain, though they could not see her watching at all.

The door suddenly opened, letting in a burst of music to break the silence. Lily didn't want to be found hiding from her own party, so she drew the curtain closer around her, holding her breath.

She peeked out to see her mother and Lady Heath, whispering together like girls as they poured out a brandy from the sideboard.

'Cheers to you, Stella,' Lady Heath said, holding up her snifter. 'This must be such a proud night.'

'Indeed it is, Eleanor,' her mother said, with deep satisfaction in her voice. She sat down on one of the velvet sofas, her silvery skirts draped around her. 'I've put all I had into my children and Lily looked so well standing up there tonight.'

'She will be an excellent duchess.'

'Thanks to you.' Stella reached into her beaded evening bag and took out a slim box she handed to Lady Heath. 'You have been such a good friend to us. This is just a small token—there will be more after the wedding.'

Lady Heath opened it, and Lily saw the sparkle of a diamond brooch in the lamplight. A satisfied smile spread across Lady Heath's lips. 'You are too sweet, Stella. But making Lily a duchess has absolutely been my pleasure.'

They laughed and clinked glasses again. Lily sat back on the window seat cushions, a cold pit forming in her stomach. The golden glow of her dance with Aidan was fading, replaced by the terrible feeling of having been... sold.

She looked out the window to where she thought she saw Lady Rannock, but the garden was empty.

Chapter Sixteen

Aidan resisted the urge to tap on the desk like an impatient schoolboy. It would never do, not in a business meeting with his future father-in-law, but it was a bright, sunny day as the gardeners cleared away last night's party and he had much work to do on the farms. He'd glimpsed Lily herself riding out early that morning, galloping away in her green habit, and he would have loved to be with her.

But first, this terrible necessity. The reminder of what he had to do for Lily.

Mr Wilkins sat across from him, a stack of papers in front of him that he perused slowly with a shrewd frown, lawyers to either side of them. The affable man of the party was gone, the hard-headed businessman in his place.

Aidan wished he could match Coleman, that paperwork could hold his attention. After all, this was his future on the table, his and Lily's. And Roderick's. But being a man of action for years was a hard habit to shake off.

'I am sure you cannot mean for the Duke to ask his wife whenever he requires funds,' Aidan's lawyer—or rather his mother's lawyer—Mr Greville of the City, said with great indignation.

'Women do keep control of their own fortunes in America, Mr Greville,' Mr Wilkins said with a tight smile. 'My daughter is an intelligent lady so I can't see why that should be any different here. She does come with a generous dowry. Very generous. Railroad shares, mine stocks. It's all there in the paperwork.'

Mr Greville opened his mouth to retort, but Aidan held his hand up. 'Mr Wilkins,' he said, 'I have great respect for you and for Lily. It's true this estate is not yet as prosperous as it once was, but I want to change all that, with Lily's help. I assure you I am no fortune hunter.'

Coleman studied him carefully for a moment, before giving a tiny nod. 'But I have no doubt money is needed here. Your mother has been showing me around in the last few days. This is a very large house and the agricultural downturn looks to be going on for the long term. My daughter is used to…certain comforts.'

Aidan nodded, uncomfortable at the reminder that what he could give Lily was in many ways not as fine as what she had come from. Her fine Worth gowns, her jewels, her mother's many remarks about heating and plumbing and artworks—he could give her none of that. And it made him angry at himself. His fiancée's family thought him only a fortune hunter, when he agreed a lady should have her independence. He wanted Lily to be happy in her new life, that was all. If only they saw that!

'I want to make her happy,' he said simply, but he worried about whether he could really do that. Roderick was going to be a great deal of work for a very long time. For the first time, he looked beyond his own happiness at finding her and wondered if she could really be happy there. If he was doing what was right for her.

'And the Duke has no wish to put the great burdens of running an estate such as this onto his wife,' Mr Greville said. 'Especially one not accustomed to it. Men run such things here.'

Mr Wilkins nodded. 'That makes sense. But I won't leave my daughter unprotected in a country not her own. I still insist on separate settlements, but in these proportions. And Lily's allowance, of course, is hers to do with as she wishes. My wife assures me a duchess has much need of fine clothes and such.' He reached for a paper and scribbled a line of columns.

An hour later, the cold, hard facts of the money all laid out and signed, Aidan was released from the library. That sense of disquiet, of fear that he could not give Lily all she deserved, haunted him. He needed to get outside, to blow the doubts out of his mind. His future in-laws thought ill of him, thought him a gold-digger. He left the lawyers and Mr Wilkins finishing and strode across the hall, intent on getting away, on being alone. Being free of Roderick, of money, of everything, just for a moment. The old restlessness had taken hold of him and he knew it wouldn't be shaken away easily. That anger burned.

'Oh, Aidan!' he heard Lily call from beyond the open door of the Yellow Drawing Room where the wedding gifts were being displayed. 'Do come and see the vase Lady Paul sent—it's quite delightfully hideous.'

'Later, Lily,' he said brusquely, not slowing his path towards the door. He knew he couldn't face her now, not with those doubts clouding his mind, clouding their future. He couldn't laugh and smile and examine strange wedding gifts, not yet. He slammed out of the front door, past the impassive footmen. 'Later.'

* * *

Lily stared after Aidan as the door slammed loudly behind him. Would he turn back, look at her? But he didn't and she felt so cold all over again. Was he so angry that the money didn't go the way he hoped? Was he thinking of calling it all off?

'The lawyers were here this morning, Lily dear,' the Duchess said. 'Such things are bound to make anyone cross, especially a man like Aidan. He is such a *doer*, you know, not one for dull indoor meetings.'

The lawyers. Of course. For the settlement. She remembered the smug satisfaction of Lady Heath and her mother at a job well done and now Aidan had to face the same thing with her father. She knew her father wouldn't make it easy, either. Not when it came to money. He wouldn't spare anyone's pride.

Money. How she wished she lived in a little cottage somewhere! But then she would be someone else and Aidan would be someone else, and they couldn't escape who they really were. He needed her money. That was the cold, hard truth. Would it drive him back to Lady Rannock in the end?

'Lily, come and look at this,' Violet called and Lily turned back to her sisters, who were helping the Duchess unpack all the gifts that were pouring in. She made herself smile, not to put a pall over her sisters' excitement. Not to let the Duchess see how she really felt.

She went to study the clock Violet held up, a confection of porcelain cupids and lambs cavorting around an ivory face and gilded hands. 'It's from Mother's family in South Carolina,' Violet said. 'Where do you think they found it?'

'Probably dug it out of an attic, after hiding it from the Yankees or something,' Lily said with a laugh. She

watched as Violet found a space for the clock among the
silver candlesticks, the Sèvres tea service, the red leather
seating chart from Lady Heath so she could conduct her
own proper dinner parties, the gilt punchbowl engraved
with the Lennox arms. There was even a gift from the
Prince and Princess of Wales, matching dressing cases
fitted with enamelled bottles and pots and brushes, their
initials in gold on the green leather. They sat beside Lady
Paul's hideous mosaic vase.

Lily stopped to study a small silver statue, an image
of Diana the huntress. It looked familiar and, when she
peered closer, she saw it was an exact copy of the goddess who crowned the folly in the garden.

She reached for the card.

*To Aidan, with such brilliant memories, much af-
fection and hope for the future,
Your Melisande, The Rannocks*

Your Melisande. To Aidan, not to the Duke of Lennox. Not to her, Lily. She curled her hands into tight
fists to resist tearing the card apart, knocking the statue
to the floor.

'What's wrong?' Rose asked, so worried, so observant.

Lily remembered seeing her strolling the gardens with
Lord James, and dancing with him at the party, and she
didn't want anything to mar her sister's happiness. 'Not
a thing, Rose darling. Tell me, what do you think of this
punchbowl?'

As they examined the table of gifts, Stella swept in
with a bright smile and another jewel case in her hands.

'Another gift delivered, Mrs Wilkins?' the Duchess said. She wrinkled her nose at Lady Paul's vase and

nudged it to the back of the table. 'Roderick shall sag under the weight!'

'Yes, people *have* been generous, haven't they? So kind,' Stella said. 'But this is a special gift, Lily, from your father and me, and it just arrived.'

Lily and the twins watched as their mother opened the box with a flourish and light burst forth as if she had released the sun.

'A tiara!' Violet gasped.

'Not just any tiara. It once belonged to an English queen, they say.' Stella lifted it out from its satin cushion and Lily saw it was a floral diadem, an intricate pattern of flowers and leaves that built up to a crest. All perfect, pure white diamonds with sapphires and rubies at the centre of each bloom.

'Good heavens,' the Duchess murmured. 'It will be perfect when you are Mistress of the Robes, Lily.'

'Oh, no,' Lily whispered. Just the prospect of being a duchess was intimidating enough; she didn't want to think about being the foremost royal attendant, too. But her mother was already carefully placing the tiara on Lily's head, turning her towards a silver-framed mirror, another gift. 'It does suit you, darlin'.'

Lily stared at herself. She wasn't sure it *did* suit her. It seemed to weigh her down, pressing her lower and lower into the Axminster carpet. She remembered Aidan storming out of the house without a backward glance and she sank even further.

'Oh, do let me try it,' Violet begged and Lily happily removed it and crowned her sister with it instead. It gleamed in Violet's red curls and she didn't seem weighed down by it at all. She strolled the length of the room, giving regal waves that made Rose giggle. What a fine duchess her outspoken sister would make! 'I shall take your photograph wearing it, Lil.'

'I feel terribly inadequate now, my dear Lily, but there is this,' the Duchess said, gesturing to an open box marked Garrard's on the far end of the table. Resting there was another tiara, a meander pattern in old diamonds. There was also a necklace and earrings, not nearly as sparkling as Stella's gift, but lovely. 'The Lennox diamonds. They could use a good cleaning, I dare say. I wore the necklace at your party last night, but now they are yours.'

Lily reached out and touched the earrings, recognising the pieces from so many of the portraits around the house. She supposed she, too, would have to be painted in them. The old and the new, like crossroads in front of her. She couldn't go back now. She would have to find a way to make Aidan love her, and not just her money.

Lily leaned on the terrace balustrade, staring out at the gardens. The lawns were filled with the sound of busy gardeners, getting everything ready for the wedding day, the rush-caw of birds wheeling in the clear blue sky, but she didn't really see any of it. She was too overwhelmed by it all: the gifts, the wedding, Aidan's anger as he'd stalked out of the house.

She glanced over her shoulder at the ever-present shadow of Roderick behind her, its ancient stones and forest of chimneys, and felt almost as if she was drowning in it all. This *would* be her responsibility soon. She'd been sure she was up to it all, with Aidan beside her. But what if he was not there with her, as she had dreamed? Not really. That look on his face when he had stormed out of the house...

Was it the money? Had her father not done as Aidan

asked? Or maybe it was something more. Something like the beautiful Lady Rannock.

Was she living in some fool's paradise?

She heard a footstep and turned, expecting her mother or the Duchess, come to drag her back to open more gifts, to approve more invitations. But it was Aidan himself, smiling tentatively.

'Lily,' he said quietly. 'I've come to…well, to apologise for my churlish behaviour earlier. It was most uncalled-for. I was just in a ridiculous temper.'

Lily bit her lip. 'I do often see people leaving Papa's office looking startled. He's not an easy man to do business with, I fear.'

Aidan laughed ruefully and ran his hands through his hair, leaving it rumpled. Lily longed to run to him, to smooth those tousled waves, to kiss him, but she folded her hands tightly in front of her and stayed very still.

'That he is,' Aidan said. 'But I suppose he didn't become "King Coal" by being soft, or by being careless as my own father was. And he loves you—he wants you to be happy. As I do.'

Lily smiled. Maybe happiness *was* possible here, after all? Did she dare hope? 'Yes, I know.'

'And do you think you might be happy here?'

Lily hesitated, not sure how to answer. She glanced over the busy lawns, the summer house.

Aidan shook his head, looking a bit sad now. 'Would you walk with me? Perhaps we could go to see the chapel.'

'The chapel?'

'Yes. It's where we'll be married, after all, and you haven't had the chance to even look at it yet.'

Lily's mother had pressed for a grand London wedding, or even something at fashionable St Thomas Church in New York, but the Duchess insisted all Dukes of Lennox had wed at Roderick itself. Lily herself loved the idea of a country wedding, but it was true she hadn't yet seen the chapel. And Aidan did look so eager to make amends, it quite tugged at her heart.

'I'd like that,' she said and they walked together down the terrace steps through the gardens, past the roses and the herb hedges, the hurrying gardeners.

'Do all grand houses in England have their own chapels, then?' she asked.

'Not all, of course. Most were knocked down or changed to drawing rooms or something during the Reformation. But Lennox Dukes, as I think I mentioned, were once Catholics and never quite got over it, I think. We're all christened and married there.'

Lily thought of babies with Aidan's green eyes, and Lady Paul's loud insistence that Americans were good at birthing sons, and blushed.

They climbed up a rather steep, grassy hill beyond the lake and Aidan took her hand to help her up. It felt so strong in hers, so steady.

'There it is,' he said, pointing to a building in a clearing, set amid a churchyard of ancient mausoleums and tilting, weathered stones. It was very old and very charming, all mellow grey stone with a square Norman bell tower and covered porch, just as she imagined an English church should be. They made their way up a flagstone pathway and Aidan pulled open the heavy, creaking, carved wood door.

A rush of cold air, scented with smoke and beeswax and roses, rushed out. It felt like a magical place, ancient, out of a fairy story or tales of King Arthur, and Lily held her breath as she stepped inside.

She saw right away it would be the perfect place to be

married, where so many couples had begun their lives together before. The ceiling was arched, lined with age-darkened beams, while the walls were painted a pale celestial blue that matched the carpet runner under her feet. Pale blue velvet cushions lined the pews and a blue altar cloth, embroidered with gold, was draped under an old silver cross. Stained-glass windows were interspersed with brass and marble memorials to past Dukes. At the other end was a gallery high overhead, with an organ and choir lofts.

Lily ran her fingertips over the polished back of a pew. 'It's so perfect,' she whispered.

Aidan smiled and his shoulders seemed to relax as if he was relieved. 'Then you approve of the wedding plans?'

'Oh, yes,' she said, feeling for the first time that the wedding was indeed hers—hers and Aidan's. It was only what would come after it that was a small, nagging doubt at the back of her mind. 'It will be quite beautiful.'

Chapter Seventeen

'Oh, Doris, aren't we nearly done?' Lily beseeched, standing very still as she and two other maids fluttered around her. 'It feels as if we've been here for hours.'

'And so we have, Miss Lily, but what did you expect?' Doris said, pinning and tucking and clucking. 'It's your wedding day!'

Her wedding day. Lily couldn't believe it had already come. So quickly, in a blur of preparations so vast there had been hardly a moment to be alone with Aidan. When she was with him, her doubts faded; when they were apart, when the ducal duties reigned supreme, she wasn't sure.

But now it was all too late. In just an hour, she would be his wife. If her gown was ever finished.

She forced herself to stand statuelike as another ruffle was tucked into place.

'She's in a terrible hurry to see her bridegroom!' Violet teased, as she straightened her own hat. She and Rose, 'helping' by sitting about and rearranging Lily's dressing table, looked so pretty in their bridesmaids' dresses of white silk with blue sashes, shepherdess' straw bonnets with blue streamers to match. They also wore matching lockets engraved with the Lennox crest, gifts from Aidan.

'Of course she is, who could help it? He's so handsome,' Rose said.

'As handsome as your Lord James?' Violet teased some more, making Rose blush. 'He's sure to be here today, watching you walk up the aisle! You must be sure to throw your bouquet Rose's way, Lily.'

'We're just friends, Vi,' Rose answered, fiddling with Lily's silver brushes. 'He loans me books.'

Lily remembered when once she, too, had considered Lord James. It all felt so far away, such a long time ago. Ever since she had danced with Aidan she had thought only of him. But did *he* think only of her? Or did her money stand in the way—and Lady Rannock?

'All right, Miss Lily, now you can look,' Doris said and turned her towards the full-length looking glass.

'Oh…' Lily sighed. 'Is that really me?' The gown was from Worth, of course, made to her mother's design and Lily's measurements at top speed, sent from Paris and escorted by its own tailor to perfect it. It was heavy, creamy white satin with asymmetrical ruffles of Valenciennes lace, beaded with seed pearls in patterns of lilies across the skirt and on the tight sleeves. A six-foot train fell in pleats from the shoulders, so weighty it seemed to drag her backwards. *Perfect for presentation at Court,* her mother had said.

Doris had carefully curled and pinned her hair, crowned with her mother's tiara gift to anchor the long, tulle veil that billowed around her like a cloud.

'Oh, Lily…' Rose sighed.

'I doubt this stuffy old house has ever seen such a beautiful bride,' Violet said. 'Let me get my camera!'

They were finished just in time, for there was a loud knock at the door and one of the maids let Lily's father in.

'Well, now, I knew my girls were pretty,' he said, hugging the twins. Rose straightened his gardenia buttonhole. 'But who are these three beauties?'

'Oh, Papa,' Lily said. She tried not to cry as he carefully kissed her powdered cheek. 'I'm so glad you're here.'

'Where else would I ever be on my first baby's wedding day?' he said. He smiled gently as he touched the lacy edge of her veil and Lily thought of her parents' own marriage, the distance between them. Surely it hadn't always been thus? Her mother had said she loved her rough miner husband at first. Surely Lily could avoid such a fate, if she always held on to the memory of their beginning and how sweet it *could* be?

'Now, Lily Marie,' he said. 'You're sure this is what you want? All this duking business?'

Lily smiled. 'I do want Aidan. He's a good man, Papa, I'm sure of it.' She thought of Lady Rannock and the Diana statue, but she shook such doubts away. They had no place on this day, no place in her mind.

'Then he must be, because I know how smart my girl is. Just know this isn't *all* you have. You have me and your sisters, and your home in America. And I've made sure you're as safe as can be here. Good man or not, cash in the bank is what we should rely on.'

Lily swallowed hard. She didn't want to think about 'cash in the bank' and how much Aidan needed that, any more than she wanted to think about Lady Rannock and the past. This day was about the future. 'I know, Papa.'

He offered her his arm and Lily took it, glad of its familiar strength as they made their slow way down the corridors and the grand staircase. Doris and the twins carefully lifted her heavy train, guiding it past the potted palms and arrangements of pink and white roses everywhere, the servants having gathered to watch her walk past. Even though the Roderick Castle chapel was only across the rose garden, a carriage waited to convey them there, its top lowered and bedecked in more roses.

The bells tolled merrily at the chapel, which looked so different in the daylight, so bright and welcoming. The Bishop who was to perform the ceremony stood on the covered porch, along with Lily's mother. Stella was resplendent in sky-blue brocade edged with black lace and she dabbed at her eyes with a lacy handkerchief beneath the tulle veil of her hat.

'Such a splendid, sunny day, my darlin',' she said as she watched Lily alight, Rose straightening the train behind her. 'Happy is the bride the sun shines on!'

'I do hope you're right, Mother,' Lily said. But there *was* something glorious about the light through her veil, the warmth on her satin-covered shoulders. Something hopeful in it all. She could surely make her life what she wished it now. She was free. She could help her sisters. And Lady Rannock would soon be gone.

'Of course I am! You're going to be a duchess. What could be more splendid?' She straightened the tulle folds of Lily's veil and sniffled. 'Now, I shall go to my seat and the bells will cease tolling. That's when you'll hear the organ fanfare and begin your procession. Don't let your father walk too fast. Isn't that right, Bishop?'

'Indeed it is, Mrs Wilkins. The music was certainly well chosen. If only my offices had *you* to organise them!' He offered his arm to escort her into the church.

Lily took a deep breath and waited as her skirt was smoothed, her bouquet of gardenias from the Roderick hothouse handed to her by the housekeeper. It seemed an age before the bells quieted and they heard the organ. The twins walked ahead of her and her father led her to the blue-carpeted aisle. He did try to walk too fast, ahead of the music's rhythm, and she had to press her fingers into his sleeve to slow him down.

The church was a bower of flowers, every pew decorated with sprays of pink and white roses trailing white satin bows, the walls lined with potted palms, arches of gardenias and roses echoing the soaring ceiling. The congregation, all satins and lace and feathered hats, stood on tiptoe to peer past the arrangements and watch the bride approach. Lily could hardly breathe, everything looked so hazy behind her veil.

The sunlight poured from the high windows, red, blue, green, gold, and fell on Aidan as he watched her walk towards him. His hair gleamed like old gold and that wonderful smile touched his lips.

She could see no one else then, her sniffling mother, the serenely smiling Duchess with Lord Shelton on her arm, Lady Rannock with her beautiful face hidden behind a pink lace veil standing with Shelton's tall cousin. Lily could see only Aidan. Her soon-to-be husband.

They reached him at last, and her father passed her gloved hand to Aidan. Hers trembled, but his was steady, warm. Reassuring. She saw the sun gleam of his smile through her veil and was suddenly sure she was in the right place.

'Dearly beloved,' the Bishop said as they stepped forward towards the altar, into their new life.

'To the bride and bridegroom!' Lord Shelton said, raising his glass high. 'To many happy days to come.'

'And to you and my mother,' Aidan said, with an answering tilt of his own glass. 'We're sure to have another wedding in the Roderick chapel before the year is out and I shall be the one giving the bride away. To the future Lady Shelton!'

'Oh, Aidan, really,' the Duchess said with a laugh. The champagne had been flowing freely during the wedding breakfast and even she was bright-eyed and giggling. 'I am too old to be called a *bride*.'

'But so you shall be, Mama. Though I doubt anyone could ever be lovelier than my own bride today.' He reached for Lily's hand and raised it to his lips for a lingering kiss, making her blush and everyone else cheer.

She studied the White Drawing Room, which had been set up with several small, round tables and gilt chairs for the wedding breakfast, all draped in pink damask cloths and decorated with silver vases of pink and white roses. Over the bridal table was an arch of ferns and gardenias, their scent heady and thick in the air. Plates of salmon mousse and eggs Drumkilbo—the Queen's favourite, the chef had insisted—lobster patties and chicken pâté had been served and cleared, the tiered white sugar-laced cake cut.

It was all so grand, so lovely, but all Lily really wanted was for it to be over. To be alone with Aidan.

She thought of the wedding night ahead of them, of the fumbling explanations of the marriage act from her mother, the secret books she'd read late at night, the whispers of married friends. It had all sounded so strange before and a little frightening. But if it was with Aidan...

She looked up at him. He was laughing at another toast, his hair tousled, his cravat a little crooked. The curve of his lips made her remember their kisses and she turned away to take a gulp of champagne.

As she looked up, her gaze caught Lady Rannock's.

She frowned a bit as she looked at Aidan, as if, just like Lily herself, she saw only him in the crowded room.

'Lily, darling, would you like another bit of cake?' her mother said, distracting her from her doubts. 'It's good luck, you see.'

At last, it was time to change into her going-away outfit. Lily slipped away from the noisy crowd with her sisters to make her way upstairs to the Queen's Chamber. When they returned from Brighton, she knew her wardrobe would have been packed up and moved to the Duchess's Suite, adjoining Aidan's.

Lily made her way automatically to her chamber, where Doris waited to help her change. She felt cold, as if the sunny day outside had suddenly turned cloudy.

'Is something wrong, Miss Lily?' Doris asked as she unfastened the heavy train and let Lily slump forward, freed of its weight, though she was sure she could still feel it, dragging her back and back. 'You do look pale.'

'A headache from that tiara, that's all,' Lily murmured. 'And maybe too much champagne.'

'You'll have to get used to tiaras now.'

'I suppose I will.' Lily watched as Doris removed the diamond shackles and put it away in its case, next to the one holding the Lennox diamonds. They would follow her always now. 'Oh, Doris, I am glad you're staying here! No French *mademoiselle* could have done such a fine job with me today.'

'It's nothing at all, Miss Lily. I like my job. And you're easy to work for, I must say! You should hear some of the stories the visiting lady's maids tell below stairs when they've had a sherry or two.'

'Do tell, Doris!' Lily said, eager to be distracted from her doubts and fears.

As she helped Lily out of the elaborate gown and into the bright blue silk and velvet suit, she told her stories of ladies throwing hairbrushes when they were dissatisfied, stepping over maids who'd fallen and twisted their ankles, hidden flasks of brandy in evening bags and second-hand markets.

'And that Lady Rannock's maid—it does sound as if the lady makes life heavy going,' Doris said as she pinned on Lily's wide-brimmed blue hat.

'How so?' Lily murmured.

'They say her husband is a drunkard,' Doris whispered. 'And he neglects her something awful! And then she takes it out on her maid, throwing things at her, threatening to sack her. But she pays well.'

'I shall have to remember to increase your wages, then, Doris,' Lily said, appalled. If Lady Rannock was so unhappy in her marriage, no wonder she looked so wistfully at Aidan.

The twins burst in, crying that everyone was ready on the drive to see the bridal couple off. Lily took up her bouquet and pressed it into Rose's hands as Violet took a photo of their parents.

'I won't toss it, darling Rose,' Lily whispered in her sister's ear. 'It must be yours, if you truly care for Lord James.'

Rose's hazel eyes shimmered and Lily knew that, whatever happened next, she had done right by her sisters. 'Oh, Lily! If only I can be as happy as I see you are today.'

Lily hugged her close, just as she had ever since the girls were babies. Their future was both secure and free now, she'd seen to that. 'You will be even happier, you and Violet. I just know it.'

And she would be happy, too. She came from tough

stock; she would look ahead just as her mother and father had. She would make a bright future. Perhaps she could even make Aidan love her. Lady Rannock, no matter her present unhappiness, could only be in the past, surely. Lily was the future. She was the Duchess. Aidan's Duchess.

Pasting a bright smile on her face, she made her way downstairs to the farewell kisses of her sobbing mother, the still-smiling Duchess and a satisfied Lady Heath, who had done her task so well. Near the door, she met with Lady Rannock, and Lily nodded as she shook her hand. 'Thank you for the lovely Diana,' she said. 'It was so thoughtful of you to make your gift a tiny part of Roderick.'

Lady Rannock smiled, her golden hair gleaming. It was hard to imagine that anyone so beautiful could be unhappy, Lily thought, or giving up something she desired. 'I'm sure Aidan will share all the history of this place with you. It is quite special.'

Lily nodded and stepped through the door into the sunshine. Aidan waited for her there on the marble front steps. He took her hand in his and she couldn't think of anything else. They dashed towards the flower-bedecked carriage, between the lines of servants tossing confetti over their heads. Lily couldn't help but laugh, especially when Aidan swung her up into his arms to place her on the velvet carriage seat.

He climbed in beside her, pressed close, warm and safe. The door closed behind them and they lurched forward, turning towards the Roderick Halt station where their train waited. The silence was deafening after the noise and tumult of the day and Lily felt suddenly shy with him. Her husband.

'Alone at last,' he said hoarsely and wrapped his arm

around her waist to draw her even closer. His kiss reassured her as nothing else ever could. 'I thought the day would never end.'

Chapter Eighteen

Lily stared out the window of her suite at the Grand Hotel, watching the night gather in and lights blink on at the sea pier below. There were still people there, lingering to listen to the last of the music on the bandstand or eat one more cone of sugar floss or rock candy, watching the pale shadows in the dusk. She almost wished she could climb down and join them, rather than face what might happen on this, her wedding night.

But she also longed to stay right where she was and see *exactly* what would happen next.

'If only Aidan were here now,' she whispered. When he was with her, everything seemed just as it should. Yet, as the minutes ticked past, she became more and more nervous.

She turned away from the scene outside and studied her bedchamber. All of the hotel, only a few years old, lived up to its name—grand. Right on the edge of the seashore, it was all white scrolls and furbelows, like a wedding cake. The lobby was sumptuous red brocade and golden curtains, potted palms and scented arrangements of roses in brass vases, with a 'vertical omnibus' hydraulic lift to sweep them up to their suites.

It had been about an hour since Doris had helped her change clothes and left her, and she couldn't hear any noise at all from beyond the connecting door to Aidan's chamber. Lily glanced at herself in the mirror, smoothing the diaphanous silk folds of her rose-embroidered peignoir, sent by Worth along with the wedding gown. Her dark hair fell over her shoulders, carefully brushed into shining waves.

She sat down gently on the edge of the turned-back bed, running her fingertips over the soft damask sheets. After what seemed like an hour, but could only have been a few minutes, the connecting door between their chambers opened and Aidan slipped inside, his dark blue dressing gown blending into the night darkness, his hair gleaming gold.

'Hello, Wife,' he said with a gentle smile.

'Hello, Husband,' she whispered as he sat down beside her and took her hand.

He watched her carefully, his eyes such a dark green, like a stormy sea. She felt she could fall into them and be lost, like diving deep to emerge into a new world, a place of such unimaginable beauty, only found with him.

They lay back slowly on the mattress, the soft blankets and cool sheets billowing around them, enveloping them. He rolled onto his side next to her and he reached out his palm to cradle her cheek. His long fingers slid into her loose hair, wrapping it around his wrist, binding them together. Slowly, slowly, as if in a dream, he cupped his fingers to the nape of her neck and drew her even closer.

Her eyes closed tightly as he kissed her, his lips sliding softly over hers, and she tasted the champagne and cake of their wedding feast. And beneath, she tasted that dark, delicious sensation that was only Aidan. It was intoxicating, full of need. He tasted like life itself.

Their tongues tangled, all artifice and hesitation and shyness melting away in sheer need and raw desire that washed away everything else. His title, Roderick Castle, her family, their past and future—none of it mattered when he kissed her.

Through the shimmery, blurry haze of lust and tenderness, she felt his hands in her hair, combing free the last of the pins until it fell around them in a dark cloud. With a deep groan, his lips slid from hers and he buried his face in her hair, to the soft curve where her shoulder met her neck, nuzzling there. He drew her peignoir away from her, letting it drift to the floor.

'Lily, Lily,' he whispered against her bare skin. 'You are so very beautiful.'

'Not as beautiful as you,' she whispered back. She reached out hungrily for him, pulling him on top of her so she could kiss him again, could press her starving lips to his cheek, his bare throat, to the smooth, golden skin revealed by his loosened dressing gown. He tasted of salt, sunshine, mint and wine. She held on to him so tightly, closing her eyes, to absorb all of him. His heartbeat, her breath, the vibrant strength of him.

He *was* beautiful, she thought, every part of him, body and soul. She needed him beyond all words, all rational thought.

'Lily,' he muttered. His lips trailed down her bare neck, the tip of his tongue swirling in the hollow at its base. He kissed the soft swell of her breast. She gasped at the warm waves of pleasure that followed his mouth, his touch.

She wove her fingers into his hair, holding him close.

'I want to see all of you,' he said.

Lily nodded mutely, arching her back so he could draw away her thin silk chemise. It drifted down like a whisper, leaving her bare before him as she had never been with any man before.

For a long, still moment, he stared at her avidly, and she couldn't breathe. Did she look…all right? Were her breasts too small, too large? Would he find her pretty?

'So beautiful,' he said roughly, erasing all her doubts. 'Lily, you are perfect.'

She laughed and drew him back down to her. His lips closed over her tender nipple, drawing, licking, so shocking, until she moaned in sheer delight.

Her eyes closed and she pushed back his dressing gown until he was as bare as she was. She closed her arms around him, sliding her palms down the groove of his spine, feeling the taut muscles of his shoulders. But it wasn't nearly enough.

She wanted him in every way she had ever read about in forbidden books, or heard whispers of among married ladies. *Only* him.

'Please, Aidan,' she whispered. 'Please, make love to me. Make me your wife.'

He raised himself to his elbows on either side of her. His eyes were burning with a desire to match hers. And she knew, in that moment, they belonged to one another.

'Yes,' he said. 'Oh, Lily. My darling.' He pushed away his dressing gown to join her clothes, abandoned on the floor, and took her in his arms again.

At last, they lay together, she wearing only her white silk wedding stockings. He knelt above her, tracing his fingertips over her knees, her thighs, to the bare skin just above. Lily thought she might snap from the ache, the tension. She felt so damp at her very core, so heavy with need.

Then, at last, at last, he touched her *there*. His fingers

combed through the wet curls and then pressed forward to circle that one aching, throbbing point.

Lily cried out, shocked and delighted. 'Now, Aidan, please!'

He lowered himself over her, bracing his palms to either side of her, holding her his willing captive. His lips caught hers in a passionate kiss, a kiss that blotted out everything else. There was no doubt or fear, just the knowledge that tonight they belonged only to each other.

She wrapped her legs around his lean hips, arching up into him, her naked skin sliding against his and making her sob with need.

His moans aroused her, his warm breath on her ear making her shiver.

'I'm so sorry,' he gasped. 'I have to…'

She nodded and tilted back her head as she felt his manhood press against her, sliding slowly, so slowly, deep inside of her. She bit her lip against the sudden, stinging pain.

'I'm sorry,' he whispered again.

'No, no, I…' But already the sting was fading away. As they lay still together, that pain curled away, leaving only bright pleasure.

He pulled slowly back and drove forward again, a bit deeper still, and that pleasure burst free like a bright comet. Every thrust, every movement, every moan and sigh, drove that pleasure higher and higher. She was blinded by the burst of light.

He suddenly arched taut above her, shouting her name, and something in her mind exploded into blue, white and red flames that seemed to consume her from within.

Then all was darkness. When she opened her eyes, she found herself curled in the crumpled sheets, Aidan stretched beside her, his chest heaving for breath. His arm was heavy around her waist, holding her close. His eyes were closed, his hair tumbled over his brow.

'Aidan…' she whispered.

'Shhh,' he said, not opening his eyes. He just drew her even closer, until they were curled together. 'Just sleep for a moment, wife of mine.'

Wife. Lily closed her eyes and happily snuggled into the curves and angles of his body. She wished she could stay there, for ever and ever.

Aidan held Lily as she slept, listening to her soft breath, smelling her flowered perfume blended with the salt breeze from the window. The candles had gone out, but the moon was bright, the glow of lights from the beach pier making the scene dreamlike.

He had never imagined he could feel this way about a woman. That with her he could find the feeling of home he had travelled the whole world seeking. Her sweetness, her smile, her care and concern—she was special.

How could he ever be worthy of her?

He drew her closer, pressing a gentle kiss to her cheek. She murmured softly, a tiny frown on her brow as if she was dreaming. Did she worry about the future, as he did?

He *never* wanted her to worry, never to have a single pain or regret. He would make sure she never would, not with him.

'Just sleep peacefully now, my dear,' he whispered. 'Sleep safely with me.'

Chapter Nineteen

'I'll race you!' Lily called over her shoulder as she and Aidan clambered down the wooden steps to the stony beach below. She plucked off her shoes and lifted the hem of her white linen skirt to run towards the beckoning water. He wore no hat and the sun shone on his hair, on his wide smile. How free he looked, how young and beautiful! And it made *her* feel free, too, so gloriously, giddily happy she was sure she could take off and fly across the water.

The cold waves lapped at her feet and she yelped, making Aidan laugh. She laughed, too, and nudged him towards the water.

Was this what being married always felt like, then? She couldn't understand why she hadn't done it sooner. Being with him made everything brighter, sharper: the sea, the clear turquoise sky, the smell of roasted almonds and candy floss in the salty air, the laughter of children nearby as they paddled in the waves. It was glorious.

Aidan caught her by her waist and spun her around and around, making her laugh even harder, laugh until her sides ached. She kissed his bristled cheek and breathed deeply of his delicious smell.

'I wish we could just swim here, without messing with

those cart contraptions,' she said, gesturing to the red-painted swimming houses, where ladies swathed in long blue serge swimming costumes emerged into the greyish-purple waves. Beyond them, the pier was lively under the afternoon sun, music drifting to them on the breeze, with laughter and chatter and the clang of games.

'Would you swim all the way to France, then?' he said, his arm still looped around her waist as they stood there in the waves. 'It's just out there, see?' He gestured at the horizon with his hat. He took out the engraved pocket watch she had given him as a wedding gift, which matched the pretty enamelled watch pin he had in turn given her. 'I think we might just have time!'

'Why not? I would love to see Paris with you.' And stay as long as possible in this golden honeymoon glow. Roderick Castle and all its duties and expectations waited for them all too soon.

'And so we'll go there, one day very soon,' Aidan said. 'But for now, what about some rock candy? Or ginger beer? Not a Champs Élysées café, I know…'

Lily caught his hand in hers with a smile. 'Rock candy sounds like *exactly* what I want right now.'

They quickly put their shoes back on and joined the crowds making their way to the pier, no longer a duke and duchess, just a couple enjoying a day out. Lily gorged herself on candy floss and sugared almonds, got giddy on shandy and laughed as she watched Aidan win at the ball-toss game and hand her the tiny teddy bear prize. It was a wonderful day, almost perfect, she thought. She wished it would never end.

'Aidan! And your lovely bride,' someone called from across the plush lobby. It was Lord and Lady Orwell, Aidan's travelling friends she'd met at the engagement ball.

'David, what a surprise,' Aidan said affably, giving his friend's hand a hearty shake. 'And Cora!'

'Since Cora heard you were coming to Brighton, she wanted to see it for herself,' David said.

'And I'm so glad I did,' his wife said with a little smile beneath her beribboned straw hat. 'It's just like when I was child! Summer holidays with Nanny.'

'It makes me think a bit of Newport,' Lily said. Though the strictures of Newport had never held the glorious freedoms of the pier and the rocky beach. 'Paddling on the shore with my sisters, that sort of thing. I dare say it's nothing to adventuring down the Nile, though.'

'Oh, do have dinner with us tonight,' Cora said. 'I know it's your honeymoon, but a bit of company can't be amiss, I hope? The restaurant here at the Grand is quite nice and we can tell you more about our travels. Perhaps even a spot of gossip about your new husband, Duchess!'

Lily glanced at Aidan and could tell from his hesitation that he, too, was reluctant to give up their moments alone. But she knew very well that all too soon there would be duties, people to meet, conversations to get through; they might as well start now.

'Of course,' Lily said with a smile. She lowered her voice and whispered to Cora, 'I should certainly dearly love to hear all the gossip about Aidan from before he met me.'

Cora laughed merrily. 'Oh, my dear Duchess! I confess we *were* a bit surprised to hear he would marry and so soon after returning to Roderick. All the ladies in Egypt quite adored him! There was this Italian *marchesa*...'

Lily's smile stiffened, and she nodded. She wanted to hear a bit of gossip, true, but maybe not quite *this* much.

On the other hand, her father *did* always say information was power. And she needed all the information she could find to make her marriage work. 'That would be lovely, thank you,' she said.

It was very late, surely nearly dawn, Lily thought as she peeked past the silk curtains of the bedchamber. Even the lights of the pier were extinguished, the beach silent, the stars blinking overhead. Yet she couldn't sleep.

She turned to look at Aidan—her *husband*, how strange that still sounded!—sprawled asleep on their bed, his hair bright and tousled. How lovely it was to remember those hours in his arms, to know this was surely only the beginning. Yet how frightening, too, to look into their future and see the uncertainty.

Dinner had been more fun than she had expected, laughing with his friends over old travels, but worrying as well. Cora was a gossip, and had whispered to her about Lady Rannock. Lily was appalled at how Aidan's family must have suffered when his brother loved her, but what would happen now? She had to learn to be a duchess, to make her husband happy, and she realised suddenly she hadn't the first idea about him, really.

What *had* she got herself into?

Chapter Twenty

Lily watched as the scenery flashed past the train window, growing more country-like with every mile. Hedgerows and fields replaced towns and villages and she knew Roderick itself wouldn't be far. The sunlight and salty sea breezes of Brighton, the carefree days of wading in the cold sea, playing games on the pier and getting sick on too much candy floss as she and Aidan laughed together seemed so far away.

Aidan sat across from her in their compartment, intently going over a stack of papers that had arrived for him their last day at the Grand. Her laughing, tousled husband now seemed to disappear behind the screen of the duty-worn Duke, but she trusted he was still there. Somewhere. Surely he would come out when they were alone again? Maybe if she let her help him with those papers, let her come to see the estate as *theirs* now?

She glanced around the train carriage through the sliding doors. It was sparsely populated and everyone else was quietly going about their business, reading or dozing or, like her, staring out the windows. She thought of her father and his private railroad carriage, all blue velvet and gold swags, vases of roses and champagne glasses.

She wondered idly what Aidan would think of possessing such a thing and decided that the rugged adventurer David and Cora had told her about would scorn it altogether. Then again, Old King Coal's money was now at his disposal.

She checked the enamelled watch pinned to the lapel of her brown velvet travel suit. She thought of the night Aidan gave it to her, their wedding night, and smiled a secret little smile. Yes, her husband was surely still there, somewhere inside the Duke.

'I think we'll be at Roderick Halt station soon,' she said.

'Hmm?' He looked up at her, his eyes still hazy with distraction. 'Oh, yes, of course. Are you ready, then?'

'Ready to arrive? Yes, I suppose. I could certainly do with a cup of tea.'

He laughed and, unlike his usual sunny chuckle, it seemed harsh, humourless. 'I think you will find a great deal more than tea waiting.'

She saw what he meant as the train pulled into Roderick Halt. She'd expected the carriage from the castle to be waiting, but a large crowd jostled on the platform, which was decorated lavishly with bunting and flowers. She could hear the sound of a brass band playing and she nervously straightened her velvet hat with its spill of creamy silk roses.

'Ready?' Aidan said with a smile. At least this time it was warm and reassuring.

'I suppose I must be,' she answered. She took his arm and they stepped down from the train.

The band struck up another tune and Lily pasted a bright smile on her lips as she studied the crowd. The mayor of the village, Mr Bybee, the vicar, every shop owner she could remember and a clutch of children from the local school waving their little flags. All watching *her*.

The stationmaster stepped forward, his hand holding that of a tiny girl in white lace who offered a bouquet of red roses with a shy little curtsy.

'Welcome home, Your Grace,' he said. 'And to your fine new Duchess. This is my daughter, who is also called Lily.'

'That is certainly one of my very favourite names,' Lily said gently as she bent down to the child's level and accepted the roses. Little Lily buried her face shyly in her father's coattails, making everyone laugh.

She listened as the stationmaster and then the mayor gave long speeches of welcome and presented Aidan with the gift of a green leather cover for the local train time-table. Aidan stood close to Lily, sometimes taking her arm, always smiling, but she had the unmistakable sense that he was far away from her.

The vicar, Mr Bybee, was the last to make a speech, his flowery words taking even longer than the mayor's, but Lily had to smile at his sincerity.

'I can see my Duchess will have many friends in her new home and I thank you from the bottom of my heart for your welcome of her. I hope we shall see you all at Roderick for the autumn fête in a few weeks, where I can thank you properly.'

'Autumn fête?' Lily whispered. That sounded like something the Duchess would have to organise and over-see, and she suddenly realised that Duchess was her.

'An event that Roderick hosts every year,' Aidan an-swered. 'Don't worry, my dear, everyone there knows exactly what to do.'

But *she* did not. Before she could ask more, he was swept away to speak to the village councilmen and Mr

Bybee led Lily to the edge of the platform. 'I do hope I may call on you very soon, Your Grace, with news of all the various charities and committees the Duchess of Lennox traditionally chairs. I'm sure you must be eager to know all about your new home.'

'Indeed I am, Mr Bybee, and I'm glad I can come to you for advice,' Lily said, realising that this *was* her new home and she was meant to lead it. She would need all the advice she could find. 'I'm anxious to get to know the people.'

He beamed at her from behind his spectacles. 'Excellent, excellent! I can send word every morning about which families in our parish might need extra assistance or a personal visit that day, as I always have with the Duchess.'

Lily wondered how many people there were in the parish and how she would find them all. But she did want to help. 'That would be so kind, Mr Bybee, thank you.'

Aidan took her hand and led her towards where their carriage waited, an open landau in the Lennox green and gold, bedecked with garlands of flowers. Much to her surprise, as they took their seats, the horses were unhitched by a crowd of tenants and pulled away through the land, amid more cheering crowds. Floral arches had been erected all along the way, even over the gatehouse to the castle, and Lily laughed.

'Is this what the Queen feels like every day?' she said.

Aidan studied it all with a warier air than the awe she felt. 'It's the way when a Duke of Lennox gets married.'

Lily peeked ahead to the waiting house where the servants formed two long lines up the front stairway and the Duchess waited at the top to greet them—already dressed in her travel suit, as if she couldn't wait to depart and hand over all the duties to Lily.

Lily shivered and clutched at her bouquet. Aidan's hand, which had held hers so warmly, fell away so he could wave and she felt suddenly alone on the precipice of this strange new life. Would the man on whom she had built such tentative hopes ever come back to her now?

Chapter Twenty-One

Lily stared down at Lady Heath's leather seating chart, her eyes almost crossed from trying to figure it all out. Mrs Bright, the housekeeper, had left the copy of *Debrett's* for her to try to decipher the labyrinthine ways of aristocratic hierarchy, but even so she wasn't quite sure.

She switched around two of the cards, but noticed it still left her with a question—there were two countesses, friends of the now Dowager Duchess, coming, so which should be seated where? Was Lady A. due the seat to Aidan's left, or Lady B.? And then there were the Rannocks. And Lord Clarendon, Lord Shelton's cousin.

Lily frowned as she looked at the Rannocks' cards, left to the side on the desk for the moment. When the Duchess had written to Lily after their return from Brighton, asking if she and Lord Shelton could possibly have their engagement dinner at Roderick—'after all, it was my *dear* home for so long and, now I must bid it farewell, I do feel so sentimental'—Lily hadn't been able to say no. But now it left her with her first party to plan as Duchess of Lennox.

Lily sighed and pushed the seating chart aside for the moment to concentrate on the stack of new menus the

cook had left. She felt more sure about those, as she had
watched her mother plan twelve-course dinner parties
regularly in Newport. Yet she still wasn't certain about
English tastes and she knew it had to be perfect for her
mother-in-law.

She gave up for the moment and stared out the window. She'd had her desk moved into the Yellow Drawing Room, where she had a long view over the lawns to
the lake and the summer house, but she wondered if that
had been a good idea. It was a beautiful, gold and green
late summer day and she longed to be outside in it, away
from the endless letters and menus and Ladies A. and B.

She groaned. Would she ever be a proper duchess?
What was more, would she ever be alone with Aidan
again?

The silvery perfect days at Brighton seemed to slip
further away with every moment. Ever since their train
journey home and their carriage was pulled up the drive
to Roderick, he had been different. Strained, worried.
Distant. Their nights were glorious, filled with kisses
and caresses, silly whispers. Then in the morning he was
gone, riding out after his early breakfast, not returning
until near dinner, when they would eat at opposite ends
of the vast table. There was no time for the giggling
moments, the little jokes, like on their honeymoon. The
servants were always watching, watching, and Aidan
seemed so preoccupied.

Lily sighed and reached for the seating chart again,
as well as the little notebook full of instructions on Roderick that the Dowager Duchess had left for her before
departing for London. Surely she was just being silly?
Aidan had so much to do and so did she. She was charge
of the house now and there were hints that the Prince of

Wales wanted to come later in the season for shooting. She had to learn everything, for Aidan.

But when she tried to study the closely scribbled note-book, listing every plant in the hothouse and where the fruits were sent, every servant, every storage room, every piece of linen and where it went, she kept thinking about Brighton. About Aidan's laughter as they dashed into the sea, his hand warm in hers. Would she ever see that Aidan again?

The drawing room door opened and Aidan was there, as if summoned by her thoughts. He wore his riding clothes, his hair tousled, his cheeks reddened from the ride.

'You're home!' Lily cried happily.

'Yes, I thought I'd better make myself presentable be-fore we left for dinner at the vicarage,' he said.

'Oh, yes,' she said quietly. She'd almost forgotten. Mr Bybee had been so eager to tell her of all the work to be done at the church and village, and was so happy when they had said they would dine with him. She did need allies, and it had seemed a fairly painless way to ease herself into the social life of the neighbourhood. Now, as she looked at her husband, so handsome after his day in the fresh air, his green eyes glowing, she wished they could just stay home alone by the fire, eat their dinner off trays and just be Aidan and Lily for a while.

Not that anyone would ever be allowed to dine off trays at Roderick.

'Were you at the Halls' farm today?' she asked.

'The Home Farm fields. I'm hoping to call on the Halls tomorrow.'

Lily sighed. 'I do wish I could go with you. I'm aching for a good gallop and it would be nice to see sweet little Meg again.' Her father had sent some horses before he left for New York, replenishing their stables just as they filled the house with plasterers and painters and joiners.

'Then you should. Meg would love to see you again.' He bent to kiss her cheek and she inhaled deeply of his lemony, sunshiny scent. He seemed to bring the fresh day into the stuffy drawing room with him, the feeling of freedom.

'I have an idea I'd love to talk to them about, for a local school,' she said.

'A school?' he said, his voice surprised, though she didn't know why he should be.

'Of course. I want to do what I can to help the local people. There are so many children on the estate, a proper school would be a fine thing for them. Don't you agree?'

'Of course. But you have so many things to occupy you right now.'

'Nothing so important as the people,' she said firmly. 'I also have more ideas, if you'd like to read over them? We could maybe ride over the estate soon and see about a suitable property.' She handed him a folder of notes, hoping he would approve. 'After all, it's *our* money now, yes?'

'Yes,' he murmured as he leafed through the folder, though she couldn't see if he was happy or not. 'Our money.'

'Perhaps I will indeed go with you to the Halls', if I can get ahead on these blasted seating charts today.' She laughed. Surely she *was* becoming more English if she could curse now like an Englishwoman.

'Is this for Mama's dinner?' Aidan asked, studying her stack of cards, his sleeve brushing her bare neck above her frilled collar and making she shiver. 'Where do I sit, then?'

'Between your mother, and I don't know who, it's all

such a muddle! Lady A. or B.? Or my mother, maybe? If she can come to Roderick. Her last letter hinted she'd love to see it again before she goes back to New York. She and the twins have been so busy enjoying the last London parties.'

Aidan gave an exaggerated shudder. 'Oh, no, not both mothers!' He picked up Lady Rannock's card. 'What about Melisande?'

Lily frowned. He seemed rather too interested in sitting near his old sweetheart. 'Lady Rannock? Is that the correct seating? I've been looking at *Debrett's...*'

Aidan laughed and dropped the card. 'Never mind all that, this is just an informal dinner party at our own home. Melisande is an old friend and I hardly know Mama's countesses. But I think you should put her next to Lord Clarendon, yes?'

'Lord Clarendon?' Lily said slowly. Did he really not wish to sit next to Melisande? Or was it a feint, to distance himself? She wished she did not feel quite so in the dark about it all. 'If that's what you want.' She picked up the card and carefully slotted it into place on her chart.

'Mama is sure to pick everything apart no matter what we do,' Aidan said lightly. 'We just have to show her, show everyone, that Roderick is our home now as well as the ducal seat. We can do things in a new way, arrange them as we like. You're the Duchess now.'

'I'm the Duchess,' she whispered. She wasn't sure she believed it yet.

Aidan kissed her again and turned towards the door. 'I'd best ring for a bath before tea. Shall I order the carriage for seven?'

'Yes, of course.' The door closed behind him and the drawing room seemed to quiet again. She turned her gaze back to the garden, now gold and pink as the sun started to sink.

She pushed away the seating chart and menus, and went over to the fireplace. She stirred up the embers there, despite the warmth of the day and the fact that the footmen took their fire-setting duties very seriously. She looked up at the portrait of the young Duchess over the carved mantel, her bright green eyes, so much like Aidan's, watching everything.

Her gaze caught on the silver Diana statue, positioned between two Meissen vases. She remembered the card that came with it, Aidan and Lady Rannock in the summer house, wrapped in a past she couldn't share.

Before she could stop herself, she reached out and knocked the statue from its perch. Diana tumbled to the carpet with a loud thud, her bow snapping off.

The door opened suddenly and a maid appeared, as if waiting outside for any sign. 'Your Grace! Is everything well?'

Lily took a deep breath and smoothed her hair. She was being ridiculous and she knew it had to stop. 'Quite. I just had a bit of a clumsy accident, I'm afraid, and I broke this statue. Can you take it to Donat to be repaired?'

'Of course, Your Grace,' the maid said, wide-eyed as she swept up the unfortunate Diana.

Aidan reached for his onyx cufflinks as he finished dressing for dinner and glanced quickly into his shaving mirror. It was most odd—even after months back in England, as Duke, and now a married man, master of Roderick Castle, he didn't recognise himself in his proper evening dress. He still felt like Aidan, tramping through jungles in old dungarees and cracked boots, sleeping under the stars.

How very odd life was, he thought with a laugh. He'd never envisioned anything like this. It wasn't meant to be his destiny. When facing rampaging lions or venomous jungle snakes, he'd never been cowed. Never felt out of place. But now, dressing for a respectable dinner at the vicarage, with his wife, he felt completely displaced.

He thought of all the tenants like the Halls, of the eighty servants at Roderick. He thought of Lily. How hard she'd been working since they came home, how much everyone already seemed to love her. She deserved the best he could give her. But what did he really have? A crumbling old house and endless work. Not to mention duty dinners at vicarages.

She deserved all that was fine and beautiful. Could he give it to her? Could he, this new Aidan he was only just getting to know himself, really be worthy of her? He remembered too well the hurt look on her face when he stormed out of the house after meeting with her father before the wedding, her confusion when he cut their dinners short, pleading paperwork.

He would find a way to make it all up to her. He had to.

'Will that be all, Your Grace?' his valet asked.

Aidan glanced at the watch that had been Lily's wedding present to him and nodded. 'Oh, yes. We can't be late.'

Chapter Twenty-Two

Aidan was sure Lily was still asleep early the next morning when he made his way past the door of the Duchess's Chamber. He heard only silence beyond. The light filtering past the curtains on the corridor windows was still yellow-grey, the day barely beginning, and surely Lily wouldn't have opened her eyes. His new habit was to rise very early and see to business; he realised with surprise that he didn't yet know what Lily's 'habits' would be. They had barely landed on their feet at the estate after those giddy days at Brighton and he had to admit he wasn't sure what to do next. Lily seemed to feel the same and he didn't know how to get past that.

His previous life was very different—travelling where he liked, meeting who he liked. And his only vaguely distant idea of what being a duchess entailed came from his mother, her shopping and parties. He had a difficult time imagining that would make Lily happy. But what would? What could he do?

During the day, when he went out to examine the estate, the crumbling fences and tracks that needed to be replaced, he tried to imagine Roderick *his* way. Their way. Lily's way, really, since the money was hers. Yet he didn't know how.

To his surprise, Lily wasn't still abed, even after their dark, enjoyable hours together. *There* he did know how to make her happy, at least. She sat at the round table of the Yellow Breakfast Room, dressed in a crisp white shirtwaist and blue serge skirt, pearls at her neck and ears, her head bent over a notebook as she sipped coffee and scribbled notes.

She glanced up and smiled at him, strangely shy after what they had been doing mere hours before. She did look rather different that morning, businesslike, serious. He noticed the room, too, looked suddenly different, furniture rearranged, different paintings on the yellow and white walls.

'Good morning, Aidan,' she said, a faint pink blush staining her cheeks. 'There is coffee in the pot. Shall I ring for more toast and eggs?'

'Coffee will do.' He poured out a cup and sat down across from her, trying to peek at her notebook. What was she devising? 'You're up early today.'

'I thought I might ride out with you later. I've been corresponding with Papa's accountant…'

She had been taking over estate business? Was that what her father meant by leaving the money in her hands? 'The accountant?'

There must have been something in his tone that made her glance up at him sharply. 'Of course. It's *our* money, is it not? Our decisions on how to improve Roderick. I wanted his advice, but now I want to see it all for myself. I hope you don't object?'

Aidan was surprised. Roderick was surely his responsibility. But he had to admit he liked to see Lily's confidence growing. 'Not at all. As you say, it's your—*our* money.' He poured out more coffee, considering his next words carefully. 'What are some of your ideas?'

'As I have already mentioned, I had thought perhaps a school. For the local children. The village school must be far away, especially in the winter, and there doesn't seem enough space there. If we had our own school on the estate, we could hire our own teachers, have a curriculum that could be useful to them here at Roderick.'

'And where would this school go? Roderick is large, but there needs to be room for new farms, as well.'

Lily frowned, as if worried he might disapprove. 'It need not be large. I'm not thinking it must be Eton.' She slowly reached for the toast rack. 'You don't…mind a school, do you, Aidan? I am still learning so much and I don't think…'

He suddenly felt like a heel for making her doubt her idea. He didn't want that at all; he never wanted that for her. It was all new to him, as well. 'Not at all.'

She shuffled the pages of her notebook. 'I also noticed that many families are taking care of aged relatives, which must be difficult when everyone is working. Perhaps there could be a place, near the village, where they can join others for the day sometimes, talk, play cards, have a bit of tea, maybe listen to a lecture or two? Your mother said she liked to read to tenants' parents sometimes, but this doesn't seem like a long-term solution…'

'What a fine idea,' he said, surprised and a bit chagrined he had not thought of such a thing. His focus was always on improving the land, making the agricultural lands yield more. Maybe Roderick *could* be made theirs?

'Shall we ride out, then? I just need to change into my habit,' she said, tidying her papers. He nodded; he could tell he had a long way to go to keep up with his wife, but maybe things would work out all right after all.

Chapter Twenty-Three

Lily studied herself in the mirror and hardly recognised herself. She looked so much…older. Her eyes burned dark in her pale face, her hair heavy on her brow. Was that really her, bookish Lily Wilkins? Or was she transforming, like an insubstantial wraith, before her very eyes, into the Duchess of Lennox?

At least she knew her gown was her own, for this, the Dowager Duchess's engagement dinner. In New York, among the Knickerbocker set the Wilkins could never claim, brides wore their wedding gowns in the season after the wedding as tradition. Her mother had insisted she do the same, so Doris had trimmed the high neckline lower and shortened the sleeves, and removed the train to put away for her future Court presentation.

She wore her pearl collar necklace and the Lennox diamond tiara and earrings. She reached up and touched it, feeling the sharp, cold edges of the stones through her glove. It didn't seem to belong to her. Would it ever?

She heard the gilded clock on the wall of the Duchess's Chamber chime and realised all the guests would be down soon. The afternoon had been such a flurry of arrivals, making sure everyone was settled in their guest chambers, sending up their luggage and baths. She hadn't had a moment to be alone with Aidan in all the chaos. She'd only glimpsed him a few times, greeting his mother, laughing with the Rannocks.

She turned away from the mirror and reached for her fan. As she took up the ostrich feathers, there was a knock at the door. Hope rising in her that it might be Aidan, come to have a quiet, reassuring word, she called, 'Come in!'

But it wasn't Aidan. It was her mother, sparkling in maroon satin and a parure of rubies and topazes, her eyes shining as she kissed Lily's cheek.

'My darlin' girl,' she said happily, fairly fluffing her feathers as 'mother of the Duchess'. 'How pretty you look. So regal. I'm so very proud of you!'

Lily made herself smile. 'Thank you, Mother. I'm so glad you could be here tonight, even though the twins had to stay with Lady Heath in London. I'll miss you all so much.'

'I would never abandon my baby as she takes her first steps in such a new life! Your father does want me to return to him in New York before the winter season, but there's plenty of time for that. I'm here if you need me, though I know you do not. We did bring you up to be equal to any challenge.' She wandered about the room, studying the silver brushes on the dressing table, the flowered hangings of the ancient Duchess's bed, the porcelain shepherdesses on the mantel.

Lily wondered if she *was* equal to it all. 'What will you do before you go home, Mother?'

'Oh, travel a bit, perhaps! Violet and Rose should see more of Italy and get a little more polish. Violet is such a hoyden! Not that Rose needs polish, of course.'

'In what way?'

Stella sat down on the blue velvet sofa by the fireplace. She smoothed the black braid passementerie on her skirt. 'She tells me Lord James Grantley has proposed.'

'Proposed?' Lily cried. 'So quickly?'

Stella smiled smugly. 'Your own engagement was swift, as well, Lily. I can't stop true love in my children. I remember that from my own youthful heart!' She fluffed a needlepoint pillow. 'He's called on her often since your wedding, taken her to the theatre, out driving. Even to the British Library, which pleased her no end, though I don't think it very romantic. All those dusty books! But Rose is so happy.'

Lily sat down beside her mother, remembering her own old thoughts about the kind Lord James, her joy and worries for her sister. And that small, selfish gladness that Rose would stay in England with her. 'Will Papa agree?'

'I'm sure he will. It's not as fine as *your* match, Lord James being a younger son and all, but he suits Rose. That girl is so quiet, so buried in her studies, I've rather worried about her.'

'Yes, indeed,' Lily said softly. 'They'll do well together.'

'And now two of my girls are happy! Lily, I'm so pleased. Now, we just have to find someone for Violet.' She sighed with a frown. 'That might not be so easy. All she does is sit behind that camera all day now.'

Lily thought of Lady Heath and Stella's 'gifts' to her friend for such adept matchmaking. 'I'm sure Lady Heath can help you.'

'I'm sure she can! What a good friend Eleanor has been. Now, darlin', shall we go down? They'll be expecting you, the Duchess! Everyone says you're doing such a fine job here.'

'I hope so! You go ahead, Mother. I'll be there in only a moment.'

Stella took her hands and suddenly kissed her cheek, surprising Lily. 'Oh, my girl, I am so proud of you. You will be such a fine duchess. And maybe soon I may be a grandmother?'

Lily felt her cheeks turn hot and she looked away before she could let thoughts of what happened between her and Aidan in their quiet bedroom intrude. 'I don't know, Mother. But you will be almost the first to be told.'

Her mother patted her cheek and hurried out of the room, leaving her spicy Parisian perfume behind. Lily smoothed her hair and her gloves, fluffing up the lace of her wedding gown. A baby—would that be true one day, soon? Her own child, hers and Aidan's?

Flushed and shy, she tiptoed to the connecting door to the Duke's Chamber. He had come through it before, in the dark and quiet of night, her husband, her own. 'Aidan?' she called softly and knocked. She couldn't hear any sound from beyond. Had he already gone downstairs?

Feeling foolish, she spun around and hurried out of the chamber. Whether or not she yet felt like the Duchess, she had to make sure everything was as it should be downstairs and she shouldn't mope after her husband like a schoolgirl. She passed the rows of guest rooms—the Chinese Chamber, where the Dowager Duchess was lodged, next to Lord Shelton in the Primrose Chamber, all the Countesses and Earls, old Lady Paul. At the end of the corridor was the Mauve Room, where Lady Rannock had been lodged. Lily had thought the silvery shades of the room would suit her.

A burst of merry laughter floated from behind the closed door, the clink of glasses. Lily heard the murmur of voices, Lady Rannock's high and gleeful, and the answering tenor of a man. She could make out no words, but the tone of the chuckle sounded rather like… Aidan. But that couldn't be, could it?

She backed away, her face burning, her stomach queasy. She dashed away as fast as her heeled satin shoes could carry her, bursting out of the corridor and into the Elizabethan gallery. That heat of embarrassment turned icy cold, a chilly knife at the centre of her. Could Aidan really be with Lady Rannock?

She paused for a moment at one of the windows to catch her breath and compose herself. She pushed open the rusty old casement and let in the evening air, filled with the sweet scent of roses and cut grass, the sound of gardeners retiring for the evening. The sun was low in the sky, gilding everything.

Had she been fooling herself all these weeks? When Aidan proposed to her, when he rowed with her on the lake and made her laugh? Those golden days in Brighton? Had that all been something of a dream?

No, surely she was not as blind and silly as all that. Those days with Aidan were real. Aidan was her husband, he cared about her. They had just been buried in duties, in finding their way, since they had returned to Roderick. He was often tired, as was she. Overwhelmed. They would find themselves again.

As long as he did not find Lady Rannock first? Or find her again?

'Your Grace?' Donat said.

Lily drew as deep a breath as her stiff silk bodice would let her and made herself smile before she turned to the butler and his impassive expression.

'Yes, thank you, Donat,' she said. 'Are all the guests in the White Drawing Room? Is the Duke down yet?'

'Not yet, Your Grace. Her Grace the Dowager Duchess and Lord Shelton are there, as well as Mrs Wilkins and a few of the others.'

Lily nodded. 'Please do have a footman remind His Grace, then, and possibly bring in more sherry?'

He cleared his throat. 'The Dowager Duchess would say…'

Lily was rather tired of the servants always telling her what the previous Duchess would say. 'Sherry, Donat, thank you.'

She left the gallery and hurried down the stairs to the drawing room. It had been restored to its old ways after her wedding breakfast, every velvet hassock and marble plant stand, every portrait, back in its old spot. The Dowager Duchess and Lord Shelton were chatting with the other guests near the terrace doors, open to the lovely night, laughing over their sherry.

'Oh, Lily, my dear, I so love what you have done in here,' the Duchess said, gesturing to the one painting Lily had moved before airily kissing her cheek. Her dark green satin and chiffon gown glowed richly, just like the new emerald tiara in her hair. 'I would never have thought of that Dutch landscape there!'

'It's so beautiful, such a happy scene,' Lily said. 'I wondered if it was too dark for it on the staircase.'

'Well, it *is* kind of you to host Shellie and me for our engagement dinner here. We do so appreciate it, don't we, my dear?'

Lord Shelton, who was flirting shamelessly with Lily's mother and an auburn-haired countess, bowed low and said, 'Oh, yes, my love, quite marvellous.'

'Roderick Castle is always your home, of course,' Lily said. Would it ever feel like *her* home, too? She'd had such hopes on her wedding day. She just had to keep trying. 'Your notebook on housekeeping has been so valuable to me.'

The footman offered her a glass of sherry. As she took it she noticed Lord Rannock standing by the open doors, swaying and red-cheeked as if he had been imbibing of the sweet wine rather freely. His wife was nowhere to be seen.

The Dowager Duchess waved Lily's words away with her fan. 'I simply wanted to share all my years of work, Lily darling, all that trial and error! It should not go to waste. Of course, you are such a quick learner. American girls always are.'

'And sons!' Lady Paul shouted and banged her stick on the parquet floor. 'They're also good at having sons, I hope.'

'Of course,' Lily murmured and waved to the footmen to make sure Lady Paul had more sherry immediately.

'Now, where is my *own* son?' the Dowager Duchess asked, laughter in her voice. 'I was hoping you two would play for us on the piano before dinner.'

'Here I am, Mama,' Aidan said as he strode into the drawing room, so tall and golden and smiling. 'I am sorry to be late for your special dinner.'

He kissed Lily's cheek and she smiled, feeling warm again. He bowed over her mother's hand and Lady Paul's, making her giggle like a girl, just as Lily felt herself. Lily only then noticed Lady Rannock slipping into the drawing room behind Lord Clarendon, her slim figure sheathed in a silver lace gown that changed and shimmered with every movement. She went to her husband, who grabbed her hand hard and whispered into her ear, making her frown. Was he admonishing her for being with Aidan?

'It's quite all right, I was just chatting with your lovely

wife,' the Dowager Duchess said. 'What a breath of fresh air she has brought to old Roderick in only a few days!'

Aidan slipped his arm around Lily's waist. 'I quite agree, Mama.'

'Well, shall we go in to dinner?' his mother said. 'Shellie, darling, you will take Mrs Wilkins?'

Lily was quite sure that was her duty, but for once she was glad of her mother-in-law's authority, her easy way of managing the people around her without letting them know she did it.

Lily smiled sweetly at Lady Rannock. 'My dear Lady Rannock, will you go in with Aidan? And I am sure your husband will kindly escort me.'

'Of course, Duchess,' Lady Rannock said with a cat-that-got-the-cream smile. Lily reminded herself *she* was the Duchess now, *she* was Aidan's wife, and nothing could ever change that. Could it?

Lily studied the table in the dining room carefully, the old china with the gilt edges and Lennox coat of arms, the heavy silver, the crystal that had been a wedding gift, the arrangements of Roderick roses in low silver bowls interspersed with platters heaped with glistening fruit. The candlelight gleamed on the damask cloths, the old portraits, the satins and jewels of the guests.

It had all been going rather well, she thought. Conversation flowed, along with the fine wines her father had sent to replenish Roderick's cellars. Everything seemed bright and cheerful. And so very long. She had no time to worry about Aidan, no time to watch him smile with Lady Rannock at the other end of the table. Lady Rannock, who had somehow manoeuvred her way to a chair between Aidan and Lord Clarendon.

Lily reached for her wineglass and took a long sip,

watching as Aidan talked with Lady Rannock in the candlelight. Her mother sat across from him, but she was deep in conversation with the Bishop next to her, leaving Aidan and his old romance to bend their heads together in the candlelight, laughing softly.

'Such a pretty pair, eh?' Lord Rannock, who sat on Lily's left, slurred and she turned her head sharply to face him. She'd spent most of the course so far talking to Lord Shelton and hadn't noticed how silent Lord Rannock had become, how often his glass was filled. His eyes were bleary and red with a strangely malicious glint above his moustache.

'I beg your pardon, Lord Rannock?' she said coolly. She shook her head at the footman who approached with the decanter.

'My wife and the illustrious Duke, of course,' he said. 'So pretty.'

'I understand they are old friends.'

Lord Rannock snorted. 'Friends! That is good. She only...'

'You are quite foxed, man,' Lord Shelton said frostily, so unusual for such an affable gentleman. 'You should go outside and sober up. This is a respectable house.'

'My cousin is quite right,' Lord Clarendon said languidly. 'You're a disgrace, Rannock.'

'I've had barely a drop,' Lord Rannock protested indignantly. 'Such a prickly old house is Roderick! But we all know why my wife really loves to visit it.'

'And why is that, Lord Rannock?' Lily said tightly.

'Because she loves your husband, blast it all!' he shouted. 'Don't you see? Foolish Americans!'

Lily felt her face flame and Lord Shelton pushed back his chair to grab Lord Rannock by the arm and march him smartishly out of the room, with his cousin Lord

Clarendon's help. He then returned to his own seat with a cool, kind smile and Lily could quite see why the Dowager Duchess had decided to marry him.

But she herself felt slightly nauseous at it all.

'Lord Rannock was suddenly taken ill, nothing to worry about,' Lord Shelton announced with a gruff laugh. 'Nothing to worry about at all.'

Lady Rannock looked uncertain. 'Is he—should I…?'

'I do think you should be excused, my dear, at least for a moment. You must be so concerned,' the Dowager Duchess said sweetly. 'I think dear Clarendon is with him…'

Lady Rannock slowly laid aside her napkin and left the room, her silver lace train twisting behind her. Lily watched carefully to see if Aidan missed her, but he just smiled and went on chatting with Stella.

Lily took a deep breath and gestured for the pudding, a raspberry trifle with a Roman punch, to be brought in. Everyone returned to their hum of conversation and Lily tried to follow Lord Shelton's talk of the newest musical theatre in London. At last, after what felt like hours, Lily signalled for the ladies to depart to the White Drawing Room for their coffee, leaving the men to their port.

'My dear Lily, won't you play something for us? You have such a talent,' the Dowager Duchess said, sipping her coffee from the china that had been a wedding gift.

Lily was glad of the distraction. She shook away that cold touch of disquiet that had followed her ever since she'd watched Aidan and Lady Rannock at dinner and went to the piano. As her fingertips trailed over the cool keys, she felt herself settle into the old pleasure of the notes again.

'What would you like to hear, Your Grace?' she asked.

'Oh, Agnes, please, my dear. I do hope you will look on me quite as another mother once Mrs Wilkins has returned to America.' She settled into a brocade sofa near the piano, blocking Lily's view of Lady Rannock at the terrace doors. 'Perhaps some Chopin, or some Schubert? That piece you played with Aidan was so charming.'

Lily smiled and launched into a Chopin nocturne. She wasn't sure she could really see Agnes as a *mother*, though. She was too perfect a duchess, too all-seeing.

'Lily,' she murmured, as the younger woman's fingers lightly skipped through the chords, the music blending with the night outside. 'Roderick is certainly lucky to have you, I hope you know that. Imagine hearing music in every corner again! I was never talented at it myself. This place is coming back to life.'

Lily thought of Lady Paul's demands for baby sons and smiled wryly. 'Americans, again, Agnes?'

The Dowager Duchess laughed. 'Oh, I do admit I once imagined my son with a different sort of wife. One of those pale daughters of an earl or viscount who make their bows every Season, who could step into my duties here at Roderick so easily. But I see now a girl like that would never have done for Aidan. He is too energetic, too curious. He needs someone to help anchor him here, to hold his interest.'

Lily glanced at Lady Rannock, so still, so beautifully sad by the doors, moonlight washing over her silver gown. 'Perhaps you once had another bride in mind, one in particular?'

Agnes pursed her lips. 'I never did. And he never did care for anyone suitable.' She took a long sip of coffee. 'I tell you this, my dear. *You* are what Roderick needs. What Aidan needs. You are clever and energetic. You know what is required.'

Lily's eyes prickled and she worried she might cry. 'I wish Aidan thought that.'

'Oh, he does! I am quite sure of it, or he would never have married you. He is so independent that way. Never what you expect the son of a duke to be!' She finished her coffee and smiled. 'Lily, every marriage is always an adjustment and you have to become accustomed to our odd English ways as well as to a new husband. You just need to give it time, be patient. It will all come together for you, I know it.'

Lily nodded, hoping Agnes was right, wishing she could find that optimism in herself again. But Aidan was behaving so strangely since they had returned to Roderick. Maybe he needed to hear his mother's words, too, and to believe in himself in this world they found themselves in.

As she finished the nocturne, the men came in to join them and Lily rose from the piano to gesture to Donat to pass the coffee. Aidan was not with them, but she saw Lord Rannock had reappeared after his abrupt ejection from the dining room and she indicated to Donat to make his coffee extra-strong.

'I see my lovely wife has quite vanished,' Lord Rannock said, exhaling wine fumes onto her. Lily fell back a step.

'One can hardly blame her,' Agnes said. 'Such scenes!'

'I am sure she has gone to the ladies' withdrawing room,' Lily said tightly. She glanced at the terrace doors and saw that indeed Lady Rannock was not there.

'With the Duke to help her with her hem?' Lord Rannock tried to laugh, but hiccupped instead. 'You are so charmingly naive, you Americans. You all think your money solves everything for you, don't you?'

It had always been Lily's experience that her father's

money caused more trouble than it solved. She had imagined Aidan truly cared for her, but had all that money really just bought him for her? Was that what everyone really thought? Now that his castle roof was secure, he would run back to his old love?

'Oh, Rannock, not that again. Do sit down before you fall down,' Lord Shelton snapped, taking Lord Rannock firmly by the arm.

'Really!' snorted Lady Paul. 'You are not in your London stews now, boy.'

Lily spun away from him, from them all, and hurried to the open terrace doors. She stepped outside and leaned on the reassuringly cold, solid balustrade to stare out into the garden. She saw not the lawn, gleaming in the moonlight, stretching away like a perfect bolt of green velvet, but the seaside, at Brighton and Newport, her sisters and her mother, Roderick, all her choices. Aidan and his beautiful eyes. All she had wished for, all she was unsure of now.

She suddenly glimpsed a flash of liquid silver in the darkness, the glow of the moon catching on a silver lace gown. Lady Rannock? She'd vanished from the drawing room before her vile husband came back. Yet she was not alone now. She was hurrying towards someone in the distance, a tall, dark figure just outside the pale stone of the summer house. Aidan?

For a moment, Lily couldn't breathe. She felt so hot then freezing cold, her chest tight. The terrace seemed to shift under her feet.

But then something else took hold of her. Some steely, hard determination that had surely pushed her, some primitive sense to seize what was hers. Her husband, her house, her new life and all her hopes. It was *hers*, not Lady Rannock's, not anyone else's. And if Aidan truly did not care about her, better to know it, to take that piercing arrow to the heart and know the truth. Better to see her cards on the table.

She moved down the steps to the garden, the glowing white silk of her wedding gown floating around her, light and cloudlike now, not holding her down. She hardly seemed to be in her own body, watching herself from a distance as she made her steady way through the garden towards the summer house.

No matter what, her life would not be the same after tonight.

Aidan paced to the balustrade of the folly, staring out over the moonlit lake. He couldn't bear one more minute of port and political talk. He lit one of his cheroots and leaned against the cold stone. The night was quiet, perfectly still, almost as it had been before he came home. When he walked alone under bright foreign stars, he was searching for he knew not what. Now he knew well what he had been searching for.

He'd been searching for love. For a partner in life. For Lily. Her kindness, her serenity, her smile, her heart. She brought his home back to him again.

He turned to stare at the house, a bright beacon in the night, lit from chimneys to basement. When he was a boy, Roderick had seemed so cold, so vast and lonely. Now it actually seemed like a home, a place of music and laughter and life. And it was Lily who made it so.

He heard a soft footstep in the darkness, the swish of silk against the stone steps of the summer house. He spun around, his heart leaping like a schoolboy's at the thought that it must be Lily, come to him there. But the perfume that caught on the warm night breeze was a heavy spice, not Lily's sweet floral.

Melisande stepped into the lantern light, her silver gown sparkling, an enticing smile on her lips.

Once, when he was young and foolish, such a moment would have been all he wanted. He'd been so infatuated with her, but she had wanted a duke. His brother. Poor, deluded Edward.

'My heavens, Aidan, but you do look surprised,' she said with a laugh. 'Surely you must have known I couldn't bear silly drawing room gossip a moment longer than you ever could.'

Aidan frowned. 'How did you find me?'

'I was standing by the terrace doors and saw you walk across the garden. I wanted to leave before my dreadful husband came back.' She gestured to his cheroot. 'May I have one of those, darling?'

'Of course.' He took out his silver case and let her select one, lighting it for her. In the flare of the match, she looked hard-eyed.

'Very naughty of you to abandon your host duties,' she teased, exhaling a silvery plume. 'But I suppose your little American wife will cover for you.'

'Lily is always gracious,' he said tautly.

'And pretty. And, of course, so rich. My husband says everyone at his club whispers about what a prize she is.' She tossed down her cheroot and stepped closer to him, laying her hand lightly on his chest. He remembered when once she had stood with him, just like that, before she declared she would marry Edward, and anger took hold of him. Anger that she would do this now; anger that she would insult Lily. 'But you are surely the greater prize. A duke, for an American nobody.'

Aidan stiffened. 'Melisande...' he said warningly.

'What? We're both married now and I am always discreet. No one could expect you to be *faithful* to American dollars, you know.' She went up on tiptoe close to him. 'You have always been the most gloriously handsome man I know.'

He took her hand to start to push her away. 'I love my wife.'

Melisande laughed bitterly. 'How sweet, darling! I once thought I loved Rannock, too. For a foolish moment. It does pass.'

'I thought it was Edward you wanted back then.'

'Because I couldn't have *you*. But now you are the Duke and I can! *We* can. Don't you see?'

'And Clarendon? Everyone says he's your lover.'

She laughed. 'It's just for fun, of course! You're the only one I ever really wanted.' Before he knew what she was doing, she flung herself against him, her lips searching for his in the shadows.

A gasp echoed through the stones of the folly, soft but as loud as an explosion, tearing everything apart. Aidan pushed Melisande away and saw Lily standing on the steps behind him, as if in a nightmare. Her face was stark white, her lips parted as she stared at them.

'Lily!' he shouted, but she spun around and ran away, vanishing into the night. 'Come back!'

'Oh, let her go.' Melisande tried to catch at his sleeve and he tore away to run after his wife. 'She doesn't matter, Aidan!'

'She is the *only* thing that matters.' The only thing that had ever truly mattered in his life—or ever would. Lily was his home, his everything. He had been a fool not to see that from the very first moment he met her.

Chapter Twenty-Four

Lily slammed the door of her chamber behind her, not caring if the servants heard, or what the people gathered in the drawing room thought. She'd spent her whole life trying to be good, trying to be smart, and where had it taken her? To this house that couldn't be hers. To a husband she loved desperately, but who had never been hers. She couldn't fool herself about that any longer.

She barely remembered how she had returned from the garden. After she saw Aidan with Lady Rannock, after Lord Rannock's violent behaviour, she remembered little at all. Everything seemed like a dream. A terrible nightmare. If only she could wake up and be in her old Newport bed.

Her head pounded, and she couldn't stop shaking. She reached up and tore off the Lennox tiara, pins catching painfully in her hair. She tossed it to the carpet, biting her lip to keep from shrieking like a madwoman. The madness had to end. She had to regain some measure of control over her life. Over her heart.

She let her hair down, shaking it free over her shoulders. On her dressing table, in an elaborate silver frame which had been a wedding present, was her engagement photo with Aidan. The two of them arm in arm, smiling. How happy she looked there. How happy she *was*. She'd thought Aidan was, too, that their future would only grow brighter and brighter. That she could overcome any doubts. How foolish she had been.

She spun away and opened the armoire. She shoved aside the silks and velvets and linens of her trousseau and dragged out her valise. It wasn't part of the new green leather set stamped with a gilded coronet, but a battered old piece she'd once dragged between New York and Newport. She opened it on the bed and started tossing clothes and books into it, not knowing what she packed or where she would go. Everyone she knew, everything she had, was in this house.

The door swung slowly open and Aidan stood there. Lily froze, watching him like a deer in the woods. She trembled even more.

Aidan smiled, but then he almost stepped on the fallen tiara and that smile turned wary. Yet, to her dismay, he still looked like her beautiful, wonderful, vibrant, sunshine husband. He hadn't grown hooves and horns, which would have made things so much easier. No, he was still Aidan and she did still love him. Longed for him.

The image of Lady Rannock in his arms was still there, too, like a knife. But there was also the laughing man on the Brighton beach, the tousled hair in the wind as he raced horses with her, rowed with her on the lake. The man who had held her hand at the altar. The Duke who had ridden with her in a flower-bedecked carriage pulled by their own people to their home.

It was all there, her and Aidan. Their past, the future she'd longed for. It could have been glorious.

'How could you throw it all away?' she whispered. Her hands curled into fists on the clasp of the valise. 'How could you turn away from *us*? I knew English noblemen were said not to be faithful, but I thought you were different. Better. My brave explorer.'

'Lily. My own beautiful Lily. I promise it is nothing like you think! It was never like that. I could never have hurt Edward that way, nor you. Please, please, listen to me.' He placed the tiara on the dressing table and came slowly, carefully, to stand with her by the bed, as if approaching an easily startled fawn. Which was what she felt like, all trembling, exposed nerves.

He carefully picked up a white lawn nightdress, folded it and placed it in her valise. She drew in a deep breath. He stood so close to her, so close, and he smelled and felt just the same. But she dared not look up at him.

'Lily,' he said. He spoke quietly, calmly, but she heard the tremble in his own voice. 'I am so sorry for what you just saw. More sorry than I can ever say. If you want to leave, if you think you could never be happy here, I will let you go right now. I'll call the carriage myself. But please, won't you listen to me just for a moment? My sweet, kind Lily. Give me a chance to save my own life, for that is what you are. My whole life.'

Lily tossed one blue silk shoe into the valise, but couldn't see the other one. Her eyes were growing blurry with unshed, sad, angry tears. How she wanted to believe him! But she dared not. 'Are you going to tell me that you love her? That you always will?'

'Love Melisande! Good heavens, no. No, Lily.' He reached out at last and took her hands, keeping her from packing, holding her to him. His touch was gentle, but she couldn't break away. Didn't want to break away. His touch was just the same, so sweet and reassuring, too much a reminder of so many wonderful things.

'Once, when I was young and foolish, I thought I cared

for her,' he said. 'I asked her to marry me. But Edward, my brother, loved her as well and declared he would marry her. I could never stand in his way. Melisande, though, intended to marry him and keep me as her lover. Once, we kissed at a ball and she told me the truth—but we were seen. I will never forgive myself for that, my greatest mistake. But love her? No, never. She is not a thousandth part of the woman you are. What she did to my brother…that was unforgivable. Appalling.'

Lily blinked up at him, alarmed at what had happened in his past, how he had been deceived. But he was not that man now. He was her Aidan still, surely? The man who would stand beside her, be loyal, no matter what.

'She wants me, I suppose, because I am the Duke now,' he went on, 'but *you* are my one chance of any happiness, Lily. Your kindness and sweetness, your curiosity, your strength. I don't blame you for being angry with me—your good heart can't understand unhappiness such as Mel has, like the unhappiness *I* once had. I need you, only you. I will have no secrets from you ever again, I will work every hour of every day to make you happy. If you will just let me. Lily, Lily, I can't imagine my life without you. Please, I beg you, give me one more chance to show you how much I love you. How much I need you.'

He shook as if caught in a terrible storm, his expression stark, hopeless. She'd never seen Aidan like that and it frightened her. She threw her arms around him and held him close, both of them still trembling, but sheltered at last from the storms inside their hearts. Beat and batter as those storms would, they could no longer touch them. Lily and Aidan were together.

The past had vanished like the dark cloud it once was.

'I love you, Lily,' he said, his cheek against her tousled

hair. 'As I never imagined I could love anyone. Please let me show you that. Prove it to you.'

She looked up at him through her tears. He looked different, younger, softer. They needed each other. They always would. That was the only truth that mattered, the only truth she could always trust.

'You don't have to prove it,' she said. 'I see it now in your eyes, Aidan. I know it's true. And I love you, too. I always will.'

'Lily,' he whispered hoarsely and kissed her with all the fervour of passion and need and love that she now knew was all hers. All theirs, for ever.

Epilogue

Ten months later

Aidan paced the length of the White Drawing Room, from the fireplace roaring with warmth against the cold day to the terrace doors. The garden beyond was just starting to come back to faint green life after a long winter and the painted eyes of his ancestors' portraits seemed to watch him with disapproval at so much emotion. But he took no notice of them at all, nor of the curious glances of the servants hovering at the door.

His mind was in the Duchess's Chamber upstairs, where Lily was bringing their child into the world. He couldn't hear anything in the grand vastness of Roderick, no screams or cries, but he had seen enough in his travels to imagine all kinds of bloody scenes. And his wife was a delicate lady.

'Aidan, dear, do sit down,' his mother said from her sofa by the fireplace. She turned a page of her newspaper to the scandal columns. 'Have a brandy. Or three.'

'I can't sit down, Mama.'

'You cannot help Lily that way, you know. She has the doctor and nursing sister, as well as Rose Grantley. She'll be quite well.'

'But shouldn't it be over by now?' He stopped at the window, staring out at the terrace as if it could have some answers. There were just more hovering servants, waiting for news.

'She just felt the first pains early this morning and first babies can be slow. It will be hours yet! I took two days with you.'

'Mama, that is not helping,' he growled.

'Oh, but Lily is so dainty! I am quite sure he'll be much smaller than you.'

Aidan frowned. He remembered all the cosy winter months of sitting with Lily by that very fire, watching her grow larger, feeling the baby kick, laughing at his wife's attempts to learn to knit. How could all that sweetness end like this?

But he knew his mother was right; he couldn't help Lily now, except with his patience. Patience was something he had never had much of.

He poured out a large glass of brandy and sat down across from his mother. 'Oh, do look!' she exclaimed. 'It seems Lady Rannock has left her husband for Lord Clarendon. Shellie did worry his cousin would do something foolish, but quite to this extent—tsk-tsk.'

Aidan hardly cared about Melisande's new scandal. He saw Lily's maid, Doris, run past the doorway, but she didn't stop.

'Why will no one tell me what's happening in my own house?' he said.

'Because I am sure nothing is happening yet,' Agnes said, turning another page.

But Rose suddenly ran into the drawing room, her apron stained, her red hair straggling from its pins. Her smile, though, was radiant.

'You have a son!' she cried.

'A new Duke.' Agnes sighed happily, the scandal papers forgotten.

Aidan felt suddenly overwhelmed by raw emotion. He rose slowly to his feet, swaying. 'A son? And Lily... she's well?'

'Yes, perfectly. Just very tired, but the doctor says it was an easy birth. They're both very well and happy.'

'I must go to her,' he said, already racing out of the drawing room and up the stairs, three at a time. He had to see Lily, to *know* she was all right.

'Aidan, she's still in bed!' Rose called.

But he didn't hear her. He burst into the Duchess's Chamber, crowded with doctors, nurses, servants, warm and stuffy, thick with the cloying tang of blood and camphor, the sweetness of burning rose oil.

He could see only the bed on its dais, its pillows piled high. Lily lay against them, her cheeks damp and flushed, her hair clinging to her brow, and the most radiant smile on her face as she stared down at the bundle in her arms.

A shrieking, flailing bundle.

'Lily,' he said softly, more enraptured than he had ever been before in his life. She glanced up and held out her shaking hand to him.

'Oh, Aidan, do come say hello to him,' she said.

He went to her, his heart bursting with hope, with a fierce, overwhelming happiness he'd never dreamed of before. He took her hand and kissed it as he looked down at the baby. His son. His family.

The child was terribly red and wrinkled, his minute features fixed in a look of deep displeasure at finding himself in such a bright, crowded world. A tuft of dark hair, like Lily's, curled damply atop his head and his eyes had a hint of Lennox green.

'Isn't he so beautiful?' Lily whispered.

'A bit like an angry beetroot at the moment.' Aidan laughed. 'But I can see he will be almost as beautiful as his mother.'

'I think he looks like you when you're deep in concentration over something.' She caressed the baby's soft cheek with her fingertip and he immediately ceased wailing and stared up at her with wide, wondering eyes. 'See, he knows us!'

'So he does,' Aidan said, fascinated by his son's tiny hands, like little starfish. 'You've given me the most wonderful gift of all, Lily. My beautiful wife. My family.' He gently kissed her, marvelling at all he had now. All he had travelled the world searching for. It had all been right here the whole time. 'I am the luckiest man who has ever called Roderick Castle home...'

* * * * *

If you enjoyed this book, why not check out
Amanda McCabe's Debutantes in Paris miniseries

Secrets of a Wallflower
The Governess's Convenient Marriage
Miss Fortescue's Protector in Paris

And look out for the next book in the
Dollar Duchesses miniseries, coming soon!

Author Note

I hope you've enjoyed reading Lily and Aidan's tale as much as I enjoyed writing it! I've always loved reading about the 'dollar princesses' and how they fared in a life very different from the ones they knew in America. Some flourished and some failed miserably, but sadly not many found true love as Lily did!

A definition of 'dollar princess' I found on www. ancestry.com says, 'A "dollar princess" referred to an American heiress, often from a newly wealthy family, who married a title-rich but cash-poor British nobleman.'

These girls and their ambitious mothers were often cut off from New York high society—which was even more strict and exclusive than in Europe!—and sometimes used the help of well-connected but poor English ladies such as Lady Heath—who is based on the real-life Lady Paget—to make their way in London society. There were also books like *Titled Americans: The Real Heiresses' Guide to Marrying an Aristocrat* to assist them.

In 1895 alone, nine British noblemen—including a duke, an earl and several barons—married Americans. Some of the most famous were Jennie Jerome, who became Lady Randolph Churchill—mother of Winston; Consuelo Vanderbilt, who became Duchess of Marlborough; Frances Work, who became Lady Fermoy—an ancestor of Diana, Princess of Wales; Mary Leiter, who became Lady Curzon; Consuelo Yznaga, who became Duchess of Manchester; Nancy Langhorne, who became Lady Astor, and Kathleen Kennedy, who became Marchioness of Hartington.

Be sure to look for Violet's story next! She is a *very* reluctant noblewoman indeed!

And visit me any time at http://ammandamccabe.com

Here are some sources I enjoyed, if you'd like to know more about the lives of these extraordinary women:

Julie Ferry, *The Million Dollar Duchesses: How America's Heiresses Seduced the Aristocracy.* Arum Press, 2018

The Transatlantic Marriage Bureau. Aurum Press, 2017

Cecelia Tichi, *What Would Mrs Astor Do? The Essential Guide to the Manners and Mores of the Gilded Age.* NYU, 2019

Anne de Courcy, *The Husband Hunters: American Heiresses Who Married into the British Aristocracy.* Macmillan, 2018

Consuelo Vanderbilt Balsan, *The Glitter and the Gold.* Hodder Paperbacks, 2012

Ruth Brandon, *The Dollar Princesses.* Knopf, 1980

Amy de la Haye & Valerie D. Mendes, *The House of Worth: Portrait of an Archive*. V&A, 2014

Jane Gabin, *American Women in Gilded Age London*. University Press of Florida, 2006

Pamela Horn, *High Society: The English Social Elite 1880-1914*. Alan Sutton, 1992

Amanda Mackenzie Stuart, *Consuelo and Alva Vanderbilt*. Harper Perennial, 2010

Gail MacColl, *To Marry an English Lord*. Sidgwick & Jackson, 1989

Jane Ridley, *The Heir Apparent: A Life of Edward VII*. Random House, 2014

Anne Sebba, *American Jennie: The Remarkable Life of Lady Randolph Churchill*. WW Norton & Company, 2007